CONTENTS

THE LEGEND OF SOSEN NO TANI

Through the Well

Allison Conroe

The Legend of Sosen no Tani: Through the Well

Cover art by Lorelei Fleishman.

"Hunger, poverty, environmental degradation, economic instability, unemployment, chronic disease, drug addiction, and war, for example, persist, in spite of the analytical ability and technical brilliance that have been directed toward eradicating them. No one deliberately creates those problems, no one wants them to persist, but they persist nonetheless. That is because they are intrinsically systems problems—undesirable behavior characteristics of the system structures that produce them. They will yield only as we reclaim our intuition, stop casting blame, see the system as the source of its own problems, and find the courage and wisdom to <u>restructure</u> it."

-       Donella Meadows, Thinking in Systems

Pronunciation Index

Kairi Raynott (ka-eye-ree ray-not)
  Mato Asahi (ma-toe a-saw-hee)
  Mie (mee-yay)
Misao-dono (mee-sa-ow-doe-no)
  Ryoko (ree-o-ko)
  Tadaaki (ta-daa-kee)
  Hiroko (hee-er-o-ko)
  Aoki (a-o-kee)
  Shimizu (shee-mee-zoo)
  Saito (sigh-toe)
  Hayashi (high-ya-shee)
  Yamashita (ya-ma-sh-ta)
  Fujita (foo-jee-ta)
  Kamachi (ka-ma-chee)
  Chiyo (chee-yo)
  Minoru (mee-nor-oo)
  Hana (ha-na)
  Sora-Sensei (sor-a sen-say)
Yoshizo Takamura (yo-shee-zo ta-ka-moo-ra)
  Saru (sa-roo)
Gento Hyuga (ga-en-toe hee-you-ga)
Sakura Morai (sa-ku-ra mor-eye)
  Kenzo (ken-zo)
  Shuten doji (shoo-ten doe-jee)
Tamamo no Mae (ta-ma-moe no ma-ay)
Sutoko Tenno (soo-toe-koo ten-no)
  Kenji (ken-jee)
Mizukume Zukeran (mee-zoo-koo-may zoo-ker-an)
  Amaterasu (a-ma-ter-a-soo)
  Yatagarasu – (ya-ta-ga-ra-soo)
  Jimmu – (jee-moo)
  Inari-sama – (ee-nar-ee sa-ma)
  Kagutsuchi (ka-goot-soo-chee)

Hiryu Gongen (hee-er-yoo go-n-gen)
Sosen no Tani (so-sen no ta-nee)
Mizu no Okurimono (mee-zoo no o-
  koo-ree-mo-no)
  Nachi (na-chee)
  Wakayama (wa-ka-ya-ma)
  Kii (kee)
  Tokyo (toe-kee-yo)
  Kyoto (kee-yo-toe)
  Fuji (foo-jee)
  Monsoko (mo-n-so-ko)
  Tagama (ta-ga-ma)

PROLOGUE

Mato

A cloud of early morning mist rolled along the water's surface, coating my feet as they padded against the wooden docks. With the sun yet to fully rise, I couldn't see more than five feet in front of me through the weight of the fog, but I let instinct and muscle memory be my guide as I wound through the floating maze of earthen-walled houses making up my village. Thud. Thud. Thud.

The reverberation of my bare feet was only muted by the constant, lulling hum of the water beneath me. The rest of the town and my neighbors were still asleep. A small fish hung by its tail from my child-sized fingers, still wriggling slightly, fighting to live. I was excited to show my mother, hoping she would cook the thing for breakfast instead of serving the same old miso soup day after day. I had a nagging feeling that I had to get it to her quickly, that she was waiting on me for something important, but I couldn't remember why. Leaving the main streets of houses, restaurants, and stores behind me, I raced down one long, meandering dock until I reached a sea of lily pads. In their center floated a small, single-room kominka farmhouse. My home.

Sliding open the front door, I bounded into the room in a brash and boyish manner, not caring if anyone was still asleep.

"Mom! Dad! Look, I did it! I caught my first fish!" I boasted.

But my success was met with silence.

I scanned the room. They appeared to still be sleeping, the outlines of their bodies lying motionless beneath the comforter of the futon. I strode over to them, determined to be acknowledged. As I pulled back my mother's comforter and shook her shoulders, rolling her toward me, I expected to see her sleepy eyes blink open to greet me. But instead, what stared back at me was the stiff, cold, and emaciated corpse of what was my mother, rigor mortis locked on her face. I let go of her and jumped away. I felt my stomach churn and my body fill with dread as the realization washed over me. The fish I was holding flopped to the floor.

"Where were you? We waited for you," my father's disembodied voice echoed from the walls around me.

Suddenly, the corpses of my parents began to disintegrate to ash at my feet. The walls of my childhood home became engulfed in flames and smoke shrouded my vision. Reflexively, I held my hands over my mouth, beginning to cough while trying to breathe. "You never came."

Something clicked in the back of my brain and I heard my teacher's voice saying, "Watch your breath when you handle fire, Mato. Take a deep breath; feel the heat of the flames filling your body. Imagine when you exhale, ice freezing over every single inch," it said.

With my instinctive training kicking in, the smoke subsided almost as quickly as it began. Suddenly, I was no longer standing in my childhood home but in a scorched field devoid of human life and covered in ash. Ash was falling around me like rain.

I was no longer a young boy. My eyes burned as I struggled to see the scarred earth that stretched out before me, seeming to swallow the landscape in volcanic stone. I couldn't remember the last time I couldn't handle the effects of fire. The feeling of dread that had filled my body moments prior grew, lodging itself into a familiar place in my gut.

As I felt swirling clouds of ash land on my body, I looked down in slow terror to see it mixing with splatters of fresh blood that marked my skin like paint. I knew it was not my own. At my feet, bodies of humans lay in pools of blood, dripping from the katana I now held in my right hand. The color of blood painted the sky red as dawn began to rise around me. All I could hear was the crackling of flames and blood drip, drip, dripping from my blade onto the bodies below.

Just as the pool of nausea threatened to escape up my throat, the caw of a crow broke the silence. The black silhouette of a three-legged crow soared across the sky, bringing with it rays of warm, bright light. The crow flew low on the horizon in front of me and morphed into the figure of a girl, who began to walk toward me. As she got closer, I could see she was small in stature, with long sable-brown hair. Her eyes were dark and soft; the shape of her nose mimicked the sharp beak of the crow's. The warmth began to dissipate the knot in my stomach, filling up my body, erasing the dread.

The girl held out her hand to me. "Mato," she said, her petite lips forming a melodic sound. "You came for me."

***

I woke with a start to the sounds of crickets, birds, and shuffling feet outside. Beyond where I lay, I could hear the whispered chants of the Keepers as they filed into the temple next door. I was no longer in my childhood home of Mizu no Okurimono, but in Sosen no Tani, where I had been living for ten years now. Rolling onto my back, I peeled my eyes open to stare at the ceiling. Letting the lingering images of the dream flicker and fade behind my eyelids, I took several moments before allowing myself to stand. I thought of the three-legged crow swooping across the sky.

Yatagarasu, what were you telling me?

I usually had no trouble waking in the early mornings and actually enjoyed getting up early, but I felt made of lead as I dragged myself from my futon. Sliding open the shoji door of the temple's lodging, I could see the mist descending from the mountains, hovering between the trees as dawn broke. Next door, the Fire Keepers entered the shrine one by one in their vermillion robes, lighting candles with fresh flame to welcome the day.

I splashed water on my face in the small washroom connected to my sleeping quarters, and rinsed out my mouth. Tying my dark hair in its usual half knot, I removed my black robe from its hook on the wall and changed into my kimono and hakama, as I have done every day since first arriving in this village. Before crossing the shoji to join the procession outside, I almost forgot to grab my candle. Taking it from its place on a small wooden stool next to the door, I stepped out into the morning.

CHAPTER ONE

Kairi

As the first chirps of the uguisu bird broke the silence of dawn, I couldn't help but remember my mother's voice.

"Oo-goo-ee-soo, oo-goo-ee-soo," she once called to me playfully in a singsong voice as I screamed and ran around my grandparents' garden, my toddler legs only taking me a couple of feet but feeling like I was running miles. My mother caught up with me and scooped me into her arms and I dissolved into giggles.

"Kairi, how do you know what sound the uguisu bird makes?" She asked me.

"Because it sings its name!" I howled in high-pitched toddler excitement.

"That's right, good girl! The uguisu are always louder at Obaachan and Ojiichan's house. When you hear them, you know you are home."

"Oo-goo-ee-soo, oo-goo-ee-soo," I murmured to myself now as I pulled the last carrot up from beneath the soil. I let the familiar ache fill my chest as I thought about running around these very gardens with her almost two decades ago. After ten years away from Japan and ten years without my mother, here I was, finally home.

Wiping the sweat from my brow with the back of my forearm, I stood and turned my head upward. Above me, purple-pinkish hues of light had begun to streak across the sky, and I knew it was time to head back to the farmhouse. I hoisted my pack, filled with the morning's harvest, onto my back and began to make my way through the field in the direction of my aunt's house. A chorus of cicadas broke the silence of the early morning as my labored steps disturbed their rest.

I could already imagine the neighbors awakening angrily to the noise. *Ugh, sorry everyone,* I thought to myself as I trudged onward, the weight of the pack causing me to lean forward slightly as I walked. I had been back in Japan for a little over three months and could count on more than two hands how many times I had made an idiot out of myself as the "clumsy American."

"Are you ready?" my father had asked me the morning of my flight. I stood in the doorway of our New England farmhouse, luggage in hand and mind already boarding the plane.

"The real question is are *you* ready? You don't even have your shoes on!" I replied to him. He was supposed to drive me to the airport. He rose from his seat at our kitchen counter and took a final gulp of his coffee before coming to meet me in the entryway.

"Do you have everything you need?" he asked me. I gave him a look. He knew who he was talking to.

"I'm your daughter, aren't I?" I replied with a smile. "If anything, I am overprepared and have more than I need."

"You know I have to dad you one last time before you go. I'm not going to see you for at least the next three months," he said, pulling me into a bear hug. I felt a pang of sadness and guilt at the thought of leaving him alone in that that big old farmhouse. It would be the longest I would had ever been away from my father and the first time leaving him for more than a week after Mom had died.

"It'll be your first time back in Japan since we lost your mother. It may be hard," he told me. "I know your Aunt Mie will make you very comfortable, but if it gets to be too much and you change your mind, you know I am always a phone call away.

Even if you need to wake me up at two in the morning," my dad said.

Pulling back from his hug, I looked up to meet his eyes and asked, "What about you? Will *you* be okay by yourself for so long? You know, it's not too late to join me."

"I'll be alright, sweetheart," he replied. "Don't worry about me. You know I've got work to do. I'll be busy. Besides, I don't think I could go back right now. Too many memories, and it's not quite the same without your mom."

I nodded, swallowing the tiny bubble of apprehension that had crawled into my throat.

When I was eight, my mother passed away. We were living in Tokyo at the time; technically, I was born and raised there. My mother was from Japan and my father American. My father had longed to return to his family home in New England for some time, but tolerated Tokyo because it was my mother's dream to live there.

When I'd ask him why he lived in Tokyo if he hated the big city so much, he'd say, "Look, Kairi, if I had it my way, I'd join the simple living movement, or whatever you call it. You know, back in the day, it was just called living. Anyway, I'd get myself an old farmhouse and a rice field and call it a life. But I met your mother. And what she says goes." It was a very Dad response.

So when she passed, that is exactly what we did. The pain of her absence was too much for him to continue living in Japan, and he took the both of us back to New England to his family farmhouse a few months later—without the rice field—where I spent the remainder of my childhood and all of my teenage years in the Green Mountains of Vermont.

Now, ten years later, I had arranged to stay with my Auntie Mie, my mother's older sister, in their hometown of Nachi in Wakayama Prefecture instead of immediately going to college. I had met Auntie Mie a few times growing up, but after I moved to America when my mother passed, I had only spoken to her over the phone on the occasional holiday. The plan was for me to live with her in her house in the countryside, and help her run her small farm and antique store. I had told my father after graduating high school that I wanted to take a gap year and return to Japan to reconnect with my culture. In reality, I had been thinking a lot about my mother and missing her almost as strongly as when she had passed.

Now, I made my way back to Auntie Mie's antique store up the steep switchbacked road from the plot of land next to her house. The town of Nachi was a small village built into the side of the Kii Mountain Range and basically required hiking straight up or down the mountainside if you wanted to walk anywhere.

Ding, ding ding. A set of chimes on the door jingled sharply as I entered Mikan Antiques, finding my aunt flipping through a magazine behind the counter. She looked up at me as I entered, brushing a strand of her short black hair out of her eyes and pushing it back into its bobbed cut. She was somewhere in her early sixties and her hair had only just started graying. I could only hope I'd age with her genetics, but seeing as I had found my first gray hair just the other day at eighteen, I may have been doomed to age like my European ancestors.

She greeted me with, "Oh, great timing. Did you harvest anything for the offering?"

I walked up to her and placed a basket of freshly pulled carrots, soybeans, and daikon radishes on the wooden surface between us in response.

"Kairi, I've told you, not on the counter! I'll have to clean up the dirt," she scolded me lightly.

"Hai, sumimasen." I responded, having mastered the term for "I'm sorry" as my most frequently spoken phrase. Technically, Japanese was my first language, but Dad and I never spoke it at home in America. Now, my Japanese was clunky and out of practice. "I thought you were preparing stock for the store?" I asked her, raising an eyebrow at the magazine she held in her hands.

"Just doing some research to make sure our aesthetic is still on trend for those coming in from the city," she explained.

Beaming, she added, "I sourced a whole room full of tansu at an estate sale our neighbor was having the other day."

Suddenly intrigued, I responded, "Ooh really? Any black ones?" I loved the charm of tansu, an antique style of Japanese dresser or chest. Each was unique to the family who had previously owned it. Sometimes with a family crest, or specific details from a craftsman. My favorites were the simple, minimalist kind. I felt like they had stories to tell.

"Oh yes, there's several. I'll show you later this afternoon. First, it's time to prepare our offering and bring it up the mountain," she said, pointing at the vegetables.

We washed and prepared the carrots and radishes for offering before positioning them in a *bento* box as thin slices in the shape of flowers on top of a bed of rice and miso-grilled fish. Aunt Mie packed a thermos of hot water to make ceremonial grade matcha when we reached the shrine.

Growing up, my parents were never particularly religious. My father, being from America, had grown up Christian, but for one reason or another was not heavily invested in his faith and chose not to pass it down to me. My mother grew up practicing Shintoism, the animistic practice that honors the spirits living in all things, known as *kami*. But I was never particularly involved with honoring the kami until I arrived here in the countryside, where spirituality was much more commonplace than in the cities, even if people no longer completely knew the meaning behind what they were practicing. Here, I kept an altar with Auntie Mie to honor my mother and grandparents, and Auntie Mie took regular trips to the shrine at Nachi Falls, the town's center axis, to honor seasonal changes, harvests, and life events.

Auntie Mie preferred to walk straight to the edge of the waterfall this morning to give an offering at Hiro Jinja, the small, humble shrine at the base of the falls farther into the woods. It is said that Nachi's main shrine, the Kumano Grand Shrine, built into the side of the mountain and named after the ancient Kumano Kodo pilgrimage trail that put Nachi on the map, houses the kami of the region throughout the year, except when they return home to the Nachi Falls waterfall once a year during the Fire Festival that was set to take place in a couple of weeks. But Auntie Mie insisted, "The spirits are at the waterfall today; I can feel it." So off we went.

We bowed and clapped our hands twice, as is the custom, closing our eyes and folding our palms together to pray as we approached Hiro Shrine at the base of the Falls. Drops of water and spray from the falls flecked my face and skin as I prayed. I closed my eyes.

Kami-sama, thank you for allowing another summer to come. Thank you for bringing me back home to Japan. And thank you for allowing me to reside here at the base of your beautiful mountain with Auntie Mie while I continue to learn more about my mother, who I am, and where I am from. I don't know where she is in the universe, but I hope Mom is well and cared for. I humbly ask your guidance as I figure out what's next for me during this chapter.

"That was a long one," Aunt Mie said after I opened my eyes and bowed once more at the flowing water. "You know, drops and spray from the falls are said to be blessings of longevity and good fortune. You, my dear, just got plenty."

"I had a lot I am thankful for," I replied to her with a shrug.

When I was younger, on one of my first trips to a shrine in Tokyo, Mom taught me that it's common for people to ask for things when they pray to the gods. She warned me to never ask for material objects, or clout, as many have done for centuries, but if I needed to ask for something, it was much better to ask for things like guidance, strength, and willpower. "But," she had told me, "true spirituality comes from showing gratitude. The gods are of the land. The rivers, mountains, trees, and rice fields. They don't exist to grant our wishes; they are not genies. They simply just are. If they provide something for us, they did not have to; they don't *owe* us anything. We should always express our gratitude if we want to truly appease them."

It's one of the biggest lessons I remembered my mom passing on to me, and I tried to embody this as much as possible when we prayed to the kami. Still, I am human, and sometimes I can't help but ask for the occasional good health or for Auntie Mie to decide to take us to eat yakiniku later.

We laid out a blanket a few meters away from the falls and began to unpack small bento boxes and the thermos of water, which Auntie Mie used to begin whipping up bowls of matcha for us both. The gods would eat first, but once they were done, it was our turn. After offering both bowls of the frothy green liquid, she handed me the wide-rimmed ceramic cup and we sipped our tea thoughtfully before opening our bento. By now, it was about eight in the morning, still early enough that no other townsfolk, pilgrims, or tourists were visiting the shrine. Aunt Mie and I had woken up early to prepare the store and harvest the garden in time to hike to Nachi Falls before other people started their day.

It was a foggy morning in Nachi, and the mist rolled between the lush, green mountains before blending into the spray of the cascading water in front of us. I was struck with a feeling that time had been suspended. Staring at the powerful force of tumbling water before us, I could easily imagine that we had walked into ancient Japan that morning, the scenery untouched, wild, and elusive, looking like how history books described the Warring States era, or even prior. I took a moment to imagine that I was a part of *Inuyasha*, or *Rurouni Kenshin*— two of my favorite anime from when I was a kid, while almost instantly rolling my eyes at my own dorkiness.

"It's sad," Aunt Mie said, seemingly out of nowhere, looking up at the falls.

I looked at her, surprised by the random outburst and her sullen tone.

"It's sad to think that views like this are getting harder to find in Japan these days. Our country is so different now from even when I was a child. It's sad to think this could all disappear someday."

I didn't reply to her immediately, taking in her words. We continued to sit in silence for several moments as I mulled over my own thoughts.

"Kairi-chan," Auntie Mie turned to me, a fixed expression in her eyes. "Have you ever heard of Sosen no Tani?"

"Sosen no Tani? No, I haven't." I shook my head.

"Hmm, is that so?" Auntie Mie smirked.

In the first few days of my arrival, it had taken us some time to find our rhythm with one another, and me some time to open up. She learned that I liked stories. Whether they were ancient stories of Nachi, she and my mother's childhood, or Shinto legends, her stories bridged the ten years that I was separated from her while living in America. Curious, I leaned closer on my hands and tilted my head in her direction.

"What is it?" I asked her, taking the bait.

She smiled.

"Sosen no Tani is said to be the Land of the Ancestors. It's an old legend of Wakayama Prefecture that dates back some thousand years. Somewhere in the heart of these mountains lies a village that hasn't been found since that time. Monks and lost samurai, living all the way back in Heian and Feudal eras, hiked as pilgrims on the Kumano Kodo and lost their way. Eventually, a few returned to their hometowns speaking of a village filled with Ancestors, or so they called them. It was said that theirs was a village of people living perfectly in harmony with nature and the gods, the most efficient example of a satoyama, or sustainable village. The people took care of the earth and honored the spirits, and in turn the earth and spirits took care of them. They took care of one another, with the belief that the success of the whole community over one individual brought true prosperity. The monks and samurai shared that this made the village *rich*, its harvest bountiful, its crafts and textiles plenty, and no conflict or illness ever befell its people.

"But those who found this town could never recall how they came upon it or how they got home. The mountains were, and still are, too dangerous for humans to traverse and explore every meter. Even to this day, with all of our technology and flying drones and helicopters, remnants of this village have never been found. Some began to believe that the village exists *inside* the mountains themselves. Japan's El Dorado, some like to say, but I digress.

"The people of Sosen no Tani were called Ancestors because they are said to serve as representatives for us humans and converse directly with the gods. We are meant to follow their example to lead a long and prosperous life as a people, so that we are able to cohabitate peacefully with the gods on their land for all of time. And if we ever disrupt that cohabitation, the gods will ensure we live here no longer," Auntie Mie said. "Gosh. I wonder what they'd think of us now. Do you think we've broken that agreement yet?" she finished.

"Really?" I asked her. "So is Sosen no Tani supposed to be a real village, or is it in the spirit world?"

"It is called the Village of Ancestors because it lies on the border between both. The people there are not entirely human, but not gods like the kami, nor are they yokai, supernatural creatures," she answered.

"Hmm, that's interesting," I mused. "What made you think of that story suddenly?"

"I'm not sure. It just came across my mind, something my father told me long ago. Looking up at the beautiful *Nachi-san,* I can't help but feel the power of nature. I feel we are getting further and further away from that as humans with every generation. I worry for your generation and what comes next. We are so different from the nation my mother and even my grandmother used to describe, having moved so deep into this world of consumption and so far away from one another. Even Kii Peninsula, known for having a wet and humid climate, is somehow experiencing *drought*. I have never seen conditions so dry here before."

She shook her head, pausing a moment and getting wrapped up in her thoughts.

"That's why I am continuing to save the seeds we farm.

To save our environment, and save each other as it changes. To carry out the intentions of the ancestors. I want you to carry forward the way of our ancestors, too, no matter what comes next for you in life. And I hope I've been teaching that to you while you've stayed here," she answered me as she looked up at the falls. A distant expression played on her face that I couldn't quite read.

"Mm," I agreed. "Thank you for sharing with me. I'll do my best to live in a way that will make our ancestors proud."

Aunt Mie made her way back into town first, needing to get back in time to open the shop. I hung back, telling her I wanted to look at the view a bit longer. I was still pondering the legend of Sosen no Tani. For some reason, it had reminded me of something.

Japan's El Dorado, huh? I thought. I had learned about El Dorado during my high school days in Vermont, the Spanish conquistadors describing the hidden Amazonian city as one flourishing with gold. We learned, though (it was later discovered by an American professor at my father's alma mater, the University of Vermont), that this "gold" is now believed to be an incredibly prolific soil stewarded by humans, called terra preta, creating such agricultural abundance that the Spanish equated its worth to gold.

Scientists around the world scrambled to discover the recipe of creation for this soil as a means to combat the unhinged climate crisis and the atrocious impact of capitalism. But these endeavors did not receive much funding. Over time, the general public, and the economy, lost interest.

What *would* our ancestors think of our society today? We definitely are not living in perfect harmony with nature like in Sosen no Tani, the land Aunt Mie described. I had to wonder if the monks and samurai who found themselves in this mythical village believed it to be filled with gold, or some precious resource, like El Dorado. If they did, then I guessed it was a good thing us humans could never find it again. Surely we would destroy that too. Wouldn't we?

When I was done with my reverie, I decided to walk back over to the shrine to give one more offering to the kami. Placing one more bowl of matcha that I had made from the leftovers of our picnic on the altar, I pulled the rope, ringing the shrine's bell. Bowing and clapping my hands twice, I thanked the spirits of the land for Aunt Mie's story and asked for her longevity and happiness. I prayed for a world that would appease the gods and our ancestors, as Aunt Mie wished, a world humans wouldn't destroy but would nurture with one another. And I prayed for guidance to live my own life in a way that would help make this a reality.

At the end of my prayer, I bowed once more and turned to walk back into town. After taking a few steps back up the hill, a sudden rustling in the trees caused me to shift my attention above me. On a branch just mere feet from my head, at the edge of the woods, perched a crow. For a moment, we held each other's gaze, and I got the strangest sensation the bird was trying to tell me something. He was pretty large for a crow, coated in sleek black feathers. As I looked at him more closely, I noticed he was standing on three legs. *Three legs?* That couldn't be right. Doing a double take and looking even closer, I saw that my eyes were not mistaken; the crow had three legs.

An image of Yatagarasu, the three-legged crow god, whose symbol represented the town of Nachi and the ancient pilgrimage trail it was famous for, flashed across my mind. *Maybe he's mutated?* I thought, the skeptical American in me feeling disbelief. Seeming to read my mind, the crow cawed loudly, snapping me out of my thoughts.

In an instant, he fluttered his wings and took off from the branch he was sitting on, flying a few feet to my right and landing on a low branch a few trees away. The slightest opening between brush where he perched revealed a small footpath through the woods. It was almost as if he were trying to say *follow me.*

In the past three months, I had been up and down this hill

to Nachi-san, giving offerings to the gods with Aunt Mie enough times that at this point, I felt like I knew the area like the back of my hand. But I had never been on the trail the crow was leading me to. Remembering the famous story of Japan's first emperor, Jimmu, being led by Yatagarasu across Wakayama Prefecture and to Nachi Falls, thus creating the Kumano Kodo, I decided to follow him anyway.

Every few feet, the crow would caw again and fly forward into a new tree, leading me, slowly, farther into the woods. Oddly, I felt compelled to keep moving forward, to find out where this bird was taking me. After about fifteen minutes of this, we finally arrived at a small clearing surrounded by trees. The three-legged crow flew to the center of the clearing and swooped low to the ground before cawing once more and flying out of my sight. In the center of the clearing was what looked to be a gigantic mounded anthill of hardened clay.

I slowly walked closer to the mound, which rose easily four feet off the ground and had a wide, open mouth at the top. Peering over the edge of the mound into the hole below, I could make out the edges of an access tunnel, with water running through it. On the opposite lip of the opening, I could see a handmade ladder carved into the mud of the mound, dropping down into the tunnel below.

I remembered another lesson from school, this time my Japanese grade school, that taught us about the ancient Chinese system of digging underground tunnels and wells to transport mountain water to local farmland for irrigation, called the Karez Well System. It was said that the knowledge and engineering of creating this series of access tunnels, vertical wells, and ground canals was brought to Japan in the early Yayoi Period, around 400 BC. The underground tunnels and wells were large enough that people could move freely within them to administer repairs and collect water. Perhaps this tunnel could still be transporting water from the mountains, or even Nachi-san, to isolated villages throughout our prefecture.

After a few minutes of poking around the area and finding

nothing of immediate significance, I followed the foot trail that brought me here back toward town. I had been too scared to climb down the ladder.

Why did that crow lead me to an ancient well?

CHAPTER TWO

Kairi

I made my way back to Mikan Antiques roughly forty-five minutes after Auntie Mie returned, finding her exactly as I had earlier that morning, leaning over a magazine behind the sales counter. She looked up when I came in.

"Well, that was quite a convening with the spirits you must have had," she said.

"You could say that," I replied, moving my hand over one of the tansu in the display she had ushered out onto the main floor. She raised an eyebrow.

"Actually, the strangest thing happened—" I started. "Wait, didn't you want my help with these?" I asked suddenly, worried that she had injured herself moving the heavy furniture.

"Nah, they weren't so bad. And I'm not old yet! There's plenty of life left in me," she joked. She wasn't wrong. She was a small woman, easily under five feet tall, but still framed with lean, wiry muscle. "So, what do you think?"

"They're beautiful. You got these at the local flea market? Where was I when this happened?" I asked her, wishing I had been there to swipe one for my bedroom.

She just shrugged. "You were in the fields like you are every morning. Or maybe it was while you were at the ramen restaurant the other day," she said.

"Ugh, it's just so good," I groaned, reminiscing about the savory noodles. "Either way, I want in next time!"

She smiled at me and nodded approvingly before dipping her head back into her magazine. "Understood!"

"So, according to that magazine, is our tansu display on trend?"

"I'm actually reading the news," she replied, flipping the paper in her hands to show Wakayama Prefecture's newspaper. "Another variety of heirloom rice has gone extinct. Farmers in Nachi this season have switched to planting a new GMO variety Monsoko has been rolling out, claiming they can't keep up with farming the natural way. They're getting too old." She shook her head. "I guess this new GMO crop attracted a horde of new pests that took out the last of the heirloom variety being saved by only a few farmers left in the valley, except for my secret stash, of course. Claiming it's pest resistant, but they just ended up spraying whole new swaths of pesticides on the paddies. It makes me sick. When will we realize we are poisoning our home, poisoning ourselves?" She put one hand to her forehead, rubbing the lines that had formed between her eyebrows.

My aunt was a seed saver and a passionate gardener. Like my grandparents and the generations before them, Auntie Mie had taken over the family tradition of stewarding our subsistence garden, with a large portion of that responsibility ensuring our ancestors' seeds continued to be passed on generation after generation, season after season. "It was my most important inheritance," she told me when I first arrived. "Arguably more so than this house."

While my mom moved out to Tokyo to start an urban life as a scientist at Tokyo University, Auntie Mie had stayed in Nachi to carry forward the family legacy and ensure this knowledge wasn't lost. She has been careful to save varieties of rice, barely, and soybeans that have been passed down in our family all the way from the Edo period and has been teaching me to grow them accordingly; hoping to pass them down to someone in the family who will continue the practice through the next generation.

"It's a scary world we live in," I replied to her in the present, thinking of the unintended consequences that would come with yet another extinction. "You would think there would have been at least a town meeting about it."

"I am *sure* that there wasn't," she replied. "Although, there's been the same complaint among townsfolk for some time. A lot of the farmers in town have been complaining to the mayor for weeks that they can't afford their farms anymore with all of these subsidized varieties. I think they started to make the switch to modified seeds a couple seasons ago, and it is just taking full effect now."

"How could they do that?" I asked her.

"Well, a lot of them are getting older. I'm afraid that's just the blunt truth of it. With everyone's children and relatives now living in the city, there's no one to carry on the farm, their family businesses. Folks are getting too old to keep up with the painstaking process of farming. So they are turning to these new technologies and chemicals in an attempt to ease the burden and keep things alive."

She shook her head.

"That's awfully depressing," I replied, wondering what would happen to Auntie Mie's small garden-farm if I didn't continue to steward the family seeds going forward.

The rest of the day passed like any other, with Auntie Mie fretting over Wakayama Prefecture's ever-diminishing biodiversity, and me running back and forth between the shop and the farmhouse, helping her and puttering in the kitchen to prepare our meals. When a successful day of tansu sales from city tourists had come to a close, I made a potato and carrot curry rice for the two of us for dinner. We gulped it down gratefully.

Later, while Auntie Mie made us our nightly cup of barley tea for dessert, I sent a quick WhatsApp message to my father, letting him know I was alive and yet another day had passed safely in Japan.

Glad to hear it, kiddo. Miss ya, he fired back almost instantly. It was about seven in the morning for him back in Vermont, and I knew he had probably already been awake for hours.

Auntie Mie padded over from the kitchen and handed me a steaming cup of tea.

"How's he doing?" she asked, sitting down next to me cross-legged in the engawa corridor.

We had opened the sliding shoji doors facing the backyard and let the early summer breeze blow over our faces, cooling down our steeping tea.

"Oh, he's okay," I replied, testing a sip and resisting the urge to yank my head back when the liquid burned my tongue. "I'm sure he misses me by now. I worry about him getting lonely sometimes," I said quietly, looking out into the terraced rice fields, now illuminated with the soft glow of fireflies. The breeze rustled reed grasses in the garden, and in the distance, I could hear frogs in the fields' mud.

Auntie Mie cupped her tea in both hands thoughtfully before replying, "I'm sure he gets lonely. Any father would when their grown daughter finally goes off into the world. But he's a grown man too, you know. He'll be okay."

"He has friends in town…" I said out loud, trying to soothe my anxiety and, if I'm being honest, my guilt. "It's just, there's no family there for him. Parents have each other when their children leave. Mom isn't there to keep him company."

I could feel Auntie Mie glance at me from over the rim of her ceramic cup, but I kept my eyes focused on the darkness beyond, afraid I'd start to tear up if I made eye contact with her.

"Your mother would be very proud of you, you know," she said after a few moments in silence. "And she'd be more than okay with you leaving your father alone for a few months. She'd want you to have this time to reconnect. With me, with Japan, with *her*. With your ancestors."

This time, I did look at her, looking for reassurance in her eyes.

"You left Japan at a young age. Family is one of our strongest anchors in this world, but nothing calls to you like your homeland. And your home, my dear, is the Land of the Rising Sun."

***

Later that night, I lay my head down on my futon's pillow and thought about Auntie Mie's words.

"Your mother would be proud of you."

"She would want you to reconnect with your family, your ancestors."

"You, my dear, belong to the Land of the Rising Sun."

A few months before I left Vermont, I had felt the strangest call to return back to Japan. After years of being away, years of wanting to forget my life there and the pain I had felt from her loss, trying to blend into the very different, very American world where I now lived, I had the strangest dream of my mother. I dreamt she had become a part of a mountain. And I was meeting her in a cave where she kept a warm fire going. She was crying.

"Come home, Kairi," she said tearfully.

I went to hug her, to comfort her, and I myself was absorbed into the mountain. Every night after that, I dreamt of Japan.

Well, I made it, Mom, I thought, closing my eyes and letting my mind begin to drift into sleep. *Please help me find my way back to you .*

I opened the door to the apartment, performing my usual dance of shuffling to remove my shoes without allowing them to touch the living room floor. I squeezed my body into the farthest corner of the genkan entrance while contorting to create just enough space so that the door would still close behind me. "Tadaima!" I called into our two-bedroom apartment, announcing my return. It was a fairly large living space in Tokyo for a family of three.

"Okaeri, Kairi!" my mother called from the kitchen in the room adjacent, welcoming me home. Hanging my school bag on a hook on the wall, I pried off my loafers and moved to join her in the kitchen.

As I walked in, I could hear the sizzling of oil as she fried fresh vegetables in batter for tempura.

"Hi, Mom," I greeted her, plopping down in a chair at the kitchen table, watching her as she worked. She looked up as I came in, smiling so brightly, I couldn't help but return its warmth with my own.

"Kairi! I am so happy you are home, honey. I have so much to tell you," she said.

"Really?" I asked, unsure as to why I was beginning to feel a strange closing sensation in my throat while she talked.

"Really!" she replied in her usual bright, cheery voice. She turned once more to look at me in between dicing vegetables. Her eyebrows furrowed in concern. "Kairi, what is it dear? What's wrong?"

Was something wrong?

When I didn't immediately answer, she asked, "Are you worried about your father? Oh, don't be, sweetie; he is just fine. He's got me looking out for him, remember?" She smiled again, turning back to her work with the vegetables.

"Mom," I said, "I miss you."

Her expression softened as she looked at me. "Sweetie, I'm right here."

"I know, but—" I replied, not really sure why I had said it. "Mom, I think you're burning the food," I interrupted myself. The pan she was cooking in began to char.

She turned to look in the direction of my gaze.

"Oh, dear. You can miss me later," she answered. "But right now, I think you need to wake up."

I raised my eyebrows at her, suddenly confused. "What?"

"Wake up, Kairi."

I sat bolt upright as I awoke to the scream of our village's sirens cutting through the silence of the night, the smell of smoke surrounding me.

"Kairi!"

Auntie Mie flung back the *fusuma* doors separating our rooms, fully dressed with a sack of belongings in her hands. "Come on! We need to move. *Now,*" she commanded, yanking me to my feet with surprising strength for a sixty-year-old woman.

"What's happening?" I sputtered, noticing it was still pitch black outside.

"Let's go," she replied. "Nachi is on fire."

CHAPTER THREE

Mato

Morning ceremony had ended early, but my body didn't feel any lighter as I now stood in the open air training hall for the first session of the day. My sparring partner, Ryoko, stood across from me. A fellow Fire Keeper, and one of the first friends I had made when I arrived in Sosen no Tani, Ryoko had unfortunately been given the role of my target practice for the morning and was eyeing me apprehensively. Well, any other day, I would have called him my target, but I wasn't feeling myself this morning; my mind and my movements were about as slow as lead. He had no reason to be apprehensive of me today.

"Are you out on another assignment tonight?" Ryoko asked, keeping a respectable distance from me.

This morning's training was in hand-to-hand combat, and Ryoko and I were exercising our skills in a mix of karate, judo, and jujitsu. I nodded in reply as we sized one another up.

The mornings at the dojo were reserved for Fire Keepers to ground themselves and return to the fundamentals of our skills. No use of blades or flame is allowed during morning sparring sessions.

The Fire Keepers of Sosen no Tani were blessed with the ability to manipulate and wield fire. The legend goes that the Keepers were created of the original people in the village of Sosen no Tani. It was said that in the beginning times, the kami struggled to get along with the first prototypes of man and needed representatives to help show them the way. The people of Sosen no Tani were blessed at creation by Kagutsuchi, the god of fire. "Man cannot have life without fire," he had said. In order to guide man, he gave the original people the ability to guide fire. But only if they continued to train in the practice of wielding it. "Man may never master fire, so man's ancestors must always exercise caution in using it." And so, the Fire Keepers were born.

"I am," I responded to Ryoko's question.

"What are the oni up to now?" Ryoko asked. His words came out strained at the end as he struck in my direction.

I blocked his attack and jabbed him in the rib cage, once, before stepping out to his right-hand side. Seizing his arm and spinning in place, I lowered my center of gravity as I moved. Using his own weight against him, Ryoko stumbled off balance, falling to the ground before I answered.

"Nothing new I guess," I replied, gripping his forearm as I helped pull him to his feet. "Murder. Destruction."

He grunted like an old man, but he was only a few years older than me at twenty-five.

"You feeling alright?" he asked me. "Usually you hit a lot harder and faster than that."

I just shrugged and replied, "Didn't sleep much."

The two of us returned to our original sparring positions.

"I heard that, this time, they killed off yet another kind of ancient rice variety with a poisoned version they created. Apparently, almost instantly, half of our paddies here in Sosen no Tani dried up or were plagued with disease. So the Keepers are going to take away that poisoned new rice of theirs and find the oni who spread it," Ryoko speculated.

I nodded, confirming that my assignment later was indeed for this purpose. "Don't you get sent on these assignments too?" I asked him.

"Oh I get sent on assignment, but none as *high level* as you, super samurai," he mocked me, swinging his leg in a roundhouse kick aimed at my jaw.

I might be slow today, but I blocked his strike easily. "Don't worry. Maybe one day you'll catch up," I replied, my fist making contact with his kidneys.

CHAPTER FOUR

Mato

I spent the afternoon between training sessions like any other, helping Misao-dono in the fields. After a morning of sparring, my body had almost begun to move at full capacity again, but I found my mind was still out of it. The lingering feeling of dread that comes with a nightmare had made a home in my bones for the day, and I had a feeling I wouldn't be shaking it anytime soon. My mind's eye kept replaying the image of a three-legged crow morphing into a young woman, and I couldn't shake the image of that woman's face from my mind.

"Hey, Mato," Misao-dono said, catching my attention from where she sat on her porch. Motioning to a large stack of firewood that was piled at the edge of her farmhouse, she asked, "Haul this back to the shrine, would you?"

Misao-dono was one of Sosen no Tani's village elders and basically the community's collective mother. She was the first real relationship I formed in town outside of the Fire Keepers when I arrived ten years ago, after Elder Tadaaki, the head of the Fire Keepers found me. During my first year here, I used to find myself searching for a nearby river or lake in my free time, to remind me of home, but found myself wandering into the vegetable and rice fields instead. The day I first met her, the fields were empty except for one old woman, her small frame bent over as she plunged new rice seedlings into the soft mud. I watched her in silence momentarily, my first time ever seeing rice planted on land, but she noticed me when my stomach rumbled rather loudly. She put me to work in an instant and took me under her wing, as she has for every other child in Sosen no Tani. She has been like a second mother to me ever since. Every afternoon, during the Keepers' break between morning and afternoon training, she has had a slurry of tasks awaiting me, but I always find my feet traveling down the familiar path to her fields.

Today, I helped her load a cart full of chopped wood to haul to the shrine in preparation for the upcoming Fire Festival later this month. "Wow, the village is really going all out this year isn't it?" I remarked as I deposited a load of firewood into the cart. "It's the home of the Fire Keepers; you would think this amount of wood would be unnecessary."

"There's no fire like a true bonfire," she mused, "sages or not."

"Fair enough," I replied, hoisting another stack into the back of the cart.

"Shosho is just now upon us, but it is important that this midsummer season we begin the Fire Festival without fail. You are witness to the ways the oni have taken control of the human folk. You see how another bit of our world disappears and goes missing because of them. The Fire Festival is especially important this year because it rejuvenates and re-invigorates the kami during a time when our crops are most susceptible to disease and drought. The demons in the human world have made this even worse, and so we must keep our culture alive more than ever. We must make this year's fire bigger than ever."

Our people disappear with it. A flash of my mother's dead face, lying pale and lifeless on her futon as it had appeared in my dream, my father beside her, flickered behind my eyes.

"You're not wrong," I said softly.

She eyed me thoughtfully, reading my face.

"Another assignment tonight?" she guessed.

"Yes," I replied, moving to assemble another stack of firewood to carry.

"What is it this time?" she asked.

"I'm sure you've heard. The humans, er, oni, have erased

yet another ancient variety of Inari-sama's rice. I'm sure they're close to falling ill by now," I said.

"What will they have you do?"

"Burn them down, of course. We—well, really I—am to burn the fields infected with the poisoned, unnatural variety. The rest of the Keepers are to find information on the ones responsible and slaughter whatever demons are drawn out by the flames," I answered.

"I see," she said thoughtfully, sucking the air between her teeth. Misao-dono was one of the most vocal in our community, having lived longer than most of us and was a young girl when the humans abandoned the natural ways. Her opinion had heavy weight in the village. Recently, she had been in disagreement with the Keepers, arguing against our methods of flushing out the demons with fire. The two of us had debated it many times, and she was always more than ready to argue with me about the best ways of handling things; today, she remained quiet.

While nothing in this world is entirely good nor evil, including the kami of our land, oni are particularly well known to lean heavier in the direction of death, destruction, and chaos at all costs. While we had close ties with humans for thousands of years, they, too, have a degree of darkness in them. And in the last two hundred years alone, that darkness has been fed substantially, weakening them, making them more susceptible to the influence of demons than the rest of us other beings.

Because of them, I watched my whole town and my parents waste away before my eyes with nothing I could do to help. I was the only survivor. With nothing left in the village, I was brought to the Fire Keepers in Sosen no Tani where I was initiated, where I was allowed to act on the death and destruction I had witnessed. Being a Fire Keeper meant that I would never have to sit idly by while my loved ones died in front of my eyes again.

I stayed silent as I hauled another batch of wood to the cart waiting next to Misao-dono's house. I could feel her eyes on me, but I kept my head down, not wanting to speak. Instead of the usual anger I felt at mention of the oni taking more of our own, I felt a strange sense of doubt tugging at the back of my mind, and the image of the girl's face surrounded by white light from my dream flashed again across my eyes.

"What is it Mato?" Misao-dono asked, still watching me closely. "You appear to have something on your mind." Besides Elder Tadaaki, she was perhaps the only person I shared everything with.

"It appears Yatagarasu has a message for me, but I'm not quite sure what it is," I told her finally, after some deliberation. "He came to me in a dream last night and transformed into a woman."

"Well, that ought to be a new Kabuki drama," Misao-dono joked.

I just looked at her.

"I'm sorry. Please continue," she said, clearing her voice.

Around us, farmers worked to plant rice and flood their fields. I bent low and hoisted another stack of wood in my arms before continuing.

"The dream was a nightmare of…old memories. But then, Yatagarasu arrived, showing me the face of a woman whom I have never met. And I felt at peace."

"Hmm." Misao-dono mused. She took a moment to ponder my words before speaking. "Time will tell, Mato, dear. But it looks like he may have something coming for you."

CHAPTER FIVE

Mato

We left the Fire Keepers' Temple at midnight. Donned in black with our katanas at our hips, we left the village silently, guided by nothing but torchlight. Making our way out of the village and over to the human realm, we entered the tunnels through the well one by one.

The plan was to divide and conquer, each leaving the tunnels through a different entry point. I was to go to one of the villages where the new rice had been planted, with a good half of the group sent to neighboring villages where the seed was also being spread. The plan was simple: We were to burn the fields seeded with poisonous rice, save the humans from eating it, and hopefully restore some life back into our own fields. We also suspected that, through the fire, we would flush out some of the demons behind this new wave of extinction. Killing them was a priority.

For thousands of years, humans listened to the Ancestors and kami by reading their environment. When typhoons, landslides, or fires plagued the land, the people knew their actions were creating imbalance in the spirit world and were harming their ancestors. In response, they took actions to appease us; offering food and rice for what we may have lost, holding ceremonies as signs of respect. They learned they needed to stop or change their actions, so that we all may live in coexistence.

But somewhere along the way, under the influence of the

oni, they have stopped paying attention.

We light fires in hopes that the ones who are not controlled by their own darkness can heed our warnings and maybe stop the destruction that has been snowballing for centuries. The Fire Keepers have factions of Ancestors and yokai all across the island who wield different elements than fire, such as water and earth. They have been setting these warnings with us, going on assignments as well, trying to exterminate as many demons as they can find in an effort to preserve our land and our lives. But we are still waiting for the humans to answer our call to action. At least we can kill some demons out of it.

When the time came for each of us to split off, we said nothing, silently extracting ourselves from the whole of the group, each member knowing their role. At my turn, I hoisted myself up through the lip of the well, extinguishing the ball of fire in my hand before I came into contact with the open air. When I emerged from the tunnels, I stepped into a quiet forest just outside the main town. I moved quietly and quickly through the brush, the occasional night creature taking issue with my invasion but never putting up enough protest to blow my cover. I crept silently along the edge of the village, following the mental map in my mind that the Keepers had prepared for me to find the fields.

When I found them, I waited. Settling in a nearby grouping of brush, I nestled my way in with the spiders and crouched low. Time passed and I remained still. I could feel the cool breeze on my face and smell the dampness of plants that always seemed more prominent in the nighttime. In the distance, I could hear frogs talking with one another in the rice fields. I felt an unexpected pang of guilt at the destruction I was about to do to their home. *But if we don't fight back, if we don't put a stop to this, there will be no home for any of them,* I thought.

In the distance, a shooting star streaked across the sky, breaking me from my thoughts and reigniting my resolve. It was time.

In a flash, I stepped out from my cover in the reeds.

Flicking my wrist, my katana swirled with the colors of blue, orange, and yellow, igniting to the tip in flames. With one single slash of my sword at the young rice seedlings, I set the first field ablaze. And then I ran, setting the next four terraced fields below it burning as I went, causing a chain reaction. At the end of the final field, I extinguished my sword and jumped to the roof of a nearby kura storage shed. Crouching low, ready to spring if I needed to, I relied on my black kimono to shield me from the night and took the opportunity to survey the area for what came next.

Pretty shortly after the flames had caught hold of surrounding brush and trees from the fields, I caught a dark shadow escape from the center of the field and attempt to move downhill, where I knew there was a river at the base of the valley. In an instant, I had leapt from my position on the roof and sprinted after the dark mass. Catching up to it fairly quickly, I used the height of a nearby building's roof to jump in front of it, unsheathing my katana as it hurtled to a stop in front of me.

I could see the creature was an ugly little thing, with a red body and small horns on its head. Most demons usually served a more powerful, more cunning master, and I knew it was the same for even this small fry. I would have considered asking the thing some questions, except that it would have been pointless. These types of oni were unintelligent beings, operating mainly as malevolent energy and at the wills of others. Before the thing even knew what was happening, I sliced it in two in a diagonal slash.

Villagers were beginning to awaken to the destruction, and soon the town's warning bell would sound. It was time to make my exit. I sheathed my sword and began retracing my steps, heading back uphill until I reached the head of the trail that would take me back to the tunnels. I moved quickly, the flames bending around me, leaving me unsinged. While no being of the spirit world or human world, except maybe Kagutsuchi, could tame fire, the flames do recognize those who respect it. And as a Keeper, I had been trained to build up an unusually high tolerance to its effects.

I was yards away from the trailhead when I felt the hairs on the back of my neck stand up and heat beginning to burn at the edge of my palms—a sensation that often happened when demons were near. I ducked and rolled just as a sword sliced the air where I had been standing. Drawing and igniting my sword as I got to my feet, I spun-slashed horizontally at the demon. The thing avoided my sword by mere centimeters. I locked my eyes on the demon that had sought me out.

"Where are you going, samurai?" the voice of an old man asked.

It *looked* like an old man, at least. An old farmer, frail with a hunched back, wearing a nighttime kimono and spectacles. The creature was masking itself, as oni often do, in the body of a human who had likely fallen prey to its influence and was long dead. I could smell the underlying scent of rotting flesh, and I guessed that this demon was an amanojaku; not a large-sized demon in stature, but one much more cunning than the small creature I cut down earlier. They are said to have the ability to peer into one's heart and twist it.

Amanojaku are often the source behind a human's misdeeds, tricking our weak-willed cousins if they sense that even the slightest bit of anger, sadness, you name it, has taken hold in their heart. They then manipulate the human, instigating them to carry out evil acts.

At some point in this process, the human's soul is pushed out of the body and the human dies in its fight against the amanojaku. They are wretched creatures who seek chaos and destruction, and over time, more and more humans have become weak enough to become their prey.

"It appears I am leaving too soon," I replied, keeping my eyes fixed steadily on the demon, katana raised in a defensive position. I could see the gleam of the demon's own blade extending in his right hand, reflecting the fire of mine, although it wouldn't be visible to the human eye.

"It seems as though I have you to thank for this rude wakeup," it drawled. "And the destruction of my fields. One should never disrespect their elders like this."

That was enough talking. I rolled my eyes.

These creatures always have huge egos and love to hear themselves speak. They also use words to confuse their opponent, stall, or sway their opinions to tilt the scales in their favor. It worked on many who were weak at heart.

It would never work on a Fire Keeper.

I was suspecting this was one of the old farmers who had planted the poisonous rice. Something in the human's soul probably wasn't happy with his own crops, or failing success on his farm, before he fell prey to the amanojaku and resorted to planting this insidious variety.

In a second, I had changed my stance from defensive to offensive and swung at the creature, slicing the stomach of the old man's body open. In a matter of seconds, the sacred flames from my blade incinerated the flesh of the human suit.

Out from the wound poured the red, oily form of the amanojaku. His skin was blistered, much like that of the small oni from earlier, as if it was melting off from the fire itself. Out from his snaggletoothed mouth snaked a long, pointed tongue.

It hissed at me, clearly displeased that I had wrecked its new home. Wasn't so talkative anymore, either. It sliced its now fully visible blade in my direction, but I was already moving. Dodging its attack and closing the distance between us.

We began to duel.

CHAPTER SIX

Kairi

I tried to focus my thoughts as I gathered my possessions. In a split second, I opted to grab my phone, its charger, my passport, and a photo of my parents and me that had been taken when we lived in Tokyo. Auntie Mie had two bags slung over her shoulder. "They're emergency go bags!" she told me, tossing one in my direction. "They have all the food, water, and spare clothing we will need in the week to come. In Japan, you always have an emergency bag prepared."

I nodded, thrusting the few items I'd grabbed into the open pouch of the bag she'd tossed me.

"I also made sure to grab the family's seed stock. The heirloom rice, soybeans, radishes, everything is here in my bag. This is our family's inheritance; we can't risk it dying here," she added.

A brief thought flashed across my mind that not many people in this day and age, when deciding what to grab in an emergency, would go out of their way to save the seeds from their garden.

"We have responsibility to our ancestors," she said.

In under a minute, we were out of the house and running into the street with the other villagers. The sky was a swath of gray smoke, a terrifying orange glow the size of a mountain illuminating the townscape and rice fields below. Between the sirens, our mayor's voice echoed across the village loudspeakers. "Evacuate immediately. Wildfire is spreading across Nachi.

Evacuate immediately."

We looked at Auntie Mie's car parked under the carport to the right of the house, but taking one glance down the mountain showed switchback roads backed up with traffic as far as the eye could see. It would be faster to run down the mountain.

"There's no time to evacuate!" Auntie Mie yelled above the noise.

"Where are we supposed to go?!" I shouted in return, frantically trying to remember the hazard maps I had studied before arriving in Japan in case of a moment like this.

I could feel the heat permeating the air around us, oppressive and closing us in. I was starting to imagine what it must feel like to be cooked in an oven and immediately regretted the thought. How could it have been that just hours before, Auntie Mie and I were sitting on the engawa, feeling the breeze cool our faces.

Around us, neighbors came running out of their homes. "To the river!" they shouted. Auntie Mie and I looked at each other for only a moment before taking off downhill in the direction of flowing water that ran from Nachi falls, through the base of the mountain. She could move a lot quicker than I had expected. I guess it was a lifetime of growing up on a mountainside, farming, and being nourished by homegrown food.

As we ran, the smoke grew denser and so did the heat. Although we were running downhill, I could feel my lungs begin to burn, but I kept moving forward. The closer we got to the river, the closer the fire came. Every few yards, Auntie Mie stopped at each of our neighbors' houses, banging on the doors and calling inside for anyone who had not managed to evacuate.

"We don't have time to check every house! We need to go!" I yelled to her as she pushed her way into the house of Hiroko-san, an elderly neighbor of ours who used a wheelchair.

Still wedging her way through the door, she whirled around on me with a ferocity I had yet to see from her.

"We *must* help our neighbors!" she cried back. "If we are a not a community in times like these, then *why* have one at all? *We must help each other!*"

Finally, after giving the front door one final shove with her hip, it gave way and she disappeared into the house. I grumbled a few curse words in English under my breath and ran in after her. Guilt gnawed at me; I knew the neighbor she was looking for likely could not get out of the house by herself, but survival and the desperate need to protect my family, to prevent yet another one of my loved ones from dying, had overridden my morality. *She's brave,* I thought to myself as I pushed my way in after her.

The image of my mother, lying almost lifeless in her hospital bed, squeezing my small hand while I cried and giving me the most warmth-filled smile, flooded my mind. It was not lost on me, even in this split second of a moment, how courageous the women of my mother's family were; they didn't fear death.

But I did.

When I entered the small four-room home, it was hard to see clearly. Smoke was beginning to waft through the windows and clouded the space before me. Tendrils of flame had globbed onto the back of Hiroko-san's house, licking up the walls and almost entirely consuming the kitchen. I pulled my cotton sleep shirt, which I hadn't had time to change out of, up over my mouth to mask the fumes, looking around frantically for my aunt and Hiroko-san. "Auntie Mie!" I called, not knowing where to look. Suddenly, a beam in the back right corner of the kitchen fell, succumbing to the pressure of the flames, and crashed horizontally across the stove, laying directly on top of the hose that funneled gas to the burners. That wasn't good.

The flames crackled loudly and as they spread across the house, wood and other materials popped and crumbled to the floor. Somewhere beneath the noise, I heard Auntie Mie call back, "Over here!"

The sound had come to my left. Stepping out of the genkan, I pulled open the nearest shoji door to my left to find my aunt struggling to hoist Hiroko-san out of her bed and into her wheelchair. "Kairi! Quick, help me lift her!" she called.

Hiroko-san was making small pained noises, and I couldn't tell if it was from the movement or if she was crying. I dashed across the room and looped my shoulder under Hiroko-san's arm, opposite from Auntie Mie. Together, we lifted her up out of her bed and into the wheelchair that sat directly next to it. After setting her down as gently as we could, I was finally were able to make out the soft words she was mumbling.

"Thank you. Thank you. Thank you," she said over and over again. I had to fight hard to temper the lump that rose in my throat and focus on finding a way out of the house.

"We might need to carry her out!" I called to Auntie Mie over the noise. She looked up at me and nodded in agreement. "There's too much rubble to push the wheelchair!" I thought of the gas line on the stove, engulfed in flame, knowing It was only a matter of time. "Whatever we do, we need to move quickly or else this house is going to—"

The remainder of my warning was drowned out by a deep, ear-splitting eruption that I felt through the entirety of my body. A bright light washed over the room, blotting out the image of my aunt and Hiroko-san in front of me, and it felt as though two incredibly powerful hands shoved hard against my back. My feet left the floor.

***

When I awoke, the worst headache imaginable rocked against my skull. Opening my eyes, I fought to see through a blur of smoke and tears, the smoke stinging my eyes so badly, my tear overcompensated by producing a constant stream. My lungs burned in a way that even as an asthmatic I had never experienced, and I felt as if they were going to burst into flame within my chest. I struggled to make sense of my surroundings: images of the night sky, blotted out by plumes of smoke, and the bright orange glow of flames, thirty feet tall, swirled in my vision. All I could hear was a shrill ringing in my ears. I felt a pressure against my back. Pushing myself to my feet, I watched boards of wood and various household objects, half reduced to a state of ash, tumble off of me.

When my vision finally began to clear, I realized I had been lying in the ruins of Hiroko-san's house. The gas stove must have blown. I was buried under debris. Where was Hiroko-san? Where was Auntie Mie? I called to them but could barely hear the sound of my own voice over the ringing. My throat was hoarse and dry and I nearly choked as I croaked out the words, but I kept calling. I needed to find my aunt. She had to be here somewhere. We needed to leave—*together*.

Moving out of sheer force of will and desperation, I ripped up various pieces of rubble and debris from Hiroko-san's house. Wildly searching for her, for Auntie Mie, for any sign of life. But I found nothing. Not even a body. Pausing long enough to pant and look around frantically, I shouted, "Please, someone, you have to help me! They're trapped!" But there was no one around to hear me. Just the flames, which were starting to engulf the land around me on all sides. We were starting to lose our way out.

I wasn't leaving here without Auntie Mie. We were leaving together. I resumed my search with even greater resolve, throwing aside debris, checking under every board, every block of cement, every piece of rubble. She had to be *somewhere.* But still, there was nothing. *"NO!"* I cried out, mildly hyperventilating and frustratedly kicking the remains of Hiroko-san's bedframe.

Kairi, MOVE. My mother's voice echoed through my head. *Move NOW. You are to leave NOW.*

Surely I must be lacking serious amounts of oxygen to be imagining my mother's voice. But I felt my feet slowly moving against their will, turning away from the ruins of Hiroko-san's house, turning away from my aunt, and carrying me forward.

RUN, Kairi, while you still can, she said.

No, I thought, desperation keeping me in place.

You have to, my mother's voice replied.

Pivoting on my heel, I could see an opening in the field of flames that was beginning to surround me. Confused, my feet took me there.

"But what about Auntie Mie?!" I protested out loud to myself as I ran forward, through the only path not engulfed in flames. The fire was burning so high at this point that I could not even tell what direction I was running in, if I was still headed toward the river or not.

You are not meant to join me today. Now GO, my mother's voice demanded.

I obeyed. Running on sheer adrenaline and need for survival, I let my instincts take over.

As I ran, paved road eventually gave way to forest floor. I could see herds of deer fleeing with me, small animals that were just as unlucky as I was. After some time, what could have been all but ten minutes or ten hours, I found myself at the clearing the three-legged crow had taken me to just earlier this morning. I was near Nachi Falls.

I tried to take a deep breath in and coughed harshly instead, the pain in my lungs causing me to stumble over my own feet, nearly falling to the ground. I didn't think I could run much farther. Just feet ahead of me, I could make out the lip of the well through the fog.

With the flames and smoke closing in all around me, I had one final idea. Remembering water flowing in the tunnels below, I hoped that maybe, just maybe, the thousand-year-old tunnel could keep me insulated from the flames. I had no idea if scientifically that would actually be the outcome or if I'd just be baked like pottery in an earthen kiln, but I had to try.

Gathering all of my strength, I propelled myself forward once more, leaping into the mouth of the well, not bothering to find the ladder to carry me down onto the footpaths. My body plummeted into a pool of cool, flowing water. It felt like heaven. And then everything went black.

CHAPTER SEVEN

Mato

The demon recoiled as its blade slashed the empty air where I was previously standing.

"Mouthy, but not very fast," I chided.

The creature turned to me, its red face becoming somehow even redder with anger. It struck at me overhand, but I beat aside its blade. Now defenseless, the amanojaku shot its barbed tongue out at my face. I dodged the strike and grabbed the creature's tongue with my left hand in one motion. In an instant, I pulled the demon off-balance toward me as I backhanded my blade in a reverse cut through its neck, severing its head.

I tossed the thing disgustedly to the side. I wiped my hand along my pants and the back of my blade along my forearm, the stench of demon blood soaking into the black fabric of my kimono. By now, I could fully hear alarms blaring throughout the village, and in the distance, the townspeople were running frantically from their homes. I could hear the screaming and crying. This was the part I never wanted to stay for.

It was time I get going. I tried not to think about who else wouldn't be escaping this evening as I broke out into a jog. Turning on my heel, I ran back to the tunnels, officially late to my next destination. That freaking demon took up too much of my time.

***

By the time I jumped back into the well, I was fully lacquered in the blood of the amanojaku and feeling mildly nauseous. Maybe it was the consistent scent of rotting flesh that filled my nostrils as long as this blood stayed on me, or it was the screaming in my ears of the townspeople, mostly elderly, who struggled to flee their homes from the fire. The fire that *I* set. It was getting hard to tell.

Keepers train with fire so frequently, most of us learn how to manipulate it from childhood. We've trained our lungs to withstand the smoke and our skin to tolerate the heat. As the original humans, we were born with close ties to fire. Man cannot live without flame, but we were trained to respect it, so it does not burn or hurt us in the way it does our human cousins.

The image from my dream earlier that morning started to come back to me, of human bodies lying at my feet, my katana covered in their blood. I had killed every last one of them.

I landed in the tunnels silently, careful not to disturb even a single drop of water. Instantly, images of my dream and sensations of nausea were replaced with the electric buzz of adrenaline—someone was in the tunnel. I couldn't smell any demons beyond what was coating my own clothing, but I was filled with the instinctual knowing that someone or something was close by. Once again, I froze and drew my sword in a defensive position, taking stock of my surroundings while I moved forward. Every instinct in my body was burning for me to light my sword in flame, to *see* what was around me, but I held off. Whoever was here tonight, if they weren't aware of my presence already, I sure wasn't going to be the one to tell them.

Moving back in the direction of Sosen no Tani, my sword extinguished, I walked cautiously along the tunnel's footpath. To my right, in the center of the tunnel, I could hear the water flowing as I walked farther downstream. Not more than ten meters into the tunnel, the smooth trickling noise that filled the canal was replaced with the sound of water lapping against a shoreline—or in this case, a solid object obstructing its path. In the darkness ahead of me, I could just barely make out the black mass of something lying still in the middle of the footpath, its form half in and half out of the flowing water. Finally, I decided to ignite my sword.

As flame lit up the interior of the tunnel, I braced myself for confrontation. But what I saw instead was nothing short of surprising. With legs dangling into the water, the body of a girl lay in front of me. I froze outright, momentarily shocked. I paused to smell the air. She was human.

Momentarily recovering from my shock, I moved forward, holding the light closer to her. Shock turned into disbelief before finally morphing into the kind of surprise that is not actually surprise at all. Here, lying in the middle of the tunnel to Sosen no Tani, was a human girl, the same girl Yatagarasu had shown to me in my dream the night before. And most importantly, she was alive.

CHAPTER EIGHT

Mato

"Misao-dono," I said as I entered the old woman's kominka. Sliding closed the exterior door behind me, I saw her sitting on her heels next to the sunken floor hearth in the main gathering room. She raked a ladle through a pot of soup that hung over the fire. I entered, removing my sandals.

"Ah, Mato, I'm so glad you're here." She greeted me warmly, like it was any other day. "I've got a favor to ask of you, I'm afraid. We've got a huge centipede problem recently; it's quite unsettling."

I couldn't help my face scrunching up instinctually in disgust.

"But first, I assume you have more *pressing* matters to attend to," she clucked her lips.

Was she teasing me?

"Are you coming to check on the young woman?" she asked me.

"Ah… yes," I replied, slightly thrown by the change in subject, not to mention her delivery.

Shortly after finding the girl in the tunnels the two nights before, I had carried her back to Sosen no Tani. I had sensed no demonic influence from the girl; she appeared to be completely human, not yet controlled by an oni. It was the first time I had ever seen a human who fully controlled themselves.

I decided to take her straight to Misao-dono's house upon returning to the village. It was common for her home to be filled with people from time to time: villagers who were sick or injured, travelers who were passing through. Even the occasionally well-behaved yokai would make a visit. You could always count on her house for a warm meal and soft bed if you needed it. Being a local healer and respected village leader, I was sure that if anyone could heal the girl, it would be her.

It wasn't until after I was sure she was taken care of that I mentioned the incident to the Keepers. I knew Misao-dono, a force of a woman, could handle any unwanted guests if they decided to pay the girl a visit. I still wasn't sure why I immediately hesitated to fill the Keepers in on what had happened, but I found myself feeling vaguely protective of her. Assuming it had something to do with Yatagarasu's dream, I had resolved myself to pay no mind to it—not getting attached to the idea that it was anything special.

The Keepers, I wagered, might be suspicious of the girl and her sudden appearance in the tunnels. A justifiable fear and one that I myself shared, but at the same time was feeling strangely wary of. In my dream, the three-legged crow showed her to me surrounded by bright light. I was filled with a feeling of warmth that had melted any dread, anxiousness, and despair from my body. I was convinced he was trying to tell me that whatever she was here for, whatever she symbolized, was positive. I was far from thinking humans were good, but I felt this one was here for some sort of good reason. And we needed her alive and conscious to find out what that was. And how she got in. There was no better person to make that happen than Misao-dono.

"Is she awake?" I asked Misao-dono.

"Still resting from the other night, though she appears to be alright. Seems to have inhaled a lot of smoke. Likely passed out from a lack of oxygen. It also looks like she may have suffered a head injury, too. It's a good thing you found the poor thing when you did; she easily could have drowned in the well or gotten frostbite. Not to mention what could have happened if we let that head injury sit," she said.

"What did you give her? To treat the injuries?" I asked her.

"Oh you know," she winked at me, in classic Misao-dono fashion. "One of my signature tinctures of mountain herbs that I used to cook up for you Keeper boys when you were young —helps soothe the lungs from smoke damage. When you kids were training and weren't quite used to the exposure yet, I used to bring this to the Elders to give to you with your meals. Helped build your tolerance and stamina," she said. "And for the head injury, not much to be done about that but wait and see. She didn't appear to have any extensive damage. The human brain is a fragile thing that must heal itself on its own. I'm sure some fresh air from the mountains of Sosen no Tani will be medicine enough."

She paused thoughtfully, ladling a spoonful of stew into a ceramic bowl. "She will need to rest for a good while. She should be waking up soon and will have the mother of all headaches to contend with when she does, I'm sure. I imagine she'll be quite hungry too," Misao-dono continued, handing me a tray of food.

Mountain vegetable and wild boar stew simmered in the ceramic bowl, and a fire-roasted trout sat next to it, still crackling from the heat. Small bowls of pickle surrounded the meal, with a freshly urushi-laquered bowl holding a steaming mound of rice. A mug of dark-colored oolong tea steeped in the top right-hand corner, a pair of chopsticks balanced neatly along the front edge of the tray.

"Could you please bring this to the young lady resting down the hall?" she asked me.

I nodded obediently.

"Thank you, Mato, dear. Now please go run that to her before it gets cold. Second room on the left!"

Bowing my head, I carried the tray of food down the hall. When I slid open the shoji door to the room Misao-dono had noted, I saw the young woman lying between the comforters of a futon on the tatami floor. She was still asleep as I slid the door shut behind me, and she didn't stir at my arrival. Lowering myself to my knees silently, I carefully placed the tray of food on the floor between the futon and me. After a moment of internal debate, my curiosity got the better of me, and I stole the opportunity to take a closer look at her.

I could see Misao-dono had bandaged a gash above her left eyebrow; a clean white cloth rested below the bangs on her forehead. *What was this girl doing in the well? And where did she come from?* I could tell she was around my age or maybe slightly younger, probably about eighteen or nineteen. She looked *different* than the women of what I understood to be modern day Japan, but she was most definitely human. Long strands of sable-colored hair fanned across her pillow, closer to brown in color than the ink-black that most Japanese were known for. Her skin was noticeably lighter than mine, pale and smooth like undisturbed snow when it has just fallen, with eyes shaped like almonds and petite, rose-colored lips. Her nose was thin and sharp, considerably taller than that of most Japanese, reminding me of Yatagarasu's beak as he had transformed in my dream. She was... distinctive looking. I wasn't sure if she would be considered beautiful by society's standards, but there was something uniquely appealing about her and I felt my face flush with heat.

I had never really *seen* a true human before, one subject to their own free will and not controlled by a demon. I felt the image of my parents' emaciated bodies linger in the back of my mind, but I could not imagine this girl being guilty of the same crimes the rest of the humans were. I could not imagine her turning a blind eye to such damage and destruction. I thought of the warmth in her eyes as she had grabbed my hands in the dream. Could it be possible that she wasn't guilty of those things?

Just as I started to realize that I might have been staring for too long, the girl began to stir slightly, slowly blinking her eyes open to meet mine. I felt the flush in my face deepen as her dark eyes fixed on mine, but I held her gaze. I felt the same familiar sense of warmth that had washed over me in my dream flood my body through my limbs. I tried to push it away.

"You're awake. Please don't strain yourself, but there's

food here for you when you're ready. I think it's mountain vegetable soup. I'll get Misao-dono," I found myself saying to her, feeling frustrated by how flustered I was feeling, trying hard not to show it.

As I moved to stand, I looked over at her again briefly. Her eyes looked a little unfocused and she looked groggy. She stared at me softly for a second before scrunching her face in pain and moving a hand to grab the back of her head. She groaned.

I removed myself from the room to find Misao-dono still huddled over the hearth.

"Misao-dono, your guest is awake. She seems to be in a good amount of pain."

"Oh! Thank you, Mato. I'll go check on her," she said, standing and wiping her hands off on her kimono. "Please go find Hako out back; he'll point you to where the centipedes are."

I felt an involuntary chill run down my spine at the mention of the centipedes, which I had entirely forgotten about until now, but I pushed it aside, nodding obediently. Just as I was about to slide the door of the engawa open to meet Hako in the yard, I paused for a moment in the doorframe, turning back inside the house once more.

"I'm sorry if this is rude to ask, Misao-dono, but how *do* you think a human wound up in that well?" I tried to ask as her as casually as possible.

"Now that indeed, my boy, is the question," was all she said before setting off down the hallway and disappearing into the guest room.

CHAPTER NINE

Kairi

Opening my eyes felt like peeling apart superglue. Next to me, I heard the gentle sounds of dishes clinking together. Through my bleary vision, I could make out the figure of a young man placing a wooden tray onto the floor. It took several moments before his face came into focus, and I realized that he was staring at me.

A set of dark, cool eyes looked at me curiously. When I stared back at him, I expected him to look away, embarrassed, like any other Japanese man would. But he held my gaze calmly, with a soft expression that stirred something in my chest briefly. Through my bleary vision, I noticed a few things instantaneously. His skin was darker than mine, a healthy tan that accentuated the curve of his high cheekbones and sharp angles of his jawlines. A thick mop of black hair sat on his head, half tied into a bun, the rest barely brushing the tops of his shoulders. He was shockingly attractive, much more than any J-Pop star or actor I had ever seen, and he couldn't have been older than twenty.

"You're awake. Please don't strain yourself, but there's food here for you when you're ready. I think it's mountain vegetable soup. I'll get Misao-dono." The young man spoke softly, looking away from me.

The distraction of this beautiful stranger was a welcome one until the pain returned to my head. I had opened my mouth to respond when a sharp, throbbing stab pierced the back of my head so suddenly, it took my breath away. I groaned and grasped at the back of my skull reflexively. I heard him get up and slide the door shut behind him. Where was I? What had happened? Was I at a neighbor's house? I didn't know we had any neighbors who looked like *that*…

Moments later, I heard it open again, and I opened my eyes between the throbbing long enough to see an older woman enter the room.

"Oh, you're finally awake!" the old woman said warmly, coming to my side. She was one of the more strapping women I had seen in Japan, carrying more weight than most people I had met, and looked to be about in her seventies. She wore an old-fashioned cotton kimono with her grayish-white hair pinned up on the top of her head by a pair of chopsticks. The woman had a homey presence about her; like she could have been my grandmother, and I felt myself relaxing almost prematurely, though I had no idea who she was.

"How's your head, dear? It seems like you've been through quite a bit."

Looking at the room around her, I could see I was lying on a futon on tatami floors in what looked to be an old Japanese farmhouse. The walls were made of clay and interspersed with wooden beams. The room was dressed with sparse antiques, with an old scroll and ikebana flower arrangement hanging in a tokonoma alcove in the corner. On either side of me, pale light filtered through white-papered shoji doors, dimly illuminating the room. Above me, I could see impressive, smoke-stained beams give way to a thatched roof. Thatched roof? I had no idea any houses with thatched roofing still existed in Nachi.

"Let's get some light into this dingy room," the woman said cheerfully and flung back a set of doors on the opposite side of the room. The pale shoji opened to reveal a beautiful rural landscape just beyond the house's engawa, with terraced rice fields leading across a valley and up the side of the jagged mountains in the distance. The fields were dotted with numerous old farmhouses, all with thatched roofs like the one above me. Seriously. Where was I?

I opened my mouth again to ask the woman this very question, but when I started to speak, my throat felt like sandpaper and a horrible burning sensation threatened to consume my lungs. I let out a horrific croaking sound and devolved into a fit of coughing. The old woman swooped around to the side of my futon and held a small mug of tea up to my lips, encouraging me to "Drink, drink," in soft, soothing tones. "Don't try to speak, dear. Your lungs have been put through the wringer."

I gulped down more of the tea gratefully, relieved to feel the soothing hot liquid coat my throat, until what she said occurred to me. I was put through the wringer?

Nachi was on fire.

The memory came flooding back to me: being woken up in the middle of the night, fleeing our home, waking up in the rubble after Hiroko-san's house exploded, running through the burning village, and jumping into that ancient well after being separated from Auntie Mie. Auntie Mie!

Where was she? Was she alive, was she safe? Did someone find her? And how did I survive? How did I get out of the well? What happened to Nachi? What happened to the fire?

The old woman could see all of these questions on my face and held up her hand knowingly. "Don't worry, dear. I'll tell you where you are and what you need to know. Save that voice of yours for after. My name is Misao Minamoto, village Elder and local healer. You can call me Misao. After our boy, Mato, found you in the well, he brought you back with us here... to our village. Sosen no Tani."

I sat in shock for several moments with Misao's words hanging in the air. *But Sosen no Tani is the land of the ancestors. It's a legend, not a real place,* I wanted to say. What I got out instead was, "Land... of... ancestors..." in an awful-sounding rasp. But Misao perked right up.

"Yes! That's right! I can't believe you remember us! Barely

any humans do nowadays," she said. Pure joy and surprise were written on her features. She looked like she was about to go on a tangent before glancing again at my face. She cleared her throat. "Right, yes. You are in Sosen no Tani. The land of the Ancestors."

Am I— "Dead?" I rasped again.

"Oh goodness, no, my child. You are not dead. And neither are we. You looked close to it when Mato brought you here, though." She looked at my face again and shook her head, seating herself next to me on the futon. "I'm sorry; I'm confusing you. It's just… something as peculiar as this hasn't happened in this village in centuries. You'll have to forgive us; we're all a little shaken up. And I know you are as well. Let me start over."

***

I tried keep my thoughts together as Misao explained what had happened. She told me that the town of Nachi, in the human realm, had caught fire, and Mato, the young man who had brought me food when I awoke, had found me unconscious in the well that the three-legged crow had led me to the morning before. I had suffered from excessive exposure to smoke and had hit my head at some point—likely why my head hurt beyond any hangover I had ever experienced in my high-school rebellion days. I had been asleep for two full days. She said that the well I had found was one of many that connect Sosen no Tani to the human realm.

The woman, Misao-dono—as I remembered was the respectful way the boy had addressed her—then went on to tell me about Sosen no Tani. It turned out that Auntie Mie's legend had been largely true; it was, in fact, a real place, and yes, we were in the spirit realm, but no, none of us were dead. She made it clear to me that this was not the Afterlife, the place we really go to when we die. I would not see my mother here.

My human ancestors in Japan dug the well systems thousands of years ago and used them in collaboration with the Ancestors of Sosen no Tani. But, as the spirits and the humans became more separated from one another, Misao-dono said the spiritual beings all went into hiding through the wells, for reasons she didn't explain, only using them as an access point between our world and theirs.

When she finished her explanation, she sat back on her heels and sighed, waiting for my response. I, on the other hand, still wasn't convinced that I wasn't dead. So much had happened in a mere forty-eight hours. I found myself clutching the back of my head, the intense throbbing I felt when I first awoke coming back to me now as my emotions swirled.

"My girl, I know this is a lot to take in, but I have to ask... how did you get in that well?"

"I ran... to the well..." I started, interrupting myself with a fit of coughing.

"Easy," she said, "You don't have to tell me now; we can talk more when you're—"

" ..basically on instinct—" I cut her off, clearing my throat. "I knew there was water in the well and I was about to be ... burned alive. I was looking for my aunt..." I trailed off.

Remembering the urgency I had felt before the shock of Misao-dono's story hit me, I sat up so fast, my vision blurred at the edges, and I nearly passed out for the second time. Panicking, I looked at Misao-dono like she was supposed to know exactly what I was thinking. She stared back at me, momentarily bewildered.

"My aunt and I...got separated," I started again, fighting back another fit of coughing from the scratching in my throat. "I looked for her... I looked and I looked and I couldn't *find* her," I said, tears threatening to burn my eyes. "I didn't want to leave her. I wasn't going to leave, but I heard a voice that told me to *move.*"

The image of my aunt helping Hiroko-san before being engulfed in the bright white light of the explosion imbedded itself in my brain. Did she make it out?

"Where's my aunt? Do you know what happened to her?" I asked desperately, grabbing hold of Misao-dono's arm.

She placed her free hand on top of mine gently, but firmly, and looked me in the eyes when she said, "I'm sorry, child, but I'm afraid I don't know who you're speaking of. There's no one else here but you. I'm afraid I don't know what happened to your aunt."

She can't be dead.

"I-I need to find her," I said, my voice shaking. "I need to make sure she's okay; I need to go find her!" I said, forcing myself to my feet.

The second my legs straightened, they almost instantly buckled beneath me, and I felt myself careening to the ground. Misao-dono caught me—she was as sturdy as she looked—and gently laid me back on the futon.

"I can't ... lose another family member," I pleaded to her desperately. She looked back at me with sympathy and a touch of concern in her eyes. "I need to go home," I told her, the tears I had been holding back starting to spill from my eyes.

"I know, dear. You've been through so much," she replied in soothing tones. "But you're not going anywhere until you can stand. It's important that you rest. I'm sure your aunt would want you to focus on regaining your strength."

As much as I had wanted to hear it, I respected her for not trying to tell me my aunt was likely okay.

"But I'm afraid, child," she continued, "we don't quite know how to get you home. You weren't supposed to have come here in the first place."

"What do you mean?" I asked.

"For centuries, after we became separate from the humans, plenty have wandered into the well, but none were able to cross over to our side. Somehow, you were able to find your way here."

"Jumping into the well was literally my last-ditch attempt to survive, and I was on the verge of passing out," I told her. "I didn't even think I was going to make it. I had no *idea* it was some sort of... portal."

"How did you become separated from your aunt?" Misao-

61

dono asked me.

"We were trying to evacuate the village," I responded, feeling the lump rise again in my throat. "She was trying to help our elderly neighbor evacuate when the house we were in blew up," I continued. "I stayed behind and searched for her in the rubble after being knocked out for what could have been minutes, hours, I don't know. But I couldn't find her. And I didn't want to leave her behind, but a voice in my head started telling me to move. And before I knew what I was doing, I found myself jumping into the well. It all goes black after that," I told her.

Misao-dono took in my story thoughtfully before saying, "Well, I would expect nothing less from a brave woman."

"What?" I asked.

"Your aunt," she said. "I just mean that she sounds brave."

"She is," I said. "She was the one who told me about this place—Sosen no Tani—before that crow led me to the well anyway," I said out loud, partially to myself.

Misao-dono's gaze had been fixed on the floor pensively, but she jerked her head up abruptly at my words.

"You said a crow led you to the well?"

"Uhm, yeah. It had three legs and it appeared out of nowhere and took me to the well the morning before the fire," I said, realizing that I might have said too much to a stranger who claimed to live within a mythical world filled with gods, demons, and other beings. My father would be so ashamed of me; where were my survival instincts?!

My father.

The anxious feeling in my stomach nearly doubled. He must be so worried about me; I'm sure the fire had made at least prefectural news by now. He hadn't heard from me in at least forty-eight hours. I couldn't bear the thought of him thinking he had lost the rest of his family.

I needed to get back to Nachi.

I turned back to Misao-dono frantically, about to ask her if I had been carrying anything when I was found, and almost missed the expression on her face.

"Yatagarasu," she mumbled under her breath in recognition.

"Who?" I asked her.

"Oh nothing, dear."

I was too distracted to press her further. "Was I carrying anything with me when that guy—uh, Mato—found me? Like my phone?"

"Your what?" she asked me.

"Phone? Like a cell phone? Do you know what cell phones are in the spirit realm?" I asked her.

She shook her head. "My girl, I have no idea what you are talking about. But we did find whatever this is," she said, digging within her *obi*, the belt that held her kimono in place, and holding out my smartphone to me. "I've never *seen* anything like this before. Is this, perhaps, what you call a *phone*?"

"Yes! Thank you!" I said, snatching it out of her hand.

I waited for it to turn on, but after several attempts, the screen remained black. I guess this made sense, considering it had been buried in rubble with me at one point, drowned in water for who knows how long, and then supposedly was now in another dimension entirely. I guess, with no way to reach back home, I would stay here for the time being—until I could walk, at least. But as soon as I was rested, I would find some way back through the well I came in from and find Auntie Mie.

Misao-dono stared at the screen with me expectantly.

"What does this thing you call a phone do?" Misao-dono asked as I gave up with a sigh and set it beside me on the tatami mat. I would see if there was a bowl of rice I could throw it in later.

"It lets me contact anyone, anywhere in the world, at any time, but it looks like I may have broken it," I replied.

Her eyes widened. "What magic! The humans can *do* that now?" she asked.

I nodded.

"You wouldn't happen to have a bowl of rice I could put it in, do you?" I asked her.

Staring at me, now truly perplexed, she asked, "What would that do?"

"It might help me fix it," I mumbled, clutching the back of my head once more in pain.

"That can't be good," I heard her mutter under her breath. I meant to ask her about the rest of my belongings, and the survival pack Auntie Mie had thrown me, but suddenly my eyelids were feeling heavy and I felt myself leaning back into the futon's pillow.

"It's time for you to rest," she said, helping me to lay back down in my futon. "And maybe if you are feeling up to it this afternoon, I can show you around town."

"Sure," I mumbled, all of a sudden feeling very sleepy.

"My girl, I don't think I've gotten your name," Misao-dono said.

"It's Kairi," I replied before shutting my eyes. "My name is Kairi."

CHAPTER TEN

Mato

I left Misao-dono's house after exterminating a particularly revolting nest of centipedes from the back corner of her washroom, and made my way to the Fire Temple. There had been at least thirty of the creepy beasts wedged into a corner near the house's latrine. I couldn't even begin to imagine stumbling into them in the middle of the night.

I had seen some pretty disgusting things as a Fire Keeper—hunting and exterminating demons often led to a lot of nightmarish sights of gore and ichor when we naturally completed the exterminating part. But as for mukade, the name of this particularly nasty breed of centipede, I would definitely be feeling vulnerable the next time I went to use the bathroom.

It had been a weird forty-eight hours. As far as I was aware, the last time a human had entered the realm of Sosen no Tani was well before my time, and things were tense around the village now, to say the least. The Elders had called an emergency meeting this evening amongst the Fire Keepers and village leaders regarding the arrival of the girl. Elder Tadaaki had made it a point to call me back to the Temple early, requiring I sit in on the Council of Elders, a prior meeting of Fire Keeper leadership before they spoke with the rest of the community.

I didn't know why, but I'd had an uneasy feeling in my stomach since I had arrived back at the Temple, after leaving the human girl at Misao-dono's house. When I told Elder Tadaaki what had happened, and about my message from Yatagarasu, his brow had furrowed in concern. I had gone to the convening room to report back in, as was required upon returning from a mission, and pulled him aside, away from the ears of the more volatile Elders. He knew as well as I did that the Keepers would be highly suspicious of the girl, entering our village while we were out on an operation, something that hadn't been done by a human in hundreds of years. I knew they would want to keep her here, skeptical of what information she could bring back to the human realm. I didn't blame them for mistrusting her—I myself didn't trust her—but, on the other hand, I was also grappling with the strangest instinct to keep her safe. A human, of all creatures, whom I had never met.

Elder Tadaaki had summoned the Council in private regarding the news of the human's arrival. The Keepers had agreed to leave her in Misao-dono's care for the time being, with the intention of talking to her as soon as she was awake. Now that the girl had woken up, the Council would want to meet her.

Misao-dono's house was located down in the valley along the river. It was an uphill climb for me as I made my way back through the village, up switchback roads, to the Fire Temple and Yatagarasu's shrine, which sat on the side of the mountain. As I climbed the stone steps, I bowed before crossing through the torii gate to the shrine first. In the courtyard, older, more experienced Keepers sparred in pairs of two, the gravel crunching beneath their bamboo sandals, the sound of grunts and the bite of metal echoing out over the mountain as katana swords clashed together. I dodged blasts of fire as I made my way to the Temple's entrance at the other side of the courtyard.

Removing my sandals at the entrance to the Temple, I padded in split-toed tabi socks down the long wooden corridors. Crossing the veranda from the main hall, where younger Keepers tumbled through judo drills on tatami mats, to the west wing, where the Keepers practiced their spiritual studies, my scenery changed from one of war to one of solitude. As I walked through the familiar maze of the Temple, I became keenly aware of the babbling brook that flowed beneath the open-air corridors, leading to a small koi pond and interior garden. The scene reminded me of the floating docks back home in Lake Hakone, calming the mix of emotions I was feeling in anticipation of the night's discussion.

I knocked softly outside the shoji doors of Elder Tadaaki's living quarters. Sliding them open softly after hearing his grunt of approval, I bowed respectfully upon entering the room. Turning to slide the door closed behind me, I found Elder Tadaaki sitting on his heels, studying a scroll thoughtfully while sipping a cup of green tea.

"Mato," he greeted me.

"Yes, Tadaaki Sensei," I responded.

He was a short but powerful man, with a leanly muscled frame and skin that had just barely started to show his age. His hair, whatever remained of it, had grayed considerably, the top of his head mostly bald now. Elder Tadaaki always wore a calm, collected expression. For as long as I could remember of him, it been hard to figure out what he was truly thinking. Nothing ever seemed to faze him. But I had come to take well educated guesses over time, as I had gotten to know my master better.

"How is the human?" he asked, not bothering to lift his eyes from the scroll.

"Alive, sir," I responded. Although Elder Tadaaki was my master, he was like a second father to me, but Fire Keeper code of respect prevented me from addressing him informally.

"Mm," he nodded. "And how is the Fire Keeper?" he asked, meaning me.

"Fine, sir," I answered unconvincingly, momentarily thrown by his question.

"I see," he replied, sounding as though he knew better.

"The human, uh, girl is awake."

At that, he lifted his head to look at my face.

"What is it?" I asked him.

"Nothing. Just that this will likely be a much shorter meeting than we thought. Come," he said, rising to his feet without ever putting down the scroll or the cup of tea. Fire

Keepers had immense kinesthetic control no matter what their age, and Elder Tadaaki was well past sixty. "We have a situation to handle."

Placing his tea on a low standing table, he kept the scroll in his hand as he pushed open the shoji door, not bothering to see if I'd follow. I did, naturally, trailing him down the corridor on his left side flank. We were in the section of the Temple where space was reserved for Fire Keepers to practice their spiritual studies in Buddhism, Shintoism, and ethics. Among all of the numerous, massive rooms in the Temple, all sparsely decorated and lined with tatami mats, there was a library filled with books, and numerous gardens for contemplation. While the west wing of the temple was filled with rooms for sparring, weaponry, and martial arts training, the east end was all about Zen, where spiritual ceremony and rituals were held. The east end even connected to the main hall, where the statue of Buddha was enshrined and included a raised pathway to Yatagarasu's shrine as well.

Elder Tadaaki slowed his pace when we reached the exterior door to the Elders' convening room, glancing at me once over his shoulder before pushing it open. I steeled myself for the debate ahead. A group of twelve masters sat in seiza position, seated on their heels, on the tatami mat floor. They sat in two rows of six, facing one another, and were made up of an equal number of men and women, all dressed in a mix of black and vermillion robes.

"Tadaaki-san, Mato-kun, so nice of you to join us," Elder Yamashita said while we bowed before entering the room. He was a man who would have looked to be in his eighties if I hadn't known that he was much older. He had embodied the definition of 'sweet ojiichan' or grandfather, for as long as I could remember.

"Yes, so nice of you to arrive, albeit *late*," Elder Hayashi said in a clipped tone. He, on the other hand, was not nearly as old as Elder Yamashita, and not nearly as kind. He had chosen the path of the spiritual scholars amongst the Keepers but was a complete cynic.

Elder Tadaaki didn't even blink, taking command of the room as he strode past him to sit next to Elder Ryu, the head of the Keepers' spiritual sect, at the Council's head.

"My esteemed brethren, so lovely of you to invite us here. Now, we have limited time before our convening with the village elders, so I suggest we get started right away," Elder Tadaaki said.

His failure to rise to the bait caused an infuriated twitch at the corner of Elder Hayashi's mouth. I smiled to myself as I made my way to sit in the back of the room, as was my place as the youngest member in attendance. Not once in my ten years of life at Sosen no Tani had I ever seen Elder Tadaaki lose his composure. He was the type to not be shaken easily.

I remembered the day he found me, wandering solemnly into what was left of my childhood home, gazing out at the desolate scene with his same, impassively calm face. He found me holding a vigil for my family and neighbors who had died, sending them off onto the lake in wooden boats after lighting the boats aflame. I had learned a fun trick when I about eight years old, where I could create a spark from thin air by snapping my fingers; I was the only one in my town who could do it. I remember creating that spark to light the boats then. His footsteps were silent on the creaking docks and I remember looking up from my work, surprised, to see him approaching. When our eyes met, he announced, "You have a gift with flame."

"Excuse me?" I had asked. "Can I help you?"

"What are you doing?" he asked me calmly, studying the scene before him.

"Putting my family... and my village to rest," I replied numbly.

"What happened here?" He surveyed the area.

"Humans," I answered. "They polluted the lake in their world. One by one, everyone started getting sick. And the fish started dying. We had nothing left to eat. Before I knew it, most people were gone. All except me."

"And why is that?" Elder Tadaaki asked.

"I don't know," I answered, tears welling up in my eyes.

"I think I might," Elder Tadaaki had responded, but I had ignored him at the time, losing myself to emotion.

"But I'll never forgive them. Those humans took my *home* from me. They took my *family.* I couldn't save them. *I did nothing,*" I cried, burying my face in my hands, the flames extinguishing.

"Come with me, child," Elder Tadaaki had replied evenly, taking my hands from my face and placing them in his own. "And I will teach you how to do something about the demons who call themselves humans."

"Mato-kun," Elder Tadaaki called to me now as I was taking my seat, snapping me from the memory. "Up here." He motioned to the space next to him.

Without so much as raising an eyebrow, I moved to join him.

"You're our special guest today, after all," he clarified, a sarcastic smirk on his face.

"Now let's get started," Elder Saito said. She was a short and serious woman who never seemed to show any emotion. She sat in the middle of the room in her vermillion robes; her role was often to play mediator during the Council.

This wasn't my first time in attendance at a Council of Elders. Usually, junior Keepers were not permitted entry, as the meeting was only for the leading masters, the most experienced in rank and oldest in years to discuss the high-level, serious matters of the Fire Keepers. I was invited to my first Council of Elders when I was a child, at ten, having just arrived after Elder Tadaaki brought me back to Sosen no Tani with him. Since then, I had been invited back to one more meeting regarding my unusual progress as a Keeper just two years after my initiation. The Elders had discussed crafting a more advanced training program for me.

And here I sat, a third time at the Council, because of the discovery of this girl. This was probably some sort of record for someone of my position.

"Do you have news of the human?" An Elder in the back of the room asked me.

I felt all eyes in the room turn to look at me. I looked to Elder Tadaaki and he nodded his approval.

"I visited Misao-dono's today," I replied, "where the human is being housed. The girl is still alive. And she woke up during my visit."

I felt the room collectively take a bated breath.

"Then we must interrogate her at once!" Elder Hayashi demanded.

"Mato-kun," Elder Aoki interrupted, holding her hand up to silence Elder Hayashi. She was fairly young for an Elder, looking to be in her fifties in human years. She wore vermillion robes and seemed to be more levelheaded and forgiving than some of the older Elders in the room. Elder Hayashi let out a huff of breath.

"Can you describe the girl as you found her two eves ago?"

"Yes, ma'am," I replied. "I had completed my mission of setting fire to the infected rice fields in the human village and had just re-entered the well to return. I sensed that another being was in the well when I entered, but I didn't light my sword until I was right next to it; I wanted to keep an element of surprise in the case that I would need to defend myself. When I lit my sword, I saw the girl lying halfway out of the flowing water, with her torso and head on the footpath. She was unconscious, but I sensed no demonic aura or influence from her. She was entirely pure, a human who still controlled herself. And she was bleeding from shallow wounds on her arms and legs. I lifted her over my shoulder and carried her back to Sosen no Tani, to Misao-dono's."

"And why did you bring her to Misao-dono's instead of straight to the Council?" Elder Hayashi eyed me.

"She was injured. And rather than let her die, I thought any information we could get from her on how she found this place would be most useful to the Keepers. Misao-dono was the best resource to get her to a state where she could speak again. A human has not crossed into the spirit world in hundreds of years, as is my understanding. I figured we couldn't learn how that happened if she were dead. Erm, sir," I replied matter-of-factly.

"And how likely is it, do you believe, this girl to be a spy for the demons? Or a harm to our village?" Elder Yamashita spoke up.

"I agree that the timing of her arrival is to be considered," Elder Tadaaki spoke before me. "But I believe it is highly unlikely. Mato, share with them what you shared with me."

I looked at him briefly before continuing.

"The night before the girl appeared in the well, before the Keepers went out on assignment to stop the spread of infected rice, I had a dream. In the dream, I was a child again. And I was reliving some of my life's worst memories. I watched my parents die for a second time before finding myself in a burning field covered in ash with the bodies of humans at my feet. I remember the metallic scent of blood was strong and even in a dream, I felt like I was going to be sick. Suddenly, a three-legged crow flew across the sky above me and the scene was covered in warm, white light. The crow morphed into the image of a girl who walked toward me and took my feeling of sickness away. The girl looked exactly like the human I found later that next night in the well."

The room filled with murmurs.

Before anyone had the chance to speak up, Elder Tadaaki continued, "It was no coincidence that Mato saw a three-legged crow that turned into the image of a human girl who somehow shows up in town just hours later. Yatagarasu—and therefore Amaterasu-sama—has sent Mato, has sent us, a message. And I believe this girl is meant to help us deliver it."

An Elder in the back of the room chimed in. "The boy said at the beginning of the dream, he felt pain and suffering, reliving his worst memories. We know the oni thrive off of pain and anguish and use it to manipulate the will of their prey. How do we know this wasn't just a demon influencing Mato-kun, trying to get him to accept the human as bait?"

"Come on now, Elder Shimizu. Even for you, that feels a bit far-fetched. When have we ever heard of a demon being able to influence a Fire Keeper?" Elder Aoki rebutted.

"When was the last time we heard of a human entering Sosen no Tani?" The Elder, Shimizu, shot back.

Elder Saito held up her hands to silence the room.

"Elder Tadaaki, please continue with your theory."

"I believe we need to treat this girl with the utmost hospitality and respect. We know Yatagarasu, through the incarnation of a three-legged crow, is the messenger for Amaterasu-sama, one of the original gods. Yatagarasu has appeared for thousands of years to guide both kami, Ancestors, and humans alike. Our relations with the humans have been estranged for some time. And the destruction to our lands, our peoples, *their* peoples have been worsening at alarming rates in the last two hundred years alone as the demons advance their will over the humans, increasingly causing more chaos and suffering by the hour. We need to treat this human girl with the kindness we would any cousin, any kin, any neighbor who has come to us. And hear what she has to say."

This time, I was all-out staring at Elder Tadaaki. For all the years I had known him, I did not expect the full support he was showing now on behalf of a human.

The Elders in the room were silent as they mulled over his statement.

"That isn't to say," he continued, "we do not proceed with caution. This world is becoming ever more volatile and strange by the minute. We need to be careful to protect ourselves and ensure we are interpreting Yatagarasu's message correctly."

Some of the Elders still looked unconvinced.

"I mean, what say you, Elder Ryu? You are the head of all spiritual matters. What do you think of Mato's dream?" Elder Tadaaki asked the sage.

Elder Ryu's face was impassive as she considered the

information. She was a quiet woman whose eyes held as much depth as they did steel. She chose her words carefully, and only spoke when she knew it carried value – a trait not commonly shared for the rest of the vermillion-robed Keepers. She had no hair on her head, preferring instead to shave it down to the skin, and although she was likely one of the oldest of all the Elders, her face had not aged a day past forty. She sat in silence for several moments, weighing her words.

"I believe your theory to be plausible, Elder Tadaaki," she finally replied.

"I propose as soon as the girl can walk, we summon her to the Council to learn about her purpose and motives in Sosen no Tani. Until then, she can continue to reside at Misao-dono's house and receive treatment for her wounds. We will proceed forward with caution. And we *will not* disclose the details of Keepers' strategic and protective methods due to the security risk it could present. Are we in agreement?" Elder Yamashita asked.

Around the room, each Elder gave a firm nod in assent.

"Then it is decided. The human shall be brought to the Council as soon as she is well enough to walk, for further questioning. Mato, you shall be her guide and bridge to the Council, since Yatagarasu has blessed you with this message. But you shall be monitored closely, by chance a demon is attempting to influence you, should your objectivity change." Elder Saito declared the final ruling.

I looked at Elder Tadaaki, who didn't return my glance but placed both of his hands on the mats in front of him and bowed. Wordlessly, I followed his actions.

"Mato-kun, we expect you to notify the Council as soon as you are given word of her able condition," Elder Saito continued. "We will then convene a meeting at once. The Council is now dismissed."

I nodded in assent. Slowly, in order from the front to the back of the room, each Elder bowed before the group and rose to leave, bowing once more in the archway before making their final exit. Elder Saito and Elder Yamashita led the departures, followed by Elder Tadaaki and Elder Ryu as the most distinguished Elders of the martial and spiritual sects respectively. I stayed put. Regardless of being permitted to sit with Elder Tadaaki at the front of the room, I would still be the last to leave as the most junior Keeper present.

When it was finally my turn to take my leave, I bowed to the empty space where the Elders had previously sat, standing and walking slowly to the shoji door. Facing the interior of the room and bowing once more again, I shut the shoji door behind me. Whether I liked it or not, the girl was my responsibility now.

CHAPTER ELEVEN

Kairi

When I awoke for the second time in Misao-dono's guestroom, I awoke from what felt like the deepest sleep of my life. I had slept for another six hours, and the late afternoon light had fallen over the room. After testing my weight tentatively, I found I was able to stand without the incessant throbbing in my head or swooping, vertigo vision. My throat still felt as though someone had thoroughly rubbed it raw with sandpaper and I felt mild dizziness if I moved my head around quickly, but overall, I was feeling a million times better. I would have to take things slow, but I could function again. The more I could move, the sooner I could focus on getting home.

Sometime between jumping in the well and waking in Sosen no Tani, Misao-dono must have dressed me in one of her spare yukata cotton robes, as I noticed the casual, indigo-colored kimono wrapped around me when I pushed off the covers. The thought of someone, anyone, redressing me while I was unconscious made me feel mildly nauseous, but the clothes I was wearing back in Nachi must have been filthy, singed, and soaked from the water in the well. It couldn't be helped.

I padded out into the hallway of the engawa in a pair of woven slippers I found by the end of the futon, and found a small fire burning in the sunken hearth at the center of the living room. Just at the sight of it, I instinctively felt the need to retch and cough at the same time.

"You're up!" I heard Misao-dono's voice from somewhere

in the dark, cavernous house. "Oh, I'm sorry, dear; I'm sure that fire's a wholly unwelcome sight now that you're awake and moving."

She emerged from the left-hand side of the room, where the shadows obscured an earthen-floored kitchen. "Unfortunately for you, these earthen houses are dark and our only option for illumination beyond the sun is fire," she said apologetically, taking me by the shoulders and gingerly steering me toward the front of the house. She pushed open the outer sliding door and sat me down on the exterior porch. Just like the view from my guest room, I could see terraced rice fields dotting the steep slopes of the mountains beyond, with numerous thatched-roof homes sprinkled throughout. The sun appeared to be starting its descent behind the mountains and a warm peach-colored tint filled the sky. A breeze gently blew across my face. Any reaction I was having from the fire started to fade.

Misao-dono disappeared for a moment before returning with a pot of bancha green tea. "Here, dear. Have a cup of tea and enjoy the view. Let's take a moment to make sure you feel well enough, and then maybe we can go on a short walk around town," she told me.

"Sure." I nodded, taking a sip of the steaming bancha.

"How do you feel?" she asked.

"A lot better," I answered honestly. "My head barely hurts now, and I'm only a little dizzy if I move too fast. My body feels like it just went through the most intense workout of its life, but other than that, I feel fine. Oh, and my throat still feels like it's made of glass." I replied, clearing it ungracefully.

"That's great news. You heal quickly, Kairi-chan," Misao-dono responded, the term of endearment sounding as though it had come from my aunt herself. "That's a good thing—means you have strong genes."

"I guess," I responded politely. "My aunt has great genes —she may as well be in peak physical condition, even as she gets older. She's grown up in the mountains and has eaten homegrown vegetables her whole life. She walks everywhere and takes a hike to the waterfall in my town at least once a day, every day. She barely looks like she's aged; she still even has muscle definition!" I replied.

"Ah yes. Living in the mountains and eating homegrown food is a feat not so many humans nowadays can claim, I've heard," Misao-dono said. "It sounds as though your aunt and I would be good friends."

I looked over at her thoughtfully. "I think you're right." I smiled.

"Now, what do you say we get walking?" she asked, taking my empty cup of tea from me. "I have a village to show you."

With a slow and steady pace, Misao-dono led me from the porch of her farmhouse out into the rice fields by the base of the mountains. The village of Sosen no Tani was spread along the side of a mountain, its agriculture fields nestled in the crook of a valley between two mountain ranges. The rice fields and main cropland was predominantly farmed in the flatland of the valley, with the majority of homes and village housing built along switchback roads up the side of the mountain. When we reached the center of the rice fields, we were far enough away from Misao-dono's house that I could see a full three-hundred-sixty view around me. I turned my body slowly to take in the scenery.

The town was stunning; the glassy, reflective surface of flooded rice fields created the illusion that the base of the mountains gave way to sky. Along the mountainside, I could see idyllic farmhouses, and in the center, a concentrated grouping of old-fashioned machiya townhouses made up a main street. Toward the top of the mountain, overlooking the valley below, stood two large, elegant-looking structures—a vermillion-colored shrine and wood-stained temple. I felt as though I had been transported back in time, which in a sense, I guess I had been. But at the same time, I had a gnawing sense that the whole place was vaguely familiar.

Turning my body slowly to the right, I scanned the mountainside for what I suspected I might see next. In the distance stood a tall red three-tiered pagoda, and just beyond it, the largest uninterrupted waterfall in what would have been Japan. I whirled around to Misao-dono and exclaimed, "We're in Nachi!"

"No, my dear. We're in Sosen no Tani," she frowned.

I just looked at her dumbly for a second before continuing, "But that's Nachi Falls! And over there," I said, pointing to the shrine and temple on the hill, "is the Kumano Shrine, and the Nachikatsuura Temple! This is Nachi, but in the past!"

"Ah, I see what you're getting at," Misao-dono replied after a moment. "In the human world, you call this place Nachi. But in the spirit world, it is called Sosen no Tani, or Valley of the Ancestors for which it was named. As I mentioned to you briefly when you first woke up, we are the original people. And therefore, we and the humans are connected. Our world and the human world are connected. The Ancestors, along with other kami, yokai, and even demons, used to live alongside the humans. As I told you, we built the well systems from which you arrived, collaboratively. Therefore, we share the same land. This is the spirit-world counterpart to Nachi Falls," Misao-dono explained.

"That makes a lot more sense," I replied, taking in everything around me. We continued walking slowly as I thought about her words.

"You mentioned that our lands are connected," I pointed out.

"That's right," she replied. "What happens to your land happens to ours in a roundabout way, and vice versa."

"If that's true, and our worlds are connected, then why does Sosen no Tani appear to be stuck in the past? It feels like we're back in the Edo period. Shouldn't it look developed like modern-day Nachi? Or is it just an inherent, supernatural rule of the spirit world to stay as mythical-looking and authentic as all manga, movies, and folklore like to portray?"

"A great question," Misao-dono commented. "Though you lost me at the last part. Remember I told you that the spirit world separated from the human world some time ago and we went into hiding?"

I nodded.

"Well, that happened at the end of the Edo period. Our world had been developing and progressing alongside that of the human realm since ancient times. In the thirty-fourth season of Shosho, in the two-hundred and fiftieth year of Edo, it was as if the spirit world froze in time, and suddenly the humans were no longer able to see us. We became separate from them, and as their world *progressed,* if you want to call it that, it changed, but ours stood still. What humans do with their portion of this land still impacts us, but no longer looks exactly the same. Hence why our village does not look burned to a crisp after the fire that took place in theirs."

I winced a little at the bluntness of her words. The thirty-fourth season of Shosho. I reached back into my mind to see if I could remember what part of the calendar year this would translate to in modern times. Remembering one afternoon when I had gotten bored while manning Mikan Antiques, I had found an old calendar my aunt kept on the seventy-two seasons, an old Japanese seasonal calendar that broke down the seasons we understood as fall, spring, winter, and summer into an even more complex description, dividing them into seventy-two different microseasons. If I remembered correctly, Shosho would be sometime around the beginning of July. And if the Edo period began in the year of 1603, two-hundred and fifty years into Edo would have meant the year was 1853.

Why did the beginning of July in 1853 sound so familiar? I stayed quiet for several moments as I dug around in my brain to see what was ringing a bell. Suddenly, a history lesson from my AP World History class in high school came back to me.

"Oh!" I said aloud, snapping my fingers. "July 8, 1853 was the date Commodore Matthew Perry sailed into Tokyo's—erm, Edo's—harbor from America and demanded Japan reopen after centuries of isolation. He blew up several buildings and all but forced Japan to reopen to trade with the West and undergo industrialization!" I recited as if reading aloud from a textbook, a method that would have made my AP World History teacher proud.

"I'm afraid that's right, Kairi," Misao-dono said gravely. "That—*man,* as you call him—was the catalyst for the separation of the humans from the Ancestors, from the spirit world, and from the land. It is why we still practice the old ways today, and why your kind do not," she said with finality.

I opened my mouth to ask her more, but she continued, "Now, my girl, it's been centuries since a human has come to our town. Let me show you around as our honored guest."

Misao-dono linked her arm in mine and as the sun continued its descent behind the mountains, we began our ascent up the first portion of switchback dirt roads and through the terraced rice fields. It was the beautiful time of twilight where I could hear the frogs calling to one another in the shallow water of the fields, and fireflies began to glitter in between the reeds of the baby rice seedlings.

"Misao-dono, this may be a stupid question, but do the Ancestors flood their fields with water from the falls as well?" I asked.

"My dear, there are no stupid questions," she laughed, patting my hand like an affectionate grandmother. "We actually do not flood our fields using the water from the falls as the humans do, as that would be impossible. If you notice, our falls actually runs *the opposite* direction of yours, or so I've been told. We use the wells to shunt water from the river at the top of the mountain down into the fields."

"It what?" I replied, twisting my head to take another look at Sosen no Tani's waterfall.

To my surprise and sheer confusion, I saw that she was right. The river ran *upstream* to the spirit world version of Nachi Falls and seemed to defy all gravity, flowing *upward* to the top of the mountain.

"A waterfall that runs backward?" I said aloud, not quite believing what I was seeing.

"Indeed," Misao-dono mused, tugging on my elbow and

pulling me farther up the hill.

We made our way into town slowly, taking an easy walk up the hill to give my recovering lungs a chance to keep up. As we walked, it started to truly sink in that everything she had told me was true. I was *not* in the world as I knew it anymore, and a place like Sosen no Tani actually did exist.

I was amazed by how Old World Japan must have looked, feeling like an absolute dork when I got excited over seeing farmworkers in the fields in traditional patchwork, indigo-dyed clothing, and straw pyramid hats. It really was as if I had stepped back in time into my favorite anime. With no telephone or electric wires, ugly 1980s-style vinyl homes, or paved roads filled with a variety of different Kei cars, there was a stunning cohesiveness to the village before me, allowing the unparalleled magnificence of nature to take precedence.

I took as deep of a breath as my lungs would allow. I wasn't sure if I had ever breathed truly clean air. With so much pollution all over the world in the human realm, so many of us, including myself, had asthma and other chronic conditions. I doubted anyone had asthma in Sosen no Tani.

As we made our way up the mountainside, old machiya-style townhouses began to line the dirt road on either side of us, and the streets became busier with villagers running daily errands, working storefronts, or selling their vegetables and crafts on the side of the street. I could hear the soft bells of wind chimes as they hung from the roofline of teahouses, and the bustling noise of neighbors interacting with one another. As we walked, Misao-dono kept her arm linked in mine, nodding politely to people as we passed, calling out to every third person or so in greeting. She seemed to know everyone and for some reason, I wasn't surprised.

We passed a merchant stepping outside of his *izakaya* to light the lanterns at the bar's entrance. He looked in our direction briefly and appeared as though he was going to call out something to Misao-dono, but when he saw me, he averted his eyes, lighting his lanterns in one quick flick of the wrist before darting back inside.

I had noticed he wasn't the only one to behave that way. I was beginning to see a trend amongst villagers as we passed through the town. Many would smile in greeting at Misao-dono, but when they finally noticed me, they averted their eyes with a nervous expression on their face or shuffled away from us as if I had startled them.

The first few times this happened, I thought of it as just the standard Japanese shyness that I had learned to internalize my first few years growing up in Japan, but this was starting to feel like something more. I tried to give each person we saw a polite nod, but their response walked a line of repulsion and fear.

"And here, Kairi-chan, is Sato-san's sake bar. I must say, I like to think I'm not much of a sake drinker, but for Sato-san's home-brewed sake, I find myself sneaking down here at least twice a week!" She laughed. She had been narrating our walk as we journeyed farther into the village, giving me the names of all the important shopkeepers, food vendors, and artisans, as well as a bit of town gossip, which for some reason I had assumed the Ancestors would have been above. But I guess they *are* the first humans after all.

"Misao-dono," I started, interrupting her. "Why is everyone looking at me like that? Or I guess I should say *not* looking at me?"

I felt her sigh beside me.

"In the year the human and spirit world became separated, up until that point, the humans and Ancestors had been living together collaboratively. Our role as the original people, as decided by the gods, is to guide humans, with their volatile temperament and fickle minds, to live in harmony with their environment and non-human neighbors, so that the world may maintain balance. But in the two hundred and fiftieth year of Edo, the humans turned their back on the Original Ways and began adopting exploitative, damaging habits that have destroyed both of our lands and peoples. Turning to war with one another, to war with the environment. They turned their back on *us*. It became a bloody and brutal era."

I thought of the dark and savage Bakumatsu Era, that brought the end of the Tokugawa Shogunate and thrust Japan into the new world of Meiji. In a few short years, World War I and World War II would follow. Just as I had thought back in my history classes, it was hard to believe that all of this was brought about by one man. But, I concluded now as I had back then, it must have been the catalyst for a wound that had already been festering and in turn caused infection to spread.

"Many Ancestors in Sosen no Tani feel betrayed by the humans. They don't trust them. You are the first one to step foot here in hundreds of years; they don't know what to make of you or your intentions. They don't know what to expect from you. For many, this is their first time ever *seeing* a human," Misao-dono finished.

"They think I'll hurt them?" I asked.

"In a way. They don't trust you," she replied.

"And you do?"

"It is the Original Way to care for one another, to care for one's neighbors. Being human, you are our kin after all. And just because we feel abandoned by your people does not mean we should abandon you ourselves," she replied softly.

"I'd like to show the others that you mean no harm. Are you up for one more cup of tea this evening?" she asked, coming to a stop in front of a long white hanging noren curtain in front of a building that read *Teahouse*.

I gave her a hesitant nod and followed her into the teahouse as she pushed the curtain aside.

Inside, windowless walls of the old townhouse coated the room in a blanket of darkness. Patrons sat huddled around tiny glowing fires, with tea kettles positioned on stone pedestals atop the flames, sipping steaming cups of tea and chatting softly. In the corner next to a lit candle sat a woman in a traditional kimono with a shimada hairstyle, characterized by the large bun at the back and voluminous wings on either side of her head. She played the shamisen, a long wooden string instrument that gave off eerily haunting, one-note chords, as she sat on the tatami mats.

Misao-dono flagged down the teahouse owner, who motioned for us to sit wherever we wanted. Removing our sandals and stepping up onto the tatami-matted floor, Misao-dono pulled me to an empty table in the center of the room. As we waited for the owner of the teahouse to serve us, the front sliding door where we came in opened, and in stepped a tall man in a black kimono with a sword at his waist. Swords had been banned in Japan for nearly two centuries and it was hard for me to imagine that the swords people carried here were anything more than cosplay. I gripped Misao-dono's forearm and nodded in the direction of the man.

"Is that a real sword?" I asked.

"What? Oh, of course! Why wouldn't it be?" she replied, looking in the direction of the man whose back was to us.

"Actually, I think that's Mato!" she declared happily. "Mato!" she called, all but ruining the quiet, peaceful atmosphere of the teahouse.

At the sound of his name, the boy who had brought me food earlier that morning whirled around to face our direction. The same boy who apparently had found me in the well and brought me here. The attractive stranger who, now that I thought about it, I probably owed a *thank you* for saving my life.

The boy's eyes lit up in recognition when he saw Misao-dono, but, was I wrong or did his expression darken when he saw me sitting next to her? He resumed a poker face at remarkable speed, though, and I questioned whether I had seen anything at all.

Before Mato could answer her, an old man called from the back of the room. "Misao! How many times do we gotta tell you to hush up in here! This isn't Sato-san's bar!" There was a brief pause before everyone laughed, including Misao-dono, and all continued on with their tea and conversations.

"Come here, child. What are you doing just standing by the doorway?" Misao-dono scolded, motioning Mato over to our table.

"Misao-dono," the boy greeted her with a bow, sparing a glance at me. "So you're up?" he asked stiffly, the warm confidence I had felt from him this morning replaced by something colder and more hesitant. Surely he couldn't be fearful of me too?

"Uhm, yeah," I replied, suddenly unsure of myself. "I'm feeling a lot better."

"Glad to hear it," he said curtly before turning his dark eyes to Misao-dono. "Do you think the teahouse is really the best place to bring someone who just woke up from *days'* worth of injuries?" he asked, a sarcastic edge in his voice.

"Mato, where are your manners? You know better than to question my healing methods," she replied, unphased. "Now, won't you come sit with us?"

"I'm afraid I can't, Misao-dono. I am on a run to pick up Tadaaki Sensei's favorite bancha tea and then I must return. You know he doesn't sleep well without at least one cup. Plus, you know quiet hours begin soon at the Temple."

"Oh, the trials and tribulations of the Fire Keepers. Are you really the elite warriors of this village? Or just errand boys with curfews?" Misao-dono moved to jab him playfully in the ribs.

He blocked it so quickly, I barely saw his arm move but he deflected her hand away lightly, shooting Misao-dono a look.

"Fire Keepers?" I asked.

Mato looked at Misao-dono pointedly while she answered, "Oh nothing, dear. You'll learn more about them tomorrow."

"By the way, Mato," Misao-dono continued, "this is Kairi. Kairi, I'd like you to officially meet Mato."

We bowed to one another respectfully.

"Thank you, Mato, for the food this morning," I said. "And for … you know, saving my life the other night," I said, giving him an embarrassed smile.

He looked taken aback for a moment before nodding once. "I'm glad you're feeling better, Kairi."

I felt a tingle go up my spine as he said my name.

Behind him, an old woman emerged from the kitchen and handed Mato a small package. He gave her such an unbelievably warm smile, so starkly different than the look he had given me, that I had to deliberately force myself to look away. "Thank you, as always, Fujita-san." He squeezed her hands before she turned to walk back to the kitchen.

"I must be going. Tadaaki Sensei will be wanting this," he said to Misao-dono, waving the small package of tea in his hand. He glanced over at me briefly before bowing once and ducking back out through the door.

"Such a stubborn boy," Misao-dono muttered under her breath in exasperation.

"Was he afraid of me too?" I asked Misao-dono. "But he was the one who brought me here."

"Ah, just you wait, child. You'll come to know the enigma that is Mato Asahi soon enough. Now let's have some tea and get you back to the house. In fact, bancha sounds like a delicious way to end the night. Ishii-san! Bring us some bancha!" she called to the owner.

"But didn't we just have bancha?" I protested. She ignored me.

"Misao, seriously?!" Another patron called her out. "You're yelling again?!"

Feeling suddenly emboldened, I put both of my hands flat on the tatami mat and bent my elbows and head in a bow toward the direction of the patron. "I'm very sorry for her disturbance!" I apologized formally, attempting to contribute to the joke.

There was a moment of silence while everyone took in my announcement.

Then, once again, the room devolved into laughter and a few townsfolk slid over floormats to our table and began pouring us some tea.

"Yeah, yeah, I'm coming!" Ishii-san called to Misao-dono as he brought us over a teapot of bancha.

It was the liveliest teahouse I had ever seen.

The new townsfolk who joined our table nodded politely

at me and smiled, the same look of hesitancy and fear being replaced by laughter, shy smiles, and a warm cup of tea placed in my hands.

CHAPTER TWELVE

Mato

I ducked out of the teahouse and was immediately thankful for the cover of nighttime to hide the flush that was burning my cheeks. *It had been so hot in there with all of those fires,* I told myself, ignoring the fact that heat from fire does not affect me anymore.

What was she thinking, bringing the girl to the center of the village like that just hours after she had woken up? Things were tense enough with the Keepers as it was. What would the townspeople think? What would the Elders think? Was the girl even well enough to be up and moving like that? She'd have to meet the Elders tomorrow no matter what. She could have delayed the inevitable by a few days.

I thought of the shy, warm smile the girl had offered me when she thanked me for the food—and for saving her life. I didn't think humans could show such a level of sincerity, or even feel gratitude… or be that *sweet*. I thought of how her life wouldn't have been in danger in the first place if it wasn't for her entire town being on fire. A familiar ball began to lodge itself in my stomach.

Tucking Elder Tadaaki's pouch of bancha into the front fold of my kimono, I began walking back to the Temple. I would be alerting the Keepers tonight that the human was ready to be questioned. They would summon her in the morning.

When I arrived back at the Temple, I knocked on the door of Elder Tadaaki's living quarters. He called for me to enter and motioned for me to leave the tea on a small table at the front of the room. After noticing I wasn't leaving immediately, he finally looked up at me from the calligraphy he had been practicing, and raised one eyebrow.

"Please notify the Elders that the girl is well enough to meet," I said.

"Very well," he replied, resuming his brushwork. After still noticing that I hadn't left, he didn't even bother to look up at me this time when he asked, "Is that all?"

"Er—uhm, yes sir," I replied, turning on my heel to leave.

"You know, Mato, you can talk to me about whatever is bothering you," he said softly as another stroke of ink marked his paper.

"Thank you, Tadaaki Sensei." I bowed before leaving his room.

Walking down the long corridors back to my own sleeping quarters, I kept thinking of the girl's—Kairi's—face. I had to stop referring to her like that. My mind felt agitated, and I doubted I would be able to sleep at this hour if I tried. I thought I probably should focus on spiritual studies before bed, or practice meditation; both always seemed to put me to sleep relatively quickly. I decided to take a detour into the Keepers' library near Yatagarasu's Shrine before retiring to my room for the night.

Combing the walls for a spiritual text that would be sure to knock me out, the characters for *Yatagarasu,* the three-legged crow, came into focus. I pulled the book off the shelf and lit a nearby candle with a quick snap of my fingers. Sitting down cross-legged on the tatami, I peeled open the book. Most of the text stated what I already knew: Yatagarasu was a messenger of the kami, specifically for the sun goddess Amaterasu, one of the creators of the land. He offered protection and guidance, to both humans and kami alike, and is best known for guiding Emperor Jimmu, the first emperor of Japan in the human realm, across the country, yada, yada, yada. I kept reading until I saw the line, *He has guided numerous humans to safety.*

I thought of how Yatagarasu had morphed into the form

of Kairi in my dream and how I later found her in the well that night. Maybe Yatagarasu—no, Amaterasu, more likely—had sent Kairi to us.

Was it possible that she was guided here? Just how did she get into the well? And even so, *how* was she able to cross over into the spirit realm?

I would need to find out for myself.

I closed the book promptly and blew out the candle. Pulling a black-hooded robe over my head, I left for the forest.

CHAPTER THIRTEEN

Kairi

Misao-dono and I made our way back to her kominka not long after nightfall. After Ishii-san brought us our pot of bancha —a deliciously nutty, sweet tea that I found tasted *way* better in the spirit world than the bancha I had tried back in Tokyo or Nachi—more villagers visiting the tea shop had begun to gather around our table.

After my formal apology for Misao-dono, wariness of my presence amongst the townsfolk gave way to a shy curiosity. I met a kind, older craftsman named Kamachi-san, who turned and lacquered wooden bowls for a living and wore a long beard. He asked me all sorts of questions about the current state of the human world and invited me to try wood turning sometime in his workshop. His daughter, Chiyo, had joined him for tea that evening and introduced herself to me boldly. Her husband, who was at home at the time, was a rice farmer, and the two of them worked alongside Misao-dono in the fields. Already married with a four-year-old daughter, she couldn't have been older than twenty. I was definitely in a different time period, that was for sure.

After arriving home at Misao-dono's house, we said goodnight and retired to our respective rooms. As I lay in bed, listening to Misao-dono shuffle around in the kitchen briefly before settling in one of the rooms next to mine, I thought of what a wild first day in Sosen no Tani I'd had.

After walking around all evening, my body was still sore

and bruised in many places, and I still got winded if I moved too quickly, but overall, I was amazed with how well I was feeling. Could it be that just *being* in the spirit world, in Sosen no Tani, was healing me? And to believe Sosen no Tani was the spirit realm's version of Nachi! It was amazing to think that this is what Nachi must have looked like during the Edo period. With a waterfall that ran *backward!*

I thought of how much Auntie Mie would have loved to see this. Or just hear about it. Where *was* Auntie Mie anyway? I had no idea if she was even alive. I had agreed to stay in Sosen no Tani until I was well enough to move around on my own. Our walk around town tonight had proved that I was pretty well healed. A thought occurred to me. If this *was* the spirit world's version of Nachi, then wouldn't the well be in the same location as back home?

Without a second thought, I was up. Tucking my broken cell phone into the belt of my yukata, I listened quietly at the door for any sign of life from the room next to me or in the kitchen. After hearing nothing but silence, I slid the door open and padded my way down the hall, through the dark living room. Pausing momentarily in the living room, I snatched the iron-rod poker from the sunken hearth and left through the front of the house without a sound, closing the exterior door behind me.

When I got outside, I thanked the universe for my stealth. When I was younger and had just moved into the farmhouse in Vermont, I used to scare the living hell out of my father by walking around the old, rickety wooden floors. "How can you *possibly* sneak up on me with floors like *this*, Kairi?!" he'd cry after swearing profusely. "I swear you have Indian feet." Being fresh from Japan, I didn't understand the semi-insensitive reference until I was older, with some American history classes under my belt and a few years of experience living on occupied Abenaki land. I never thought much about my ability to move quietly, but after successfully leaving Misao-dono's house of literal tree and mud, I guess he had been right.

I felt a pang in my gut thinking about him. *I'm on my way back, Dad. I'll talk to you soon.*

Nighttime in Sosen no Tani was no joke. I knew it was dark, living in the countryside with Auntie Mie, but this was *dark* dark. Nachi at least had some streetlights by the convenience stores, but 19th century spirit realm Japan had no light pollution whatsoever. Well, except for the stars. I looked up at the sky to see a full moon and some of the most stars I had ever seen in my life lighting my path ahead. It took all I had to pull my neck away from the extraordinary scene above me and carry forward. *Stay focused, Kairi.*

Moving by instinct and memory alone, I walked as quickly as my lungs would allow in the direction of the well. It took me a while with my lungs still at limited capacity, and I didn't want to push myself too hard and end up unconscious in the well again. So moving at the speed of a stark fast-walk with numerous breaks, I assumed I made a trip that should have taken about thirty minutes, tops, in about an hour. I had no idea what time it was when I arrived at the edge of the forest near the falls, but I kept going, pushing my way through the brush, trying not to think about what creatures might be lurking in the nighttime spirit world. If the legend of Sosen no Tani was true, then I'd assume the legends of things like yokai and demons were true too. And I definitely *did not* want to run into those. I gripped the iron rod in my hand tightly—it'd be my weapon for protection.

After about fifteen more minutes of stumbling over tree roots and trying my best not to scream in surprise, I made it to the opening with the well. I silently cheered in my head, fearing the whole time that I'd make it here to find nothing in its place. *Alright, here goes nothing. Auntie Mie, I'll find you soon.*

Having remembered nothing about how I got here in the first place, I figured my best bet was probably not to jump in head first, as I had last time, if I wanted to climb my way out of the well in Nachi in one piece. I had no idea how this worked, but was hoping I'd get some sort of sign as I went.

Making my way up the mounded exterior, I felt around in the darkness for at least a good five minutes. When I finally found the ladder, I positioned my feet on the first rung and prepared for a tentative descent, but paused before beginning to make my way down.

It occurred to me that it being the middle of the night and the middle of the woods, I would have no way to tell when I resurfaced if I was still in Sosen no Tani or back in Nachi. I guessed if I emerged in Nachi, the forest would be pretty bare by this point, seeing as the fire was practically licking my heels by the time I had jumped into the well the other night.

Still, to be safe, I decided to stake the iron rod I had been carrying at the base of the well, directly in front of the ladder, to use as a reference point.

Carefully making my way down into the tunnel, I was sure to land feet-first on a thin footpath that ran along the flowing water.

Now what?

Did I need to walk to another opening? Did I just need to stand here? What direction did I need to go? I took a look to either side of me.

I had no light to guide me, except maybe I could try the flashlight on my phone. Being thankful Misao-dono had done as I asked while I had been sleeping, and submerged it in a bowl of rice, I tentatively attempted to turn the device on. It powered on slowly, sluggishly, but it worked all the same. As I had suspected, there was no service in the spirit realm.

I did a silent cheer in my head and I flicked on the flashlight, illuminating the path ahead. In front of me, black water streamed steadily by. If I had jumped into the well, into the water, when I had arrived and passed out nearly on impact, the water must have carried me downstream. That meant the entrance to Nachi must be upstream from the entrance to Sosen no Tani. I turned to the right and began walking upstream.

I had no idea how long I had been carried by the water,

how many well openings I had passed, or how far apart they were from one another. But if I was carried underwater, I couldn't have gone without air for more than three minutes. Of course, at some point I had transitioned into the supernatural realm and who knows what laws of nature applied here, but I'd go on what I knew for now. After what felt like close to five to ten minutes of walking, I could see light from the moon breaking through the black of the tunnel. Holding the edge of my phone in between my teeth, I climbed hand over hand up the ladder to the surface.

Pulling myself up onto the ridge of the well, I looked around for the rod I had stuck in an attempt to discern my surroundings. After a few moments of orienting myself, I found it sticking straight up out of the dirt, directly in front of me.

My heart sank. It hadn't worked.

Which was wild, because I had definitely walked at least five minutes to a new entrance point, but here I was, at the same one I came in from. Maybe I needed to go farther.

I walked five more minutes upstream and climbed the ladder to the next opening I found. Poking my head out of the well, I shined my flashlight in front of me and once again found the rod staring back at me. What the hell? How was this possible? *It's okay,* I told myself. *I just need to figure out how this works.* Maybe just a little farther.

With a frustrated grunt, I dropped back into the tunnels. Walking five more minutes upstream, I hesitantly climbed the next ladder I found, no longer trusting my methodology, and pulled myself up onto the rim of the mound, looking around apprehensively for the iron rod. At first I saw nothing but the tree line in front of me. *Did I do it? Am I home?* Suddenly, a ball of fire blazed at the edge of the tree line and illuminated a man in black robes, standing with his arms crossed, leaning against a tree trunk. It was Mato.

"Just what *are* you doing?" he asked me quizzically.

"Damnit!" I shouted, smacking the edge of the well in front of me and dropping back into the hole.

"Wait!" I heard him call as he moved toward the well. "Ow! What the hell was that?!" Above me, I heard a scuffle and a few thuds as he tripped over the rod.

This was insanity! How was I still in Sosen no Tani? Clearly the walking method wasn't working. *Think, Kairi!* I had jumped into the water and passed out almost on impact. I must have been underwater for somewhere within three minutes before being washed onto the footpath. And somewhere within all of that, had I entered into the spirit realm. It wasn't the Afterlife, but maybe I needed to be in a pretty sorry state to transition over? It was extreme thinking, but I was desperate. I needed to get home and find my aunt and tell my father I was okay.

Without thinking about it much further, I jumped into the water and held my breath. I would need to stay underwater until I was just about to pass out. I began counting down in my head. When I reached about sixty, my injured lungs were searing in pain, but I was determined to see this through. I *had* to get home.

Abruptly, I felt a hand grab hold of the collar on my *yukata* and yank me to the surface. Mato stood there, holding a katana ablaze with fire in one hand and me in the other. I couldn't even think about how it was possible that his sword was on fire. I just started horrendously coughing instead, making a rather disgusting barking noise as he pulled me unceremoniously onto the footpath.

"Seriously. What the hell do you think you're doing?!" he commanded, much less bemused now.

"I… need… to… go… home!" I cried, sputtering and half choking on more water. I was at my wit's end. I could feel the awful sobbing noise bubbling up the back of my throat against my will as my eyes started to tear up.

"By drowning yourself?!" he echoed.

"No! I don't know! I have no idea how this works!" I shouted, frustrated. "I never wanted to be here. I just need to get home; I need to make sure my aunt is okay!"

And with that, much to my embarrassment, I devolved

into tears. I felt Mato grow silent beside me.

"You can't get back to the human realm through the water," he replied softly after several moments. "You should have been able to get there by just walking upstream and taking the next exit. But since you already tried that, I would say whatever, whoever, brought you here doesn't want you to leave yet."

"W-what?" I asked, pausing the awful crying noises I was making long enough to hear him.

"Come on; let's get out of here," he replied, pulling me to my feet. "Can you stand?"

I nodded dumbly.

"Up you go." He motioned for me to go up the ladder, letting me take the lead.

I climbed up the ladder with some effort, seeming to have a never-ending headache since I entered this town.

"How did you know I already tried walking upstream?" I asked him when he reached the mouth of the well.

"I followed you into the woods. I saw the whole thing."

"You were *watching* me?!" I asked, offended.

He looked at me levelly. "I wanted to see what you'd do. And I have to say, human, it's looking pretty suspicious on your end."

"Suspicious?" I asked, confused. "What do you suspect me of?"

He shrugged and looked away from me. "I just don't trust humans."

"Why? What have we ever done to you?" I asked him, even more offended.

Remembering what Misao-dono had told me about how the humans turned their backs on the Ancestors, it took me a second to realize that maybe we had done a lot.

Instead of answering my question, he shrugged off the long, black hooded robe he wore over his kimono. Was everything this guy wore black?

"Here; you're soaking wet. You'll catch a cold. Put this on," he said, tossing me the robe.

"Can you even catch colds in the spirit world?" I asked him.

He just looked at me.

"Fine, but turn around," I said, moving toward the tree line and positioning myself behind a bush.

I shrugged off the seeping wet yukata I was wearing and slipped on the soft, worn fabric of Mato's robe. I couldn't help but notice it smelt of sandalwood and hinoki cypress. It was delicious and oddly soothing, the scent lessening the throbbing of my headache. I tied the wet obi belt from my yukata around my waist to hold the robe in place.

"...Thanks... again," I said sheepishly as I emerged from the bushes. It was nighttime, but I could have sworn Mato's face flushed as he looked at the robe wrapped around me.

"No problem. Should we get back? And you can tell me more about why you're so desperate to get home?"

I nodded defeatedly. The urgency, panic, and desperation I had been feeling had melted away to a sad numbness. I would be stuck here for the time being. Until we figured out what whatever it was that was keeping me here wanted from me, I had to do my best to find that purpose quickly, so I could go home and find my aunt. After looking back at the well one last time, I followed Mato back through the woods toward Sosen no Tani.

***

I was silent for several minutes on our walk, but eventually said, "I feel like it's self-explanatory, but I'm not supposed to be here. I have no idea how I ended up here. I told Misao-dono all of this already, but I jumped in that well in Nachi because I was about to be burned alive. The other night, there was a massive wildfire in my hometown. My aunt and I had to evacuate in the middle of the night, leaving with nothing but the clothes on our backs and a few essentials. There was no time to leave the town, so we were running for the river. But we got caught up trying to help my elderly neighbor evacuate her house. By the time we had lifted her into her wheelchair, the fire reached a broken gas line on her property and the house exploded. We ended up getting separated. I was knocked out for, I have no idea how long, before I woke up covered in debris. I searched and searched for her in the rubble but I couldn't find her. I wasn't going to leave until I found her, but when there was almost no time left, I found myself running away from house and toward the river. I had only found it earlier that day, but by the time the flames were about to swallow me whole, I realized I was near the well. It was my last attempt at survival, and I knew there was water in the well, so I jumped in. Everything went black after that. Next thing I knew, I was waking up at Misao-dono's, looking at you."

Mato stayed quiet the whole time I was speaking. Leading our way back to the village, he gently held tree branches back for me as we walked. He said he didn't trust me but was still making sure the twigs didn't cut me or smack across my face.

"I need to go home and find my aunt. I have no idea if she's alive; I just need to know she's okay. I never meant to transition into some other realm. I thought I was going to *die.* I never even knew this place existed; I just thought Sosen no Tani was some folklore legend I had only heard about earlier that day..." I trailed off.

He was silent for several moments before replying, "I'm sorry. That you went through all of that."

"Me too. But it's not like it's your fault," I said, feeling the same level of awkwardness and discomfort that arose whenever people apologized after my mother died.

"So you said you only discovered the well earlier that morning. How did you find it?" he asked.

"Yeah... It was really weird actually, but I guess not so much in retrospect after everything that's happened. My aunt told me the legend of Sosen no Tani as we made an offering that morning to the gods of Nachi Falls. As I was walking back home, a three-legged crow flew in front of me and led me to the well."

"I thought so," Mato responded ahead of me, half to himself.

"You thought what?" I asked.

"It was Yatagarasu."

"Yataga-who? You mean the god of Kumano Shrine?" I asked.

"Kumano? Yes. Yatagarasu. I thought he may have been the one to bring you here," Mato replied casually, as if this were an everyday event. Which, maybe for him it was.

"Why would you think that?"

"Because for one thing, Yatagarasu is a three-legged crow, who likes to appear in front of humans and guide them places, and last time I checked, three-legged crows hadn't gained a significant population in the human world," he replied.

I pursed my lips at the unnecessary sarcasm.

"And because the night before I found you in the well, I had a dream of a three-legged crow who turned into a girl. And that girl looked just like you."

I stumbled momentarily at his words. Mato mindlessly put a hand out to steady me.

"Alright, that's a fair assumption," was all I could think to reply.

"And I think," he continued, removing his hand, "that Yatagarasu does not want you to leave. So he has not allowed you to go home. You should have been able to just cross back over the same way you came in. But you couldn't. Yatagarasu brought you here for a reason, and until we know what that reason is, he wants you to stay in Sosen no Tani."

I was quiet for a while, thinking it over.

"It's just a theory," he said after a while.

"Not a bad one," I replied. "If the spirit world exists, then so should all the gods, yokai, and demons. Anything could be possible at this point. And I don't think it's a coincidence that I saw a three-legged crow only an hour after learning about Sosen no Tani *and* he guided me to the well that would take me here later that night. I don't believe in coincidences."

"Then we have that in common," Mato said.

"What do you think the reason is? Why did he bring me here?" I asked him.

"Yatagarasu?" Mato asked. "I'm not sure. But I think we'll find that out soon enough."

"How can you be so relaxed about it?"

He just shrugged.

We were silent again for several minutes as we emerged back on the dirt road to Sosen no Tani. The stars were fully visible now and I allowed myself to take them in fully as we walked, seeing as I was trapped here for the time being.

"Hey," I started. "How is possible for your sword to be on fire?" We were walking side by side now that we were out of the forest.

"Oh, this?" he asked. In one flick of his wrist, the katana extinguished itself and we were surrounded by darkness.

"How are you doing that?!" I asked him incredulously.

He laughed. "I'm a Fire Keeper."

"What's that mean?"

"Do you not understand Japanese?" he teased. "You *do* have a weird accent."

"No, shut up. I understand what you said." I rolled my eyes.

He laughed again.

"Misao-dono said they were the warriors of the village… or something? Or just little boys with curfews; I can't remember which one," I replied.

"The Fire Keepers are Sosen no Tani's spiritual leaders and physical protectors," he explained. "When Sosen no Tani originated, Kagutsuchi, the god of fire, blessed the ancestors of the village with the ability to manipulate fire. As Ancestors, we were meant to be guides to humans and to show them the ways of living in harmony with nature, so that kami, yokai, and humans could all cohabitate. Since man cannot exist without fire, the Ancestors of Sosen no Tani were given the ability to control it at our will.

"We train with it since we are young children, those that

are chosen to join the Keepers. And then we choose a path, or specialty so to speak, to either become a spiritual leader or warrior. Those of us in black robes are warriors, and we set our katanas on fire when we fight. Or... in this case, need a torch. Those who wear vermillion robes are the spiritual leaders. And we're not little boys. There are girls too," he explained.

"Oh wow," I said dumbly. "Where were you when Nachi was on fire then?" I tried to joke.

He said nothing.

I silently blamed the fact that I had lived alone with my father for the last decade for cursing me with the habit of making horrendous dad jokes.

"So you guys are like the samurai of the village, but fight with actual fire," I clarified.

"I guess?" he replied, sounding unconvinced. "Though we don't follow the same rules as the human samurai. The whole code they lived by didn't make much sense. Why kill off your best warriors if they make a mistake as small as embarrassing themselves in public? So much ego with you humans."

I stayed quiet.

"The weird thing is," he continued, "I'm not originally from Sosen no Tani."

"Oh, really?" I asked. "There are more Ancestors outside of Sosen no Tani?"

He gave a curt nod. "I'm from a water village, called Mizu no Okurimono. The Ancestors there were given the ability to manipulate water, another essential resource for humans. But oddly enough, I could never do it. Even at ten years old, I could never make the water work for me. I *do* remember learning a fun trick around the age of eight, though, where I could snap my fingers and it would produce a spark. I felt so bad I couldn't use water like other kids of my village but would always act like I was special because I could create a spark out of thin air and they couldn't—to make myself feel better.

"Well, anyway, eventually, the Fire Keepers found me when I was ten and recruited me to join the Keepers. And ten years later, I've been here ever since," he said. "But why am I telling you all of this?"

I didn't know what to say, so I just shrugged. "I don't know; you tell me. For someone who claims not to trust humans, that doesn't feel like the smartest move," I pointed out sarcastically.

Now it was his turn to roll his eyes.

"You're not wrong," was all he replied.

"What's that about anyway?"

"What's what about?"

"No one trusting me. *You're* the one who brought me here."

"You'll find out soon enough," he said blandly.

"Fine," I replied, sick of everyone exhausting the phrase.

I looked over at him, but he wasn't looking at me. He was looking ahead in the distance, where Misao-dono's house and the rice fields had started to appear on the horizon.

The sun was starting to rise, and above us, the sky was painted a hazy, rose color. Mist trailed in between the mountains surrounding the valley. I craned my head behind me in the direction we had come to take a look at the waterfall. The backward-flowing water still looked unbelievably wonky to me. Like we were in a Dr. Seuss book.

"So what were *you* doing at the well tonight?" I asked him.

"I told you," Mato replied. "I wanted to see what you were doing."

"*No*," I said slowly. "You said you followed me into the woods, but that would have meant you were already out near the falls, unless you followed me from Misao-dono's house."

He laughed softly to himself. "Perceptive, I'll give you that. I was also headed to the well. I too, was trying to figure out just how you got here. I guess I just had a feeling that I needed to go there in person to get a better idea."

"Well, that makes two of us."

It was fully light out by the time we reached Misao-dono's house. She was waiting for us on the porch. As soon as we were within ear range, she called to Mato, "Yatagarasu wants her to stay, doesn't he?"

"It seems so," Mato replied.

"It's as I thought," she said, completely unbothered.

I looked between the two of them. Everyone seemed to know what was going on here except me.

"What happened to your clothes?" she asked me, raising her eyebrow like a protective mother would to a teenage daughter who had come home past curfew.

"I'm sorry for leaving without telling you, Misao-dono," I said, bowing my head respectfully, feeling the need to apologize.

"She fell in the water again," Mato answered for me. "Rather stupidly, actually. I loaned her my robe."

"Mato! No need to insult the girl," Misao-dono said lightly. "And it's no mind, child. I do not own you; you go where you please."

"By the way," Mato leaned over to whisper in my ear. "Why do you keep referring to her as Misao-dono?"

"What do you mean? That's what you call her. It's respectful," I whispered back.

"Technically, *dono* is a term of respect for women that generally only men use. I'm guessing that humans no longer use that honorific in the modern age?" He replied, laughing softly.

My cheeks flushed as I stared back at Mato in horror.

Misao-dono glared at him. "It's fine, Kairi, really. I find it endearing. Come. Let's get you dressed. We have a council to speak to."

"Council?" I asked.

"Remember us Fire Keepers?" Mato asked, waving a hand. "Well, the Elders are the leaders of the Keepers and they want to meet you."

"I see," I replied hesitantly.

"Oh, it'll be fine," Misao-dono assured me, taking me by the shoulders and guiding me up onto the engawa and into the house. "I'll come along to make sure of it. Mato, you wait outside. We'll be out shortly. Oh, and—what should she wear?" Misao-dono asked him.

"I hardly think it matters," Mato replied.

"Fine, you're no help. Stay there," Misao-dono said gruffly, closing the door in his face.

***

Misao-dono only had old, patched-up farm clothing for me to wear, a pair of lose fitting, mompei pants and a samu wrap top tied across the body with a string at the waist. It was that or wear one of Misao-dono's incredibly formal kimonos that she kept on hand in case she had a smaller-sized guest. Misao-dono thought it was best to be formal and dignified in front of the Council, but I had opted for comfort. The patchwork on the clothing indicated years of wear and tear, but painted the clothing in numerous shades of indigo with a variety of different stitching patterns. I found it rather beautiful and marveled at the work while Misao-dono pinned back half of my hair with a simple set of chopsticks and combed out the remaining strands.

"Such a pretty hair color. I've never seen anything like it," she commented. "You're not entirely Japanese are you?"

"I'm half-white," I replied. She looked at me blankly. "My father's ancestors are from the West," I rephrased.

"Fascinating," she murmured.

When we stepped back outside, Mato was sitting on the exterior porch with his back against the earthen wall of the house. He eyes had been closed, and I wondered if he had fallen asleep after staying up all night, but he opened them immediately when we stepped outside.

"You went with farm clothes? A kimono probably would have been better," he commented, pulling himself to his feet.

Misao-dono swatted him on the arm and this time, he didn't block it.

"You're a pain in my ass," she said to him.

"Come on. We're going to be late," Mato replied.

CHAPTER FOURTEEN

Kairi

Mato trailed a few paces behind us as we made our way to the Fire Keepers' Temple. He looked lost in thought, keeping his head down as he walked. I thought of what he had said to me earlier—"I don't trust humans"—after questioning me at the well. I had a suspicion the Fire Keeper Elders would feel the same.

After about thirty minutes of climbing switchback roads and a seemingly endless stretch of steep steps, we had made it to the highest point in the village, where what would have been the Kumano Shrine and Temple in Nachi presided over the town. Here, instead of tourists buying *omikuji* fortunes and emerging from the Kumano Kodo trail in the woods looking disheveled and exhausted, the grounds were filled with men and women of all different ages, some even children, sparring with one another in a mix of martial arts I couldn't recognize.

When they saw us making our way to the temple's entrance, the Keepers stopped what they were doing and unanimously bowed in our direction. With my arm still looped with Misao-dono's, I leaned over to her and whispered, "Okay seriously, what is this place? Are they a cult?"

"Shh!" She smacked my arm.

"Ow!" I whispered.

"They're bowing to Mato, not you," she replied as if it were obvious.

"What, does he have a high rank here or something?"

"Yes, for his age he does, actually."

"Oh. That makes more sense," I said, feeling my cheeks burn in embarrassment.

Mato moved in front of us as we ascended the steps to the inside of the temple. Misao-dono and I modeled his behavior, bowing when he bowed and keeping a few steps behind him.

I tried to maintain a stoic, dignified composure as we walked. Something about Misao-dono's reaction in the courtyard and the solemn, imposing interior of the temple walls silenced any snark I had left in me. But I couldn't help but find myself gazing around in awe as we moved silently through the maze of corridors. The floorboards were made of beams of cedar so wide, I could only imagine the size of the tree they came from. The interior decorations of the temple were stark, taking on a more wabi-sabi aesthetic than I had anticipated. I had never actually gone past the worship room in the Temple in Nachi. But I had imagined the halls to be as ornate as the statue of the Buddha the building was devoted to.

As we wound through the never-ending hallways, we moved in and out of a network of buildings, crossing over flowing streams leading to a small pond of koi fish in the center of a mini courtyard and numerous rock gardens. The interior rooms of one smaller building were adorned with anything from samurai swords lining the walls to an array of other various weaponry, with the next building covered floor to ceiling in books, scrolls, or soft, delicate ikebana flower vases. You couldn't say the Keepers didn't show range.

Finally, we slowed to a stop in front of a closed shoji door on the left-hand side of an open-air corridor. Mato looked at the both of us once before slowly sliding the door open. Bowing on entry, he motioned for us to follow him.

Entering into the room after Mato, I was met with a set of twelve eyes staring at me with mixed expressions of fascination, hostility, and apprehension. Twelve older men and women in black and red robes sat on the floor, sitting in two rows of six. At the front of the room sat a man in black robes; he didn't look older than his late fifties. Upon seeing us, he stood to greet us.

"Thank you, Mato, and welcome, Misao-dono. A special welcome to our honored guest," the man said with his eyes lingering on me. The words came out too thick to be fully believable.

"Please, be seated," he finished, extending his arm to the back of the room.

Mato bowed to the man respectively and took a seat beside him. I felt Misao-dono give me a supportive pat on the arm before extracting herself from me to sit along the sidewall at the back of the room. I moved quietly to the spot where the man who had greeted us pointed, directly across from him, in the middle of the two rows of Keepers.

"We thank you for taking the time to meet with us today," the same man in the black robes continued. "You may call me Elder Tadaaki. I will be facilitating this meeting in place of Saito-san. Please, state your name to the Council."

They all turned to look at me.

"Kairi Raynott, sir," I responded.

"Thank you, Kairi. I have never heard a family name such as that before. Are you not from the human island of Japan?" he asked.

"My father is from the West. My mother is from Japan. I am half-Japanese, sir," I replied.

My father had once told me if I was ever to be questioned by lawyers, or in a court of law, to keep my answers brief and straightforward, giving no further information than needed. "Anything extra you say can and will be used against you," he had told me. I felt like I was in a similar situation.

"Fascinating. Kairi, we have called you here today because, as you have likely heard, you are the first human in Sosen no Tani in centuries. We have some questions for you so that we can hopefully understand a little bit more about one another."

I stayed silent.

"Very well. Council, I will be directing the questions toward our guest. I ask that you save any additional questions or commentary until the end."

Eleven heads nodded in unison.

"Let's begin."

**

My meeting with the Council felt much more like an interrogation than a meeting driven by curiosity. Elder Tadaaki asked me questions in rapid fire about how I had arrived in Sosen no Tani, what I was doing beforehand, how I knew about the well and the legend of their village. He kept a kind voice throughout the process, but the questions came one after another and I could feel the mistrust beneath his thin veneer of politeness. I felt as though I was on trial, instinctually giving answers with only need-to-know information, unsure of what it was they were looking for from me.

"What are your intentions now that you are here in Sosen no Tani?" Elder Tadaaki asked. I didn't expect him to ask me so directly.

"To go home," I replied, keeping my hands balled in my lap and looking down at them in exhaustion.

"And why is that? Have you gotten all the information you need now that you've made it here?" I could hear the suspicion in his words.

Anger flared within me and I fought not to let it show. By now, we were at least two hours into questioning and I was well aware that I hadn't slept a wink the night beforehand. The more tired I became, the harder it was getting for me to control my emotions. I didn't ask to be here, and I didn't ask to be put on trial. But getting frustrated wasn't going to make them trust me more.

"Because my aunt may be dead and my father definitely thinks I am too by now. I need to find my family. I don't know what information I would need here," I replied calmly, letting the pain seep into my voice at the mention of my family.

"Have you not already figured out how to return to the

human realm?" Elder Tadaaki replied with an edge of doubt.

What a dumb question.

"I wouldn't still be here if I did."

"She doesn't know how to go home because she can't." Mato suddenly spoke up from his spot behind Elder Tadaaki.

I turned to look at him, surprised. I wasn't sure what the rules were in this establishment, but I'm pretty sure talking out of turn wasn't one of them.

All twelve heads of the Council turned to look at Mato as well, confirming my suspicion that he had acted out of line.

Instead of reprimanding him, Elder Tadaaki motioned to him. "Mato, please go on."

"I found the human girl in the early hours of the morning attempting to reenter the well. I had had a weird feeling that I needed to go to the tunnels, so I had left the Temple in the middle of the night. I watched her for some time as she tried to figure out how to get back to the human realm, intending to follow her if she was successful. But she kept reemerging from the well in Sosen no Tani. Even after walking for up to a mile within the tunnels. She should have found the exit and crossed over to the human world, but something would not allow her to leave."

The human girl? He knew my name well enough by now. I could feel my annoyance building, as well as a strange mix of embarrassment at his recounting of my failure. At the same time, I was glad he left out the part where I almost drowned. I could see now how my lingering around the well looked suspicious, and my theory to hold my breath to cross over looked like a suicide attempt, like a kamikaze pilot who would rather die than be captured by the enemy. It was clear the Ancestors suspected me of something, and I *was* on trial, but I had no idea of what or why.

"And what do you believe is keeping her here?" Elder Tadaaki asked Mato.

"Yatagarasu, sir," Mato replied matter-of-factly.

"Thank you, Mato," Elder Tadaaki said, holding up his

hand, indicating he had heard enough. Mato bowed his head in response.

"Girl—excuse me—Kairi," Elder Tadaaki turned back to me. "Why is it that you went to the well at such an hour?"

"I told you. All I want is to go home and make sure my aunt is okay. I had told myself earlier in the day that once I could walk on my own, I would go home and find my family. I had no idea how to cross back to the human realm and just used my best guesses. It's nothing personal, but I need to know if she's *alive*," I replied. "As you can see, like Mato said, I was unsuccessful."

"Very well. Misao-dono, I ask that you take the girl out to the hall while the Elders discuss. We will call you back in when we have made a decision," Elder Tadaaki proclaimed.

"A decision? What decision?" I whispered harshly as Misao-dono pulled me out into the hallway. She pulled the shoji door closed behind us.

"A decision for what to do with you," she replied quietly. "The Elders brought you here to determine if you are a threat to the village. They are now deciding what to do based on what you have told them."

"Don't I have a say in what they *do* with me?" I replied, releasing some of the frustration I had been feeling in the meeting, but knowing fully well that I didn't have such a say.

"Trust me, Kairi, I don't agree with their approach any more than you do. But please try to put yourself in their shoes. You are an outsider. We are a people who have fallen on hard times and unfortunately no longer trust many. They are just trying to protect their own."

I felt my anger waning slightly. I could understand not trusting an outsider in the insane world we lived in, even in another dimension of it. It seemed as though everyone was living on a live wire these days back in the human realm; with so many systems of oppression and exploitation, you never knew who you could trust.

I sighed in exasperation. "I can understand that," I said,

softening. "I just want to know *why.*"

Before Misao-dono had a chance to respond, the shoji door behind us slid open and Mato stood in its frame, beckoning us to return inside. "The Council has made their decision."

Resuming my spot in the center of the room, sitting on my heels on the tatami, I watched as Elder Tadaaki rose from his seat and cleared his throat to begin. Surely in the spirit realm, they wouldn't throw me in jail, would they? They weren't yokai.

I felt more indignant in anticipation of their answer rather than fear. I was going home no matter what they told me.

"We have decided, young human, to take you at your word. It appears, for now, that you are telling the truth. And because, as Mato shared, you have already tried to return home and could not, Yatagarasu may have greater purpose for you in our village. We will permit you to stay here until we learn what that purpose is," he finished.

I sat in silence as the room stared at me expectantly. Was I supposed to thank him? I hadn't even elected to come here. After an awkward pause while I read the faces of the other Elders around us, I jerkily bowed my head as a sign of respect and gratitude.

"Thank you, Elders," I replied evenly, recovering from my mistake.

"But you will continue to be watched by the Keepers. Mato will keep a close eye on you during your time here. And if it is agreeable to her, you are permitted to stay with Misao-dono and help her as she sees fit. During your stay here, you must contribute to the health and well-being of the community."

I snuck a quick glance at Misao-dono, who nodded approvingly. "Of course," I replied, bowing my head once more.

"And if we find you trying to contact anyone, or attempting to return home once more without our permission, your stay will be less than welcome indeed," he ended in warning.

I looked again once more to Misao-dono, raising an

eyebrow. She shook her head.

"If I may, sir," I spoke, putting on my best attempt at formal language in my clunky Japanese. "It is not hard to understand that you are suspicious of me. What I do not understand is of what or why. Are you willing to share more context with me?"

I felt the room take a bated breath. Out of the corner of my eye, I saw Misao-dono roll her eyes at my disregard of her advice, but she still smirked in surprised approval.

Elder Tadaaki looked at me for a moment quizzically, as if deciding how he should interpret my request. I half expected him to ignore it outright. But instead, he replied softly, "I guess after enduring our slew of questions so patiently, there is no harm in sharing some background.

"As you may already be aware, the humans and Ancestors have been estranged for some time. Part of our role as messengers between the humans and the gods also includes being the protectors of humans from the oni or demonic yokai. This is another role of the Fire Keepers, both to guide humans, but also to protect them from the inherent evils that threaten to throw our worlds out of balance. In partnership with humans, we maintained this balance for quite some time, but in the human year of Edo two hundred and fifty, demons were given an opportunity to gain the upper hand. A strange human man entered the shores of Japan during this year from a faraway land."

He was talking of Commodore Matthew Perry, the same event that Misao-dono had told me had begun to separate humans from the Ancestors.

"Although he was not a man at all, at least not anymore anyway. This man was being controlled by a demon and was on a path to pursue exploitation and power. While us Ancestors had been keeping a balance on the island of Honshu between the good and evil forces of the world, we were unaware of how this balance was playing out in the world around us. This human's arrival on Japanese shores spurred uncertainty, fear, and war amongst the humans, leaving an opening for other demons to follow this man's lead. The exposure of Japan to foreign systems of exploitation and pursuits of power, to advanced weaponry, and separation from life with the land exposed the weakness in our frail cousins' hearts, allowing them to be overtaken by demons so easily. The world as you know it today is one that is run mostly by demons who have taken control of human bodies, those who have become lost in spirit and mind. Lost from the ways of their ancestors. This has separated us from one another.

"And it has also led to the destruction of our lands and people in the spirit realm as well. We Ancestors, kami, yokai, and humans, share the same land whether or not we can see it. And what we do affects one another. As demons began to control more and more humans and exploit the darkness in their hearts, they have built ways of living that destroy our environment and our health. Here in Sosen no Tani, and in other ancestral towns of our realm, our fields are being lost. Our people are getting sick. We are in a fight to protect ourselves now more than ever before. And unfortunately, we have become so separated from our human cousins, we no longer can afford to trust them. We do not know them anymore.

"We were and still are concerned that you are a human under the influence of the demons as well. As far as we can sense, there is no demonic aura about you, but unfortunately, we can never be too cautious in these times. Please do not take it personally," he finished.

I stayed silent for several moments after Elder Tadaaki had finished speaking, processing his story. It was a lot to take in—the human world was being run by demons that had taken over the bodies of humans who had fallen into some sort of mental or emotional despair or anguish. And all of this was brought about by the arrival of another demon from the West, which spurred the end of Japan's isolation. It felt ridiculous. But the more I thought about it, the more it made sense. The amount of pain and suffering in the world I was raised in, spurred on by capitalism, material wealth, and commodification taking precedent over the lives and health of humans and the land felt purely evil and unbelievable at times in its own right. And it only made sense that the practices of colonization that had taken root in the West were born of this evil and opened up an opportunity for the demons within Japan, who had been isolated for centuries, to jump on board.

I wasn't sure that the Elders of the Fire Keepers had my best interests at heart, but I took my time choosing the right words before I responded.

I bowed my head to the Council and replied, "I want to thank you sincerely for sharing your story with me. I cannot imagine the pain you each have individually felt over the centuries, watching the way this has taken form. I myself have grown up in a world run by this pain and exploitation, and I had no idea the cause.

"What you said makes sense to me, and having grown up in a world that has made us so separate from one another, I can't imagine what it must be like protect your entire community of people. I, too, have watched a loved one die from the sicknesses brought on by modern human ways of life, and I tried hard to protect my aunt from the forest fire brought on by human destruction of our environment. And I failed. I can understand and respect your being wary of me. I will do my best to earn your trust."

When I raised my head, I was met with twelve speechless faces. I don't know what they expected from me, but it certainly wasn't an answer like that. Unable to help it, I snuck a glance at Mato, who was looking at me intensely, with an unreadable expression.

"Very well. I wish for the very same, Ms. Kairi," Elder Tadaaki replied. "May this be an opportunity to forge a new path between human and Ancestors yet again." He extended his hand to me. I shook it gratefully.

CHAPTER FIFTEEN

Kairi

"Otsukaresama desu!" *Good work!* Chiyo called out from the rice paddy on the terrace below me. We moved in unison, slicing new weeds that had grown between the rows of rice seedlings with a small, handheld sickle. It had been three days since my meeting with the Fire Keeper Council, where I had promised the Ancestors I would work to earn their trust, and they wasted no time holding me to my word. As soon as I had returned home from the Council, Misao-dono had thrust a sickle into my hand and a pack basket over my shoulders, claiming it was time to get to work. When I protested lightly, due to staying up the entire night beforehand, she shrugged and said, "Well, that's your fault."

Helping Misao-dono and the other farmers in Sosen no Tani had taken the form of waking up around four in the morning every day to avoid the heat of the summer afternoon. I harvested vegetables and tended to beds of daikon radish, green onion, kabocha squash, cucumbers, and soybeans. Being a little over a month away from when rice would need to be harvested, the seedlings had grown to knee height and were in the peak season of battling pests and weeds.

Each day, I worked the terraced rice paddies with Misao-dono's neighbor, Chiyo, the daughter of the woodturner, Kamachi-san, who I had met at the teahouse my first night in Sosen no Tani. She often worked alongside her husband, Minoru, but I had yet to see him in the fields at all.

"He takes care of the soy fields and our vegetable garden," she explained when I asked about him. "The rice is my passion, so I make him stay out of it," she laughed. I had seen her four-year-old daughter, Hana, a few times when she would occasionally come to help her mother in the field. Chiyo would place the sickle in her tiny hands and help her cut the occasional weed. Hana would furrow her eyebrows and stick her tongue out in concentration, but usually would run off screaming and giggling delightedly in a mad attempt to catch some paddy frog that had leapt out of the water.

Chiyo had been a helpful guide to me as well as I worked in the rice fields. I had plenty of experience with vegetables from working the garden at Auntie Mie's, but was severely lacking in the rice department. Over the last three days, she taught me how to flood the fields with irrigation, using water flowing from the tunnels in the well system, and how to detect pests like the rice bug. It was important we weeded the fields so the rice didn't end up competing with other species for nutrients.

"But the weeds are also important," Chiyo had told me. "Sometimes, they can be a distraction to pests, attracting bugs to devour the weeds instead of the rice crop. And we never want to remove anything from the natural biome of the rice paddy. Anything that grows or lives here is here for a reason. So when we cut the weeds, we make sure to release the stems and leaves back into the water, so that they may settle into the mud as sediment and give nutrients to the rice plants."

I did as she had instructed me now, slicing off the stems of weeds at the base and letting their leaf materials settle back into the water for added nutrients.

"You make good time!" Chiyo called to me from the paddy she was working on below. She paused for a moment and stood up straight to wipe her brow on the back of her forearm.

Both of our mompei pants were rolled up to our knees, our bare feet sinking deep into the mud of the rice field. I tried not to think about what leeches or other critters lived below the surface and were circling around our toes.

I took a moment to place the handle of the sickle in between my teeth, freeing my hands to adjust the tasuki sash that held the sleeves of my kimono top back. "I dare say you're a natural at this, Kairi!" Chiyo exclaimed.

I laughed out loud in disbelief. "Yeah, right. Any skill I've picked up is thanks to you." I motioned back in her direction.

I liked Chiyo. The two of us were close in age, with her only a couple of years older than me. She hadn't been fearful of me or standoffish for even a moment in the few days that I had known her, and had a headstrong feistiness about her that I appreciated.

I had made an incorrect assumption that the Edo period women of Japan would have been docile and submissive to their husbands. Chiyo was hardy, and she knew what she wanted. Minoru respected the boundaries she enforced and supported her independent spirit. It was a nice thing to see and reminded me of the relationship between my mother and father when she was alive.

Chiyo and I talked while we worked. I learned that only four years ago, she hadn't planned on getting married, but did so to support her aging father after her mother died. When I asked how she passed, she told me it was an illness. That was something we had in common and I wondered if it was an illness caused by the demons in the human realm. I smiled sadly and said, "Mine too."

We talked about how she was born and raised in Sosen no Tani and Minoru had been her childhood best friend. She saw him as nothing more than a brother until one day when she was fifteen, she had gotten too close to the edge of the forest digging up clay for her father when a stray demon stalking the town attacked her. Minoru had pushed her out of the way and took the brunt of the attack. It was his act of bravery and later, his support, when he stood by her through her mother's death, that made her see him differently.

"He was solid and sturdy and I could depend on him, but he was gentle and also patient," she smiled sweetly. Chiyo asked me about my mother and family in the human realm, why I looked so different from other Japanese humans, and my life growing up in a foreign land.

"Ehhh segoi," she said in amazement. "I've never even set foot outside of this village, let alone another continent! I wonder what the Ancestor villages are like in America," she mused.

I thought about it for a second. I imaged they'd look like many Native American settlements once did before America was colonized. Thinking about the current anguish the Ancestors in Sosen no Tani felt regarding demon destruction in the human world, there was no doubt Native American ancestors would have been super pissed for a long time.

"So, how have your first few days in Sosen no Tani been?" she asked me after we had finished weeding each of our respective paddies.

"I'm enjoying it, honestly. I love farming and gardening; personally, it relaxes me. So far it's been *fun*," I told her.

She raised her eyebrows in disbelief. "Really?"

"Definitely! There's so much to learn. And I'm in my element. I feel a little bad about saying that out loud though," I responded.

"Oh? Why's that?" Chiyo raised her eyebrows.

"My aunt was the one who taught me all I know about farming. And she could be dead. My father probably thinks *I'm* dead. I'm enjoying myself and they need me."

"Hey," Chiyo replied, putting a hand on my shoulder. "There's no use thinking like that. We've heard it all from the Keepers: The spirits are keeping you here. Until you know the reason, there's no use guilting yourself for enjoying your time. You'll see your family soon enough; nothing to do about it right now," she said matter-of-factly. "Plus, if your family loves you, imagine how much better they'd feel knowing you were safe and happy while you were gone, rather than in pain and suffering."

Strangely, her reasoning calmed me down.

"Besides, I, for one, am glad to have a *friend* out here all day," she sighed. "Not that Misao-san isn't the best company, but it's great to have a girl my age to relate to."

I lifted my eyes from the ground to take a better look at her face. She was smiling openly, her expression carefree and filled with genuine joy.

"Chiyo, can I ask why you have been so kind to me?"

"What do you mean?" she replied, suddenly confused.

"Everyone has been keeping a distance from me, like they are afraid of or disgusted by me. When the Fire Keepers told me of demons controlling humans, I understood why no one in Sosen no Tani would trust me. But you haven't treated me that way; you've been treating me like a friend. I'm grateful, but I'm wondering why," I explained.

"Listen, I don't care *what* you are; Ancestor, kami, human, or even yokai for that matter. As long as you are nice to me and my family, I will give you the same. I've never been intimidated by the labels we give each other," she replied without a second thought. "Besides, it's about time something new happened in this town. For years now, it's been all fear and anxiety. But now a human shows up that's said to be led here by kami themselves? That's exciting!"

"I guess," I laughed. "Thanks, Chiyo." I smiled.

"Don't mention it. And you seem to be useful!" she continued. "Hey, tomorrow isn't a harvest day, so there shouldn't be too much work to do around here in the morning. My father has a large order of bowls he's behind on completing and could really use some help stacking wood and cleaning up the studio. Would you mind lending him a hand tomorrow? I usually help him when I can, but Minoru will be away from the farm for the day, and I have to cover both our chores and watch Hana."

"Oh—uh, sure," I answered, slightly taken aback. "Are you sure I'd be helpful, though? I don't know the first thing about wood turning."

She laughed, a bright sound that was filled with so much self-assuredness, I wanted to doubt my own self-doubt.

"Of course! He's getting older and he needs someone

young to do a lot of the manpower. He'll show you what he needs done!"

"Um, okay. Sure. Then I'd love to," I replied.

"Great! Thank you so much, Kairi. This is a huge help! I'll let Misao-san know we are stealing you away so you don't get your wrists slapped," she giggled.

"Great. I appreciate that even more."

Suddenly, at the base of the mountain several terraces down, a tiny voice called from the porch of Chiyo's house, "Mommy! Mommy! Come down now! Daddy has lunch ready!" I cupped my hand over my eyes, straining to see Hana's silhouette against the midday sunbeams.

"Well, that's my cue." Chiyo winked at me and stood up.

"Coming dear!" she shouted back. Turning back toward me once more before she disappeared down the mountainside, she said, "I'll make sure Misao-dono tells you how to get to my father's studio. He'll be expecting you around six in the morning." And then with a wave, she was gone.

It was also time for me to return home for lunch. I made my way back to Misao-dono's house, lugging today's harvest of vegetables on my back.

Crossing the threshold through the living space and into the earthen-floored kitchen, I dropped the pack basket next to the kamado clay woodstove where Misao-dono was stoking a fire. I began unpacking the vegetables one by one.

"Just in time. I just caught some fish for lunch," she said, throwing more wood into the small opening at the base of the mud stove.

"Is that what you were up to this morning?" I asked. "Chiyo and I missed you in the fields."

"Ah, you were fine." She brushed off my flattery. "So you're helping out old Kamachi-san tomorrow, I hear?"

I stopped unloading the veggies and just looked at her. "How could you possibly know that? I just watched Chiyo return to her house on the *other* side of the paddies!"

"I have my ways," she said, brushing me off again.

"Scary," I muttered under my breath. Misao-dono seemed to know everything that went on in Sosen no Tani. She just shrugged.

"So what are we making today?"

After returning home from the Elders' Council the other morning and working in the fields, Misao-dono had cooked us a delicious lunch of rice, vegetables, grilled fish, and sauces I had never even heard of. When I asked her how she made it, she told me to watch her next time.

Since then, over the following days, I had been cooking with Misao-dono whenever I got the chance, eager to learn her recipes and improve my own skills. My father was quite the chef at home, but when left to his own devices, he mainly cooked Western food. Every now and then, he would try to cook a Japanese dish like Mom used to, but although he tried his best, it never turned out quite right. I had been learning traditional Japanese meals from Auntie Mie before the fire, but nothing beat real tradition like straight out of the Edo period.

There were so many ways to cook food that I hadn't even thought of before, using only water and fire. The sheer number of things you could ferment, salt, dry, steam, or roast were unlimited. And the variety of different foods we ate each day was more than I ate in a month on average in the human realm. Misao-dono caught so many types of freshwater fish and added mountain vegetables and animals to our meals as well, species that no longer existed in the human world or we weren't even aware of.

In just three days, eating hearty, whole meals filed with many different kinds of nutrients and spending my time working the fields, cooking, and running errands for Misao-dono had left me feeling healthier than I had maybe ever. I couldn't help but think that there was something about Sosen no Tani, too, that just made you feel better.

"I was planning to serve some pickles and grilled fish with rice, nothing fancy," Misao-dono replied. "But I really wanted to season the fish with this one herb that only grows in the mountains. Shoot! I completely forgot to forage some on my way home."

"What herb was it?" I asked.

"Mitsuba," she replied. "It grows in the forests here around the edges of town."

I didn't know it.

"Ugh, and my back is killing me now after all of that work," she said in exasperation, grabbing at her upper shoulder. "Kairi, would you be a dear and go grab some for us?"

"I'd love to Misao-dono, but I'm sorry. I don't know what mitsuba looks like or how to recognize it."

"No matter," she replied, waving her hand at me. "Go get Mato at the Temple and take him with you. He's spent plenty of hours with me foraging for plants."

"At the Temple?" I asked, suddenly feeling awkward about going out of my way to find Mato. I had only seen him once since the Council meeting, and he had been fairly quiet toward me.

"Yes, yes. He's usually outside training at this hour. Just drag him away from whatever he's doing and tell him I sent you. Now hurry up; no need to waste good firewood."

"S-sure," I nodded, stumbling forward from the light shove she planted in the center of my back.

I made my way in the direction of the Temple, using my own memory of Nachi in the human realm to guide me, along with familiarity from our trip to the Council the other day. I was still in my farm clothes and likely covered in dirt, not having had any time to change into a light kimono and wash up. I ran my fingers through my hair impatiently as I walked, brushing it out and smiling to other villagers while noting the strange looks they gave me. Why did I care about how I looked right now anyway?

When I arrived at the Temple, I found Mato outside under a wisteria-covered pavilion. He was sparring with another Fire Keeper in black robes who looked to be in his early twenties. Mato's hair was pulled back in what I had learned to be his usual half-bun style, and he and the other boy were fighting with wooden swords in a mix of martial arts.

In the heat of the day, Mato had tied back the sleeves of his kimono and I could see the tan skin of his arms flex as his muscles tensed and contracted with each movement. The look on his face was a different one from what I had seen over the past few days.

Usually, Mato looked calm and relaxed, and sometimes guarded. Now, his eyes were dark, focused, and carried a silent ferocity that I couldn't imagine him wearing prior. It sent a chill up my spine and I hesitated for a moment before approaching him.

He was moving at almost lightning speed, and while it was clear his opponent was highly skilled, it was equally clear that Mato's skill was on another level entirely. The two men circled each other in a dance of defense and offense. Mato's opponent put up a good fight, but Mato overcame him in the long run in each of their matches, every time extending his hand to pull the young man back to his feet after knocking him down.

Standing to face each other once again, Mato stood steady, with his eyes fixed levelly on the other Keeper. His hands were readied at the hilt of his wooden sword, but he made no inclination of movement until the other boy charged at him. I realized it was a game of wills, and Mato was drawing his opponent out. When his opponent finally took the initiative, the speed with which Mato struck the other Keeper was astonishing and left little to no reaction time from the boy.

I figured I would probably need to call out to him to get his attention, but instead, I found myself fixed in place, watching in awe as they moved around one another. Each movement was a mix of explosive violence and sheer controlled grace, responding to and building off one another's motions. Martial arts really was just like watching one elaborate dance.

Someone's throat cleared.

"Can I help you?"

It took me a moment to realize both Keepers had stopped

sparring and were now staring at me. Mato's opponent was sweating profusely and panting, taking the break as a clear opportunity to recover. Mato, on the other hand, had barely broken a sweat—just a thin sheen coated his skin—and he seemed as relaxed as if he had just woken up from a nap. He raised an eyebrow at me.

"Oh, uhm, hi. Sorry. I didn't mean to interrupt... this..." I said, motioning to the space in between the two of them awkwardly. "Misao-dono needs me to harvest some herbs in the forest, but I don't know what I am looking for. She told me to come get you to help me," I finished, trying to hide the sheepish edge to my voice. It was hard to not feel like a toddler while asking him for help after watching him literally defy the laws of physics with his fighting skills.

He stared at me for a moment before responding, looking as if he was sizing up his options, deciding if it was worth it to go help a helpless human or keep beating the shit out of his poor sparring partner.

"Sure, why not," he said flippantly. "Gives Ryoko here a chance to catch his breath." He clapped his hand on his opponent's back and grinned at him.

"I don't know why you're so proud of yourself," the boy, Ryoko, said between breaths. "It's not like you accomplished anything new today. It's the same thing every time."

"I'm proud on your behalf," Mato replied. "You're finally starting to catch up and actually *block* some of my strikes."

"I don't know why they keep pairing me with you anyway," Ryoko continued to no one in particular. "I'd like a partner who would actually *teach* me something rather than continuing to inflate his own ego."

Jeez, do men in all realms do this weird dick-measuring contest? I thought.

Despite their bickering, though, it was clear the two of them were fairly close. Biting back my mild annoyance, and dare I say disappointment that the spirit realm couldn't remove the most infuriating qualities of men, I said, "Well, if you two are done flirting, can we go? Misao-dono is going to be pissed if we waste all of her firewood."

Both of them stared at me blankly and I could see their cheeks beginning to flush at my insinuation.

"The *mouth* on that one," Ryoko muttered to Mato in astonishment.

Mato simply laughed.

"Ryoko meet Kairi, the human. Kairi, the human, meet Ryoko, the loser of today's sparring match."

"Jesus," I swore in English, rolling my eyes. "Nice to meet you, Ryoko. I'm sorry your sparring partner is like this. Now can we go?"

"I'm sorry. Make that Kairi, the *impatient* human. Yeah, come on now, Tiny Tiger," Mato replied, unbothered. After setting aside his wooden sword, he bowed respectfully to Ryoko before walking over to my side.

"What'd you just call me?"

"Tiny Tiger. You're smallish, angry, and have a cat-like attitude," he said matter-of-factly.

"What's that supposed to mean?" I asked again.

Ignoring me, he said, "Let's go. I've wasted Misao-dono's firewood once and I definitely don't want to be the one to do it again."

***

Mato led me up the mountain behind the back of the Temple. I had told him the herbs Misao-dono had requested, to which he had nodded and said he knew a good spot. We walked on a steady incline toward the top, carefully stepping over loose rocks and fallen branches. Like before, when Mato found me at the well a few days ago, he held the branches of trees back for me so I wouldn't scratch myself as he went ahead. Whatever play snarky-ness he had been putting on back with Ryoko was gone now, and he was back to his regular calm, reserved self. I was starting to learn he didn't get rocked easily.

"So what are we looking for?" I asked him, feeling restless with the silence.

"A green plant with green leaves," Mato said flatly.

"Well, that's all of them! How can we *identify* it?" I asked.

"Just relax, human. You wouldn't be able to spot it even if I told you. I'll show you when we reach the spot I'm thinking of."

"Fine," I muttered.

He laughed softly to himself. "Always in a rush to get things done."

God, I was being an American again, wasn't I? I rolled my eyes.

We continued walking.

"Look at you; you're like a full farmer," he said at one point, holding another tree branch back for me and letting me go in front of him.

"Yup, fresh off the fields," I replied, trying my best not to think of the layers of dirt that were probably caked around my ankles, hands, and likely on my face.

"It suits you," he said softly. I didn't know what he meant by that, but it didn't seem like it was a jab. "Do you like farming? When the Elders assigned you the job, I felt it was pretty obvious they were trying to wear you down," he added. "But I haven't heard you complain once."

"Well, we haven't really talked since the Council, so I don't know how you would have," I replied sarcastically before adding in a softer tone, "I do like it, actually. I've helped in my aunt's garden since I've been back in Japan. I think growing food is fascinating. I love being able to stick something into the soil and pull out the food I'll cook for dinner a few weeks later. I love being able to see all of that hard work pay off, to see what happens when you give a living creature time and attention. Plus, homegrown vegetables just *taste* so much better than anything you'd get at the store..." I trailed off. "And I understand why the Elders want me to work hard for Sosen no Tani. I don't mind them testing me. I understand it, actually. We fight hard to protect the people and things we love. Humans

—I guess really demons—don't have the best track record with being trustworthy. And I meant what I said about wanting the Ancestors to trust me. I'm willing to earn it in whatever way they see fit."

"That's very noble of you," Mato replied quietly.

"Not really. Feels more like a debt that needs to be paid."

"You said you've been farming since you've *been back* in Japan?" Mato asked. "Where were you before?"

"You might remember at the Council, I mentioned that I'm not fully Japanese," I replied. "Mom was Japanese and Dad is from the West. I grew up a little over half of my life in a different country, called America. I recently came back to Japan three months ago to live with my aunt."

"Your mother *was* Japanese?" Mato asked.

"She died when I was eight," I replied. "My father took me back to America after that."

He was silent for a moment.

"That must have been a really big change. Leaving Japan the first time, and coming back for the second over a decade later," he said thoughtfully. "I understand how that feels."

"Oh yeah. You said the other night you grew up in a village on a lake?" I asked him, remembering his story of being naturally gifted as a Fire Keeper but never being able to control water like the rest of his family.

"Yeah, Mizu no Okurimono," he replied. "I think it's called Lake Hakone in the human realm. I understand how it feels to leave your home after you've lost your family."

"You lost family too?" I asked him.

"Yup," he said, coming to a stop in front of a large cedar tree. I stopped abruptly next to him.

"Lost everyone. My mother, father, and little brother, gone," he said, crouching down to look over a patch of plants growing at the base of the trunk.

"How?"

"Humans polluted the lake in their realm, and it ended up polluting the lake in ours, poisoning my people. My entire village got sick and died, almost overnight. Everyone except for me," he answered.

"Everyone except you?" I repeated.

"I have no idea why," he replied, continuing to thumb through the small sprouts on the ground.

"That sucks," I said lamely. "There's not much else to say besides that just really sucks."

I always had felt awkward when people would apologize for my mother's loss, never knowing how to reply and feeling the strange need to pacify the apology. It took me a while to realize what I really wanted was just to hear my pain validated. And the opportunity to tell people about my mom and who she was.

"Sucks? What does that mean?"

I laughed, failing to remember that someone from the Edo period wouldn't know the slang. "It means that something is exceptionally shitty," I clarified.

He looked up at me, a sad smile on his face. "Yeah, you know, it really does *suck*."

"I'd love to hear about them sometime, who they were and how they made you who you are today," I added. "If you ever want to talk about them."

"Thank you, Kairi," he said. "How did your mother pass?"

"She also got sick. We're not really sure why or what caused it. But we know she was exposed to dangerous substances in her job as a scientist, trying to fight climate change at Tokyo University, so we think maybe it had something to do with that. If humans—er, demons—weren't destroying the environment, I think she'd maybe still be here."

"Well, that's something we have in common, then. The demons have both taken loved ones from us. That really sucks, Kairi." He turned to me, giving a soft smile.

I gave him one back. "Yeah, it really does."

For a moment, in his eyes, I saw the gentle stare of the boy who was looking at me so curiously when I first woke up in Misao-dono's guest room.

"Now, do you want to see what we've been looking for?" he asked, looking back at the plants he had been examining. It took me a moment to readjust.

"Oh, uh, yeah," I replied, squatting down next to him.

"This is mitsuba," he said, running his hand over a patch of small seedlings, barely five inches tall. "It's young, but do you see the three leaves here for which it's named?" he asked, running his forefinger beneath each of the three leaves on one of the plants, splayed out in a triangular formation. "Do you see the serrated edges on each of the leaves? And the blossoms on the ones that are flowering? Pay attention to these details when trying to identify it," Mato instructed.

"It looks like parsley!" I exclaimed.

"What's parsley?" he asked, sounding out the English word.

"An American herb used for seasonings," I said.

"Here; taste it. See if it's similar," he said. I waited for him to pluck the herb from its stem.

"*Not,*" he added, "before giving an offering." Out of the fold at the top of his kimono, Mato removed a small washi-paper pouch. Shaking a few tea leaves into his hand, he sprinkled them onto the earth and offered a small prayer.

"Was that in your kimono this whole time? I didn't even see you take anything with you before we left." I said.

"I always keep a small pouch of tea on me," he replied nonchalantly. "In case Elder Tadaaki needs a quick fix. Besides, we may be warriors, but a man needs to be civilized. I mean, come on."

"I didn't know you were so passionate about tea," I offered.

"Who isn't? Besides, sometimes when I'm on a mission, I need to feed myself or curb my hunger. It helps with that."

"A mission?"

"Stay focused, human," Mato said, drawing my attention back to the plant. "It's important to respect the sacrifice the plant is making to feed us. We always give something before we take, and we never take more than we need. Got it?" he asked, suddenly serious.

I nodded determinedly. "Yes, sir!"

He smiled. "Here," he said, plucking the plant from its stem and passing it to me to sample.

Looking at him apprehensively, I tentatively put the leaf in my mouth and chewed slowly after he gave me a reassuring nod.

"It *tastes* like parsley!" I exclaimed.

"Well, there you go," Mato said. "Let's harvest some more."

We spent another thirty minutes harvesting a bundle of mitsuba for Misao-dono to dry. On our way back down the mountain, Mato found a few other herbs and vegetables that he knew Misao-dono cooked with often and taught me how to identify them for future meals. He also pulled me aside to show me different types of herbal medicines that could be used to treat burns, infection, upset stomach, and even respiratory issues, in case I ever found myself in a situation where I needed them. I absorbed his lessons like a sponge, eagerly nodding and asking arguably more questions than I needed to, wanting to make sure the information stuck. I knew I liked farming, but I never guessed I'd be so invigorated by foraging. It was like finding treasure.

Mato laughed every time he pointed out a new plant and I yelled "Ooh!" in excitement from wherever I was walking a distance away. It became a game of sorts, and the two of us joked on our way down the mountain.

When we had filled the small basket I had brought with me, Mato refrained from showing me any more herbs and proceeded to lead us back down to the temple.

"Hey," I started as we reached the edge of the forest.

"What?" Mato asked, turning briefly to look at me.

"You were pretty intimidating earlier... you know, at martial arts. All ribbing between you and Ryoko aside, you're *really* good. I couldn't even see you move at times. And Ryoko never even touched you."

He shrugged and smiled politely, brushing off my

compliment. "It's something that comes naturally to me, but I still have more work to do."

"Oh, stop! What happened to all the big talk you were giving Ryoko earlier? Where's all that confidence?"

"Exactly as you said it: It was ribbing. I know I am more skilled than most of the Keepers my age, but there's always something one could be better at."

"I know the Keepers are meant to protect the village and they train with fire and katanas and martial arts, but do you guys actually... fight? Like, have you ever fought anyone before?"

"We do," he replied, watching me curiously, keeping his face impassive. "I have."

"I see," I said. "Demons?"

"Yup, a whole lot of them. Why do you ask?" He asked.

"I guess I've never watched anyone spar like that before—like, *really* spar. Even with wooden swords. I just thought it was so... fascinating. And beautiful," I said.

"Beautiful? We're learning how to kill something. And stay alive," Mato retorted.

"It was terrifying; don't get me wrong. But the way you and your partner responded to one another and how every movement had to be exact. It was like watching a dance. And not just martial arts themselves, but you specifically. Your movements were so fluid and smooth. You're really skilled. It's really impressive to see," I told him.

"Well, thanks, I guess," he said awkwardly.

"Would you mind if I came and watched you spar again sometime?" I asked.

He shrugged. "If it really interests you that much, go ahead," he said. But I caught his cheeks flushing before he turned away.

CHAPTER SIXTEEN

Mato

"Agh!" Ryoko let out a loud cough as his back slammed into the ground.

"Good, Mato," Elder Tadaaki said from where he stood watching a few feet away.

"If you would have struck him just a few inches higher in his diaphragm, the impact would have certainly knocked him out cold. Focus your breathing more."

"You're *trying* to knock me out?" Ryoko asked incredulously. "I swear you all just see me as expendable at this point," he muttered hoarsely as he pulled himself to his feet.

"You too, Ryoko," Elder Tadaaki added. "If you slowed your breathing, your mind may have found time to block his strike."

"If you say so," Ryoko mumbled, quietly enough that Elder Tadaaki didn't catch it.

But I did. I smiled ruefully at my friend.

He just rolled his eyes at me, but I saw a smirk twitch up at the corners of his mouth.

"That's enough. Ryoko, I think we've exploited you a bit too much today. Come watch with me. You could learn from observing."

"Mato, I want you to train with Yoshizo," he said, calling the older man over to us. He had been training at the edge of the courtyard. "It's time we give you more of a challenge."

Yoshizo Takamura was about ten years my senior with long, flowing black hair he kept tied in a high ponytail. His eyes were as black as obsidian and his sharp features accentuated a pair of thick eyebrows and a jawline that looked like it could cut through stone. He was both strikingly handsome—I'd admit that—and fearsomely masculine at the same time. The man always had an air of complete, serene calm about him, but in a way that made him utterly terrifying, not approachable. He was known as one of the Keepers' most elite warriors and had one of the highest kill rates of demons amongst any of us.

Elder Tadaaki must have thought pretty highly of my abilities if he thought I should be sparring with Yoshizo at this point, referring to him only as a challenge for me.

I watched as the legend of a man came to take his place across from me, standing perfectly still, keeping his hand lightly placed on the hilt of his wooden bokken. I had looked up to Yoshizo-san since I first joined the Keepers. His quiet, composed demeanor was one I often tried to emulate as I'd gotten older. Especially coming in as the angry, wounded boy that I had been when Elder Tadaaki found me. I wanted to emit such an intimidating force of character and fighting spirit that I didn't need to lift an eyebrow for others to respect me. Although he was a man of few words, we were on good enough terms, but hardly anyone heard him speak enough to say they really knew him.

I snuck a quick glance at the edge of the courtyard, where Kairi sat on a nearby rock, watching. She had made a habit of coming to watch me spar each day after she finished her work in the fields, ever since that first day she saw me spar with Ryoko. I only teased her for it a few times, but she had said she found martial arts fascinating and wanted to learn by observing.

She'd be Elder Tadaaki's perfect student, I had thought to myself when she had said that. So I let her come and watch. I was getting used to her presence, and seeing her sitting there, watching intently before I fought, was becoming oddly reassuring. Instead of feeling nervous, it felt weirdly energizing, encouraging even.

I glanced at her briefly, her big, bright eyes watching

us with curiosity. I had come to realize that girl was always so eager to absorb new information, acquire more knowledge. She'd get so excited over learning the smallest of things and was especially interested in Sosen no Tani and what she kept calling Old World Japan. I couldn't help but find it endearing.

Looking away from Kairi, I fixed my eyes back on my new opponent. Yoshizo-san and I bowed politely to one another. I had watched plenty of his sparring matches before for my own education, and I felt certain I knew how he'd begin this one.

I was wrong. I had modeled my own technique of drawing out the opponent from Yoshizo-san himself, so I had assumed we'd spend the first couple moments of this fight battling one another's wills, just gaining each other's measure. Instead, Yoshizo-san struck at me with blinding speed, taking me so off guard, I could only partially block his strike at my head. His attack with his bokken landed a glancing blow on my shoulder.

I created distance between us, backing up slightly to move out of his striking range. Our match continued in a series of strikes and counterstrikes, Yoshizo-san's expertise forcing me to use every ounce of strength, speed, and technique that I had acquired.

Before I knew it, I found myself in one of the most intense and challenging matches I had ever experienced. Occasionally, I was able to land a few blows on Yoshizo-san, but never enough to knock him down or gain the overall advantage. I had never been so pressed in my life before. Surely, if we were using real katana, I would have been flayed meat at this point. I could feel my own endurance levels waning. I needed to end this quickly.

I knew I had overextended myself when I miscalculated my next strike. Sensing the opening, Yoshizo-san hit the back of my hand, knocking my bokken out of my grasp. Instantly, he reversed his weapon and struck in an arc toward my face. Instinctively, I put my hands up, blocking the bokken before it could reach my throat. As soon as the wood made contact with my hands, I felt a surge of energy pool and release at once as I pushed the bokken away from me. Raw fire burst from my palms in a flash, incinerating Yoshizo-san's bokken, the force of the blast knocking him onto the ground. In a moment, I seized my weapon from where it had fallen on the ground and pointed it at Yoshizo-san's neck.

I halted my bokken a mere inch from Yoshizo's throat. He froze in place as he realized he had been beat. Slowly, an unreadable smile spread across his face and the two of us took a step back to bow to one another.

"Ha ha ha!" Elder Tadaaki exclaimed from the sidelines. "I'll be damned! Not bad, my boy! Not bad at all!

"In all of my years, this is the first time I have seen a Keeper use the energy of an external force to create fire instead of the energy in his own body. You need to work a bit on your blocking, but very impressive indeed," Elder Tadaaki said, amazed.

"Nicely done, Mato," Yoshizo-san said with a smile on his face. "That was incredible. Even I have never done what you just did."

It was the only emotion I had ever seen from the man and I admired the grace and strength he showed in defeat.

Man, this guy is still so cool, I thought as if I was ten years old again.

"Yoshizo, excellent work. You are both dismissed. Clean up and get some rest," Elder Tadaaki said. "I have something exciting to report to the Council."

As soon as both he and Yoshizo-san were out of sight, I let my fatigue show, dropping momentarily to my knees to catch my breath.

"Wow, I've never seen you get knocked around like that," Kairi said, trotting over to me.

I wiped the blood from my lip. "I'm not quite used to it myself," I replied. "But it's good for me."

"You're crazy," she replied. Pausing for a moment to think, she said, "You know, I can't quite tell if this Yoshizo guy was *really* skilled at martial arts, or if Ryoko is just kind of bad."

"A bit of both," I replied, the corners of my mouth quirking up into a smile.

She laughed.

Poor Ryoko. Even Kairi had caught on to my habit of joking at his expense.

"Did something happen at the end of the fight? Everybody looked really shocked, but all I saw was a flash of light," Kairi commented.

"Yeah," I said, kind of astounded, myself. "I think it did."

"In all seriousness, though, I could barely follow the two of you, you were moving so fast," Kairi said, her eyes getting bigger with excitement. I looked at her amusedly.

"Would you like to learn?"

"Who, me?" she asked, looking suddenly unsure of herself. It wasn't the Kairi I had become used to seeing.

"Who else?"

I watched her demeanor change from one of self-doubt to instant sarcasm. "You look pretty beat up. Are you sure you're in good enough shape to teach me?"

"Easy, Tiny Tiger. I'm only going to show you the basics," I replied, laughing and almost instantly had to refrain from grabbing my rib cage in pain.

"Seriously. Are you okay?"

"I'm fine. Now do you want lessons or no?"

Kairi hesitated momentarily, but she nodded and said, "Okay, if you insist."

I started by making her first practice her breathing and basic fighting stance.

"Focus on your breath while making sure your weight is evenly distributed throughout your body. Your gravity should be centered."

"I thought I'd be doing something entertaining, like getting to hit you," she replied. I could tell by now when she was joking. While it was true that she was often impatient, she actually was a very diligent and receptive learner. It was a quality I was starting to admire about her, and it was so fascinating that such a dichotomy of impatience and receptivity could exist at once in one small-sized human.

"Patience, young one," I replied.

"Oh please. I'm probably only, what, two years younger than you?"

"That's a lot of talking and not a lot of breathing," I replied, nudging the back of her knee gently.

She stumbled forward, thrown off balance.

"And not a lot of focus," I added.

She gave me a piercing glare but immediately changed her stance. I laughed. She'd probably make an excellent Keeper.

"Imagine you are breathing into every part of your body," I instructed, walking around her slowly. "Your breath is everything in martial skills. It determines your endurance, your control; it keeps your mind sharp. If you are not breathing right, you are not fighting well. And you will lose. Breath, as always, is your lifeline. Your strength, speed, power, and health, all depend on your breath."

She stayed silent as I instructed her this time. Still examining her stance, I couldn't help but notice her petite frame beneath the cotton summer kimono she wore. She was lithe but had curves in places I wasn't used to seeing from the women in my village. I felt my own breath start to shift and I forced it back into rhythm.

"Breathe through your nose constantly. Avoid breathing through your mouth if at all possible. Aim to take a maximum of seven breaths a minute."

"How on earth am I going to count that?" she suddenly retorted, breaking all concentration.

"Breathe!" I commanded, nudging the back of her left knee this time. It buckled, but her stance remained solid. She shot me a triumphant look and I had to keep myself from smiling.

I squinted at her. "Don't be petty. And don't get too confident."

She rolled her eyes, suppressing a laugh.

We continued on like this for another hour until she had to return to Misao-dono's, with me teaching her the fundamental philosophies behind martial arts while she maintained a focused stance and breathing. I instructed her to practice this breath and find her center of gravity in all of her daily movements, while she farmed, and even in just walking. "Just this alone will allow you to move better, sharpen your reflexes, and sharpen your mind," I told her.

She was incredibly mouthy during our lesson, but left almost comically determined and eager to accomplish this new skill. I shook my head, laughing to myself as she left. *What an interesting creature.*

"Hey, Mato!" Ryoko said, bounding out of the entrance and down the front steps of the Temple as I made my way back from the training yard.

"What is it?" I asked.

"That was insane! You created fire with your opponent's own energy!" he said excitedly. As he got closer to where I stood, he asked, "You were with Kairi?"

"Yeah, she just left," I replied.

"Can't say I ever quite expected humans to be like *that*, you know?"

"Like what?" I asked him.

"Relatively normal. And kind of funny, even if she can be so unbelievably rude." He shook his head.

I looked off in the direction she had gone.

"Not to mention attractive, but I guess demons *are* supposed to draw you in..." he added.

I felt a mild irritation rise up in me and cut him off. "What do you need, Ryoko?"

"Oh, right. You're on assignment. Elder Tadaaki asked that I come find you. A group of us will be leaving tonight," he replied.

"What for? Where to?" I asked, suddenly shifting my attention from thoughts of Kairi.

"Rumor has it a whole flock of demons seem to be moving into the Nachi region in the human realm. No new developments or destruction yet, but our scouts in the area have informed us that the number has been increasing drastically just in the last week alone," Ryoko said. "We're to go and flush them out; cut their numbers down before they can cause any more damage."

"In the last week, you said?" I asked.

"Correct. We leave two hours to midnight. Go get some rest. Sounds like it's going to be a long night."

"Why would they be heading to Nachi?" I asked him.

"We have no idea," Ryoko replied. "That's part of our mission tonight. If we can toy with one long enough to get it to talk and gain some kind of idea why the region's suddenly become a hot spot."

"Understood. You're coming with me?" I asked him.

"Yeah, among others. We'll break off into groups when we get there."

"Try not to get killed," I replied, punching him in the arm.

"I survive you every day, don't I?"

"Fair enough."

CHAPTER SEVENTEEN

Kairi

I had been in Sosen no Tani for almost two weeks now and had fallen into a fairly easy routine. Every morning, I helped Chiyo tend to the rice fields and vegetables with Misao-dono's help. When the work was done, sometime before or after lunch, I couldn't help but find myself eager to head to the Temple to watch Mato train. It had become a weird fixation for me, watching the skill of the Keepers as they sparred with one another.

Ever since Mato had offered to teach me some basic moves after his training was finished the other day, I found myself hooked, showing up again and again each morning after my own work in the fields was finished. Each time, we continued to build on what I had learned the day prior. Just yesterday, after multiple sessions of instructing me just to breathe and find my center of gravity, he finally began to show me some strikes and defensive blocks. I enjoyed the regular hour or so we were starting to spend together. I could still feel the heat of his fingers against my skin as he repositioned my arms, or the weight of his hands as he lightly adjusted my shoulders into the right position to strike. It was becoming hard for me to maintain my breathing during those moments.

I'm not sure when it happened, but before I knew it, it had begun to feel like Mato and I had known each other for years. He was easy to talk to, and his calm, silently snarky demeanor made it all too easy for me to pick on him, baiting me to draw out that infectious smile of his. For all the jabs and impatient complaints that I threw at him during training, he was good-natured and just as easily teased me back. It was the best feeling when I was able to make him laugh. He had this unexpectedly deep giggle that was irresistible and filled me with a sense of childish joy every time I was able to pull it out of him. Always carrying that gentle confidence and strength of his, it was becoming harder for me to stay away from him than it was to seek him out.

Training was about the only time I would see Mato most days. He didn't go out much in the evenings, like he had my first night in Sosen no Tani at the teahouse. When I had asked him what he did at night during one of our training sessions, he replied, "That's usually when I have to catch up on spiritual studies. And sometimes I go on missions," he added, sounding like he was struggling to find the right words.

"Oh, like when you go and hunt demons?" I had asked him.

"Exactly," he said.

"What do your missions usually look like? Like, what do you actually do?" I asked him.

He just laughed and said, "Nothing too exciting. Your breathing is uneven."

For as much as I was beginning to trust him, and the closer I felt we were becoming as friends, I knew just as well that there was a lot he was refraining from telling me about the Fire Keepers. *I guess that's fair enough,* I thought. I couldn't expect to earn the trust of the entire town's police force in just two weeks. But being here as long as I had now, I was beginning to really wonder what the spirits wanted with me here and when I'd be able to return to Nachi.

"Kairi are you just about ready?" Misao-dono asked, drawing me from my reverie as she slid open the door to my room.

I had just finished helping her prepare a feast-worthy dinner for the slew of townspeople who would be arriving at her house in half an hour and was now making myself presentable for the crowd. After discarding my dingy cleaning clothes and soaking in the wood-fired bath, I had slid on a simple cotton kimono and tied it in place with a neutral-toned obi belt. Misao-dono had caught me as I was attempting to tie back my hair. I was finding it much more tolerable on these hot sticky nights if it was tied into a bun or braid, but I struggled to work a simple set of chopsticks or ribbon as my only tools to contain it all.

"Give me that," Misao-dono said, snatching the ribbon out of my hand. "We'll give you a nice braid tonight," she said, suddenly invested.

I sat on my heels obediently and let the older woman do my hair. I felt a small pang of nostalgia at the memory of the last time I had let someone do this. It must have been as long ago as when I was a little girl, with my own mother braiding my hair back.

Misao-dono pulled a bone-toothed comb off of the small side table at the edge of my futon and got to work. "My, that's a whole lot of hair you've got, girl," she mumbled to herself.

I smiled.

"You know, I'm really glad that the spirits brought you here," she said between concentrated movements. "Even I get lonely in this big house sometimes. It's been really nice to have you around, like having my own daughter here again. And you're helpful too. You make quick work of those fields," she added, wrapping the ends of my hair up with the ribbon.

"Thank you Misao-dono," I said. "That means a lot to me. Honestly, you've made my time here so easy and enjoyable so far, and you've been so understanding with all that has been going on."

"It's nothing, dear." She waved my thanks away. We sat in silence for several moments.

"You said you have a daughter?" I asked her, hesitating to approach the subject. I got the feeling that this was something long in the past, and maybe a painful memory for her.

"Ah, yes. I did, you see. But she left Sosen no Tani some time ago and I haven't seen her since. I was told she too fell ill from all of the destruction the demons are causing to our land and didn't survive."

"That's terrible, Misao-dono."

"Pretty horrible, huh?"

"I lost my mother from sickness too. I'm glad that I could bring some liveliness to your house while I've been here," I added, smiling.

She patted me on the shoulder before tugging me to my feet. "There. All set, child. Chiyo and the others should be arriving soon. Let's go prepare the tea and sake and wait for them outside."

We made our way onto the front porch of the house, me carrying the tray of tea and cups freshly warmed from the fire, and Misao-dono carrying the more treasured item, the sake. The plan was for most of the village to meet at Misao-dono's house in a traditional annual feast before walking up the mountain together to the Yatagarasu's Shrine, where we would help the Fire Keepers construct large straw and cypress torches for the upcoming Fire Festival at the end of the week.

Every year, in mid-July, the town of Nachi back in the human realm always held a Fire Festival at the Kumano Grand Shrine and Kumano Temple. Large torches made of straw and sacred hinoki cypress wood were crafted and set on fire to be carried to and from Nachi Falls. It was believed that this symbolized carrying the original twelve kami of the waterfall from their seats in the shrine back home to the waterfall for rejuvenation and purification. Twelve shrine palanquins were also to be constructed to represent the twelve deities. It was a tradition that I was excited to be a part of in Sosen no Tani, considering I had missed this year's Summer Festival, with all the events of the wildfire. We were in for a lot of work, so in an effort to motivate the troops, Misao-dono held a feast large enough to feed fifty people every year, to give them strength to create the torches and palanquins with honor.

"You know we taught the humans this ceremony, right?" Misao-dono told me when I shared my excitement over the festival.

"No, I didn't," I replied. "But I guess that makes sense."

"Oh, yes. We were the ones who let the humans know the gods wanted to be brought home to the waterfall every year. It was one of the main ways to appease them and ward off famine and disaster."

"I see," I replied.

"Our Keepers take a special liking to this festival. It is rather suited to them, you know. Usually, the twelve most skilled and respected Keepers are asked to light and carry the ceremonial torches. And our most honored spiritual leaders are asked to perform ritual dances."

Now, we took our seats on the porch, ready to greet the first guests. Out of the corner of my eye, to my left, I noticed Misao-dono was taking an early start to the sake.

"Hey!" I swatted her arm away. "Those are for the guests!"

"Hush, child," she replied gruffly.

Chiyo and her family were first to arrive, with Minoru, little Hana, and her father Kamachi-san in tow. "Misao-dono! Kairi-chan!" Chiyo called to us affectionately, holding up Hana's hand to wave.

"Come, come! Please have a seat and some tea!" Misao-dono ushered them up onto the porch and into the house, where she seated them around the sunken hearth, instructing me to hand them each a cup of tea. I did as she asked.

More villagers arrived at Misao-dono's doorstep, Aoki-san from the teahouse, along with a few of the merchants I saw in the mornings along the main street. Several other farmers who lived near Misao-dono also came by. The group filed into Misao-dono's humble farmhouse and by the time we were ready to start wielding our bowls of rice, close to sixty people had crammed into her front living room and spilled out onto the front porch. Four bottles of sake had already been consumed.

I navigated the sea of seated Ancestors like I was avoiding stepping in hot lava, leaping over various legs and appendages to pass out enough rice, fish, and stew to feed the crowd. People munched on their meals happily and greeted me with a smile as I came through. Others grumbled as I briefly tripped over socked feet or accidentally knocked their sake cups off-kilter. Most of them had gotten used to seeing me daily in town by now, and no longer showed the same level of reproach they did when I had first arrived. However, more than a handful still averted their eyes when I came around to serve them.

"You're so helpful, Kairi, honestly!" a woman named Saru-san said to me. I recognized her as one of the game hunters in the village.

"It's no trouble!" I replied. "It was so helpful of *you* to supply us with the boar for tonight's stew." She laughed and brushed me off.

"She is helpful, isn't she?" Misao-dono called over the crowd.

I heard a chorus of people, who were now well into their first few cups of sake, agree.

"SO helpful!" Chiyo boasted. "She helped my father carry and store lumber to supply him through the winter for his business when he was struggling! And she's always willing to watch Hana for me when Minoru is away from the farm."

"I wasn't struggling!" Old Kamachi-san, with flushed cheeks, called indignantly over his cup of sake. "But Kairi *was* a great help," he admitted.

"She helped me pick up and clean my haul of fish the other day after it fell out of the basket while heading to market!" I heard a merchant call.

"And she offered to stitch my favorite kimono back together after she noticed it had a tear in it!" another neighbor added.

"I never thought humans could be such great neighbors!" I heard another voice chime in.

"Oh, stop it everyone! It really is no trouble; anyone would help with those things!" I replied, now thoroughly embarrassed.

I looked to Misao-dono for help, stupidly, but instead of

finding an ally, I saw something flare in her eyes.

"Say, everyone, to show our thanks to Kairi for being such an excellent guest, and to honor this beautiful example of humans and Ancestors once again living in harmony, why don't we invite Kairi to perform this year's kagura dance at the festival?"

"What?" I blurted out, completely mortified at the idea of public performance.

The room was quiet for several moments before everyone erupted at once.

"Yeah!"

"That's a great idea!"

"But she's a *human*..."

"Can humans even dance the kagura?"

"We should have thought of it sooner!"

"Will she even *be* here for the festival?"

The shouting continued for several more rounds until, eventually, the majority were in agreement.

I whirled around again on Misao-dono in bewilderment and betrayal, only to catch her wink at me.

She got the whole room drunk and then capitalized on their good mood and appreciation to solidify the towns' opinion of humans. I reminded myself to never get on her bad side.

"Come on, Kairi! Please do the kagura dance!" Little Hana bellowed from her dad's side.

"Yeah, Kairi, won't you do the kagura dance?" Chiyo emulated her daughter's puppy eyes and looked at me expectantly.

Her, too. I wouldn't get on Chiyo's bad side either.

"Alright, alright, how can I turn down such an invitation?" I said.

The room erupted in more cheers.

"Hey, crew! What say you we join the Keepers at the Temple?" Misao-dono called.

"Yeah!" the crowd cheered.

This ought to be something, I thought.

For as much alcohol as they had consumed, the townspeople cleared out of Misao-dono's house rather efficiently, forming a drunken parade, merrily making their way up the mountainside. Every now and again, I'd catch sight of various villagers stumbling and Misao-dono, their ringleader, slurring her words as she belted out the lyrics to countless folk songs the group took up in unison. Being completely sober myself, I cringed, yet couldn't help but laugh at the sight. I worried briefly about us disturbing the other neighbors, but most of the town had been at Misao-dono's anyway. And whoever hadn't joined us for food came out of their homes and joined the procession now.

Luckily, by the time we made it to the Temple, the night air and arduous walk had sobered most of the party up, leaving a light, happy buzz and just enough sobriety to seriously complete the task at hand. By now, the sun was starting to go down and we would have to work by the fireside to accomplish our task.

As we filed onto the Temple grounds, various Keepers and monks greeted us. While we had been drinking, it was clear the Keepers had been busy—no wonder none of them had joined us for our feast. Massive goblet-like torches were being constructed by groups of four Keepers per torch, with two people constructing the straw interior and two deftly weaving the sacred cypress to form the torch's exterior.

As townspeople began to pair off with Keepers and start work on the palanquins, I caught sight of Ryoko, applying the cypress wood with intense focus. I looked around, expecting to see Mato working alongside him, but he wasn't there. I did a quick scan of the courtyard, but Mato was nowhere to be seen.

"Ryoko!" I called to him, catching his attention.

"Kairi! Hey!" he replied, looking up from his work and waving his arm at me excitedly.

"Wow, these look amazing!" I walked up to the torches. Just the head of one of the goblets was easily half my height.

"Thank you!" he said, grinning at me. "They weigh over

one hundred pounds," he added, the grin falling from his face.

"Yeesh."

He grimaced.

"Hey, have you seen Mato? Isn't he here?"

Ryoko looked uncomfortable for a second, but replied, "Ah, no. He's out on assignment tonight."

"Assignment?" I asked him. "What assignment?"

Looking like he had said too much and starting to fidget slightly, Ryoko looked around nervously for help for a moment before responding to me.

I squinted at him, suspicious.

"Sorry. I thought you knew. It means he's out hunting demons."

"Oh, you mean like missions?" I asked dumbly.

"Yeah. Keepers like me and Mato, who wear the black robes, get sent out on assignments to detect and diffuse any demons that might be coming too close to Sosen no Tani in both the spirit and human realms. Or neutralize demons that are directly contributing to destruction in our realm," Ryoko explained, looking slightly more relieved that I was somewhat familiar with the idea.

"So you mean he's actually killing things right now?"

"Well, hopefully," Ryoko shrugged.

"What was his assignment?" I asked.

"That's classified."

"Fine. When does he get back?"

He shrugged again. "Whenever he completes his mission. Likely that will be sometime late tonight, or if it was a particularly tough one, early in the morning. All to say, he won't be helping us prepare for the festival tonight."

"Fair enough. Thanks, Ryoko."

"Sure. Even though now I feel like I just made some sort of grave error telling you," he muttered.

Now it was my turn to shrug. "I don't know. You tell me."

"Whatever. Want to jump in and help us on this torch?" he asked me, seeming to bounce back to his jovial self in the blink of an eye.

"Sure. What can I help with?"

I knelt down next to Ryoko, nodding to the three other Keepers working on the torch. I watched intently as Ryoko showed me how to line the cypress up side by side and weave it into place with strands of straw. When it was my turn to give it a go, Ryoko handed me the strips of cypress wood and I held them in place as he strung the straw through each strand.

"Did you know the wood comes from the sacred hinoki tree behind the Temple?" he asked me.

"No, I didn't," I replied, furrowing my brows in concentration as we switched off and he held the wood in place while I weaved.

"Easy! You don't want to tear the straw,"Ryoko said.

"Ugh, I'm sorry," I mumbled, my clumsy fingers trying to get a firm hold on the frail grass. Misao-dono has been showing me how to repair fabric and sew, but with my lack of dexterity, it looked like I hadn't developed a knack for it yet.

"Why does the wood have to be from that specific tree on the Temple grounds?" I asked.

"The wood has to be from a sacred source and blessed in order to be used in the torches. The torches are meant to re-purify the shrine and the deities. So fire in itself is purifying and burns away the old to give birth to the new, but it needs to be burnt with wholesome intention," Ryoko replied.

I stayed quiet, pondering his words.

"You mean fire isn't only for destruction?" I asked him.

"Of course not," he replied, laughing as if the answer was obvious. "Fire brings life just as easily as it takes it. Without fire, none of us could survive. Fire can burn away impurities of any substance it comes in contact with, just as it can be caused by those impurities, or rage out of control because of them. It all depends on its use, and the ability to respect its dual nature."

"Ryoko, I really think you should be wearing red robes instead of black. You're a lot wiser than you are skilled at combat," I teased him.

He rolled his eyes, "Oh, like how you're a lot more of a wise-ass than you are skilled with your fingers?"

"Exactly," I laughed at his unexpected retort. I guess I should have seen it coming from someone who had to contend with Mato's daily ribbing.

"Come on; we have like seven more of these to finish."

The rest of the night was spent in laughter and good spirits as villagers and Keepers swapped off between constructing torches and palanquins. The group decided I was a sufficient enough weaver, so I was kept on torch duty, while others painted the palanquins vermillion red and decorated them with gold charms. All in all, we finished our work late into the evening, well past midnight. As we stumbled back to our respective homes, some of us drunker and sleepier than we had been on the walk up, I pondered what Ryoko had said.

Thinking back to that awful night two weeks ago, I realized my perception of fire had changed. I thought of Mato in his training sessions. While I'd never seen him use fire while he sparred except for that one time against Yoshizo-san, he was somewhere out in the night wielding it now to fight against a whole swath of demons that had all but taken over the world.

As long as you respect its dual nature.

***

I woke up the next morning a bit later than usual. Misao-dono had given me the day off from field work, claiming that proper instruction in the Fire Festival's kagura dance was far more important. I was to make my way up to Yatagarasu's Shrine by no later than eight.

I hurried up the hill in the most formal attire I could find in Misao-dono's house, a silk kimono, with my hair tied back in a neat bun by two chopsticks, and my feet barely strapped into two *geta* platform sandals. It was the latter part of the outfit that I was struggling the most with. I tripped almost every five steps while I hurried up the hill, nearly wiping out and eliciting some strange looks and laughs from villagers.

Damnit, I thought to myself in frustration, *How is any woman supposed to get anywhere in these things?! If I can barely walk in these freaking shoes, how do they expect me to dance?!*

By the time I finally climbed the nearly endless steps to the shrine, I was already sweating profusely, and strands of my hair stuck out of place. Breathing more heavily than I wanted to admit, it took me a second to realize that there was an older Keeper standing in front of the shrine in red robes, waiting for me. I straightened up hastily when I noticed her, embarrassed by the sheer chaotic energy I was emitting.

"Are you Kairi, the human?" the older woman asked me. She was small and lean and couldn't have been older than her forties. She had a stern expression that seemed to pierce right through me as she looked me up and down.

"Why ever are you dressed like that?" she asked.

"I thought dance lessons were... formal?" I replied.

"My, you don't know anything, do you?" she sighed reproachfully. "Well, this is sure to be a lot of work. Come; let's get on it with it."

In only two hours, I had worked physically harder to master this dance than to accomplish anything I could remember in my life. Sora-Sensei, my instructor, may as well have been a drill sergeant. I don't know about spiritual, but she was severe, for sure.

The dance, in itself, was almost obviously simple. The first, preparatory, phase consisted of slow, precise movements following a circular pattern and was accompanied only by the soft sounds of a flute and the kagura bells I held in each of my hands. Then, the second half of the dance erupted into fast-paced leaps and jumps with the addition of taiko drums. I had thought I had gotten the steps down pretty quickly, especially after focusing my breath and centering my gravity from my lessons with Mato, but Sora-Sensei made it abundantly clear that I definitely hadn't.

"Stop!" she'd scream abruptly. "Your hands aren't right."

"You're ringing the bells too quickly."

"Just *look* at your right foot—no, don't actually look at it! Would it kill you to pay attention to your feet?"

Finally, after attempting to transition into the second half of the dance, Sora-Sensei had apparently had enough of my incapability and threw her hands into the air, screaming "Hopeless!" before departing from the room. The other Keepers who were playing music in the corner of the empty tatami-matted hall and had, subsequently, bore witness to all of my shame, stopped playing awkwardly and pretended to go get water.

I had never thought of myself as a dancer, but I never thought of myself as completely inept, either. Man, did Sora-san know how to destroy someone's confidence. I tugged at the hem of the kimono Sora-san had put me in, feeling the heavy fabric weighing on my neck. I had been sweating profusely through the garment like we were rehearsing in a desert.

The second I had entered the temple, Sora-Sensei required I get changed into an outfit befitting of the traditional kagura dance: a short red kimono with long, draping sleeves, and black hakama pants fastened over the top at my waist. It wasn't the traditional shrine maiden outfit I was accustomed to seeing in Japan, but then again, I wasn't a shrine maiden and it would be wrong to dress as though I was. The outfit was a blend of colors of the Keepers' robes made out of heavy silk fabric. I imagined the garment looked actually quite beautiful swirling around while the dance was being performed, but all I could feel was the stifling heat.

Later, after Sora-Sensei had regained her self-composure, she re-entered the room and explained to me that the particular dance I was performing symbolized the unity between the Keepers' two schools of thought and their aligned mission to care for humans. The dance was meant to be an offering of thanks to both the god of fire, Kagutsuchi, and Amaterasu, the sun goddess herself.

"You said Misao-dono and the other villagers appointed you to this?" Sora-Sensei asked, dripping with skepticism. She had returned to the hall whispering exasperatedly to herself that she would "fulfill her duties as a Keeper no matter what that looked like."

"Yes ma'am."

"Very well, if it can't be helped," she sighed. "Listen carefully. This is the first time we have had a human in the village in any of our lifetimes. This dance is more symbolic of unity now than ever before. You cannot risk making a misstep and bringing such disrespect to the hospitality the Ancestors have shown you. It would risk any future good relations between us and the humans."

Though a little confused by the severity of her words and the political statement I was about to make, I bowed to my teacher obediently. "I'll do my best."

"You'd better. Now let's resume."

I straightened my spine and stood up slowly, bringing the bells back into their starting position at my chest. Out of the corner of my eye, I could see the taiko drum players glance hesitantly between myself and the teacher.

"Well, what are you doing? Get on with it!" she commanded them. After a start, the flutist quickly picked up her instrument and began to play. I felt solidarity in knowing I wasn't Sora-Sensei's only victim.

Focusing intently on what Sora-Sensei had just told me, I knew I wouldn't become a good dancer overnight, but I would do my best to diligently display the respect the people of Sosen no Tani deserved. I tried to close my eyes and just listen to the flow of the music. The beginning phases of the dance were accompanied by a soft, almost dreamlike tune that floated over the room, surrounding me. I tried to swirl in sync with the notes of the melody. By the time the drums joined in, the melody had changed to something faster paced and playful.

There was a large amount of stepping, twirling, and jumping in this part of the kagura, and I was reminded of the grass dances I would watch Indigenous dancers perform during competitions back in Vermont, when the local Abenaki tribe would host festivals for First Nations and Indigenous peoples across America and Canada. My father was a board member at the tribe's nonprofit organization and would volunteer annually at the festivals, bringing me along to help as well. I remember running eagerly to the edge of the ring the dancers would compete in, eager to watch them seemingly become one with their surroundings. It looked effortless how their movements blended with the drums, as if they knew when each beat was coming.

Being so young and knowing nothing of Indigenous dancing, I had no idea if each individual dancer was skilled at their art or not, but I could feel the energy they brought to each of their dances. I resolved to be like the grass dancers I saw growing up and let myself be led by the beat of the drums, hoping my heart and intention would show through.

By the end of our practice, Sora-Sensei came up to me and threw me a towel. I caught it in my left hand and dabbed it on the back of my neck and across my forehead.

"Well, you didn't turn out to be a complete lost cause," she said.

Was she *praising* me?

"It was almost believable that you were speaking to the gods in that latter half of our session today."

"Was I supposed to be?"

After only a brief exasperated suck of her teeth, she explained, "The beginning part of the kagura is meant to prepare the dancer, which is usually a priestess or someone of spiritual power. They are presumed, when performing the kagura, to be a vessel almost for the god to speak through. The first part of the dance prepares the dancer to enter this trancelike state, with the second, more lively part meant to be performed while that person is in said trance."

"Should I be going into a trance? I have no idea how to do that," I said.

"Calm down. I have no expectations of you."

Her reply was both stinging and relieving.

"I just ask you don't offend anyone with your lack of refinement. But it looks as though we may be able to make some progress with you yet. Now off you go. I will see you here this time tomorrow."

Sora-Sensei and I practiced the Fire Festival's kagura every morning for the next four days, continuing to be relieved of my farm duties. I was determined to win her over by the end of our sessions, and on the last morning, I was able to elicit a response of "Sufficient" from her, which I considered a complete victory. I thanked a lot of my newfound muscle control and refined movements to my sessions with Mato, who I hadn't been able to train with while preparing for the dance. When I was able to rush out of practice early to the training yard, I would either have been too late and missed the Keepers' sparring sessions completely, or Mato would be out on assignment.

"I didn't know they sent him out during the day too," I told Ryoko one afternoon.

"They don't, usually," he had replied.

Something unusual must have been going on with the demons, as a lot of other Keepers were away from the Temple during the day as well. But I hadn't even seen Mato since before the night we made the torches. I was told he'd be at the Fire Festival though, as he was an integral part of the ceremony this year. The thought made me more anxious for the festival than I already was.

Now, as I bowed to Sora-Sensei at the end of my training, I left the Shrine with a strange mix of nervous anticipation. Throughout my lessons, I had learned to listen intuitively to the rhythm of the instruments. I had learned to let myself be moved by them, and to let my intentions show when I danced. I was excited to give my thanks to the people of Sosen no Tani and hoped that this offering to the gods would be a way to learn more about why I was here. But most of all, I was excited to see Mato and to show him what I had learned while he was away.

CHAPTER EIGHTEEN

Mato

There was an awful ripping sound as I severed the demon's head from its body. Watching the creature burst into flames and disappear before me, I wiped the blood from my blade on the sleeve of my kimono.

Ever since Ryoko had informed me five days ago that large amounts of demons were flocking to the Nachi area in the human realm, I had been on assignment here just about every day. There were no fires to be lit this time; the Elders had specifically informed us Keepers to infiltrate the area and try to get intel before making any moves. Only then were we allowed to start killing as we saw fit.

When I had first arrived back there, my first time since setting the fire that brought Kairi to us, Nachi was in shambles. Most of the houses were dilapidated and the once thriving rice fields were charred to a crisp. A majority of residents were living in makeshift homes above the local restaurants and convenience stores near the town's community center at the base of the valley. Or they were living in spare rooms on the Temple or Shrine grounds, which had remained unscathed. I had been careful not the light the fire near the sacred grounds, but I also knew their spiritual power alone would stave off any disaster.

The only reason I could think as to why so many demons were flooding the area was because they prayed on chaos and destruction. And Nachi was clearly a hotbed of it. It wasn't unusual for bottom-feeder demons, stragglers, to come picking over the ruins after the Keepers had set a fire or other Ancestors had caused a flood. But they were usually just that, stragglers, not droves of demons in all strengths and ranks.

Because this was a scouting mission as much as it was a culling mission, I and a few of my other brethren had been sent during the day to watch and listen. I could see them everywhere. Crawling over the debris, wearing search and rescue uniforms, making up the local fire brigade to help "extinguish any existing flames." I also saw them wearing doctors' uniforms and especially in suits, showing up and claiming to the town's residents they were there "on behalf of your insurance."

It was disgusting and unreal just how many of these worms had inhabited human bodies and taken control over the systems that were supposed to be *helping.* It was all just to stay in control and to make things worse for the villagers who had suffered damages from the fire, all while believing they were being helped. I scoffed as I watched from my various posts in the tree lines and between buildings.

On about the third day of staking things out, I had had about enough of watching this fake heroism play out. The other Keepers had found about as little information for the reason for the demons' presence as I did, and Elder Tadaaki had finally given us the okay to start taking them out. "It's simple," we had told him. "They're there because there is suffering. They are trying to prey off of it and cause even more."

That was enough for us to begin slicing their heads off. And for me to begin practicing the new technique I had learned, attempting to use the demons' energies to produce fire. I had managed to manipulate their energies only two other times, and usually when I had let myself get into desperate situations to test the limits of this new ability. I hadn't fully figured it out yet, but I had taken out at least twenty of them at this point, just two days into the gore. In the forms of elderly townspeople, young, strong first responders, and small, seemingly helpless children orphaned by the fire. They all shared the same rotting smell of human flesh with something sinister continuing to animate it.

They all shared that same cold look in their eyes that raised hairs on the back of my neck.

Now, after watching my most recent prey disintegrate before my eyes, I moved to sheathe my sword back in its scabbard when suddenly I felt a presence looming above me in the trees. Swiping my blade across the air above me in one smooth arc, I sliced a demon, masquerading as a young woman, clean in half as she jumped down from the branch she was perched on. These bastards were going to make me late.

I had spent the night in the human realm, something we didn't need to do often but was the case now, as we had to deal with the infestation discreetly. Tonight was the night of the Fire Festival back in Sosen no Tani and somewhere within the days of traveling to and from the spirit realm to the human realm, someone had informed me I had a big role to play this year due to my newly discovered technique with fire. The Keepers were so amazed by this new discovery that I had been given the honor of lighting the first torch in the festival, an acknowledgement usually given to the most skilled and accomplished Keeper. They also told me Kairi would be performing the kagura dance.

I definitely didn't plan on missing that. It had been nearly a week since I had last seen Kairi, and oddly enough, I was keenly aware of it. On the days that I was back at the Temple, I would spar per my usual training schedule before being sent back out into the field. I looked for Kairi where she usually watched at the edge of the training yard, but she hadn't been there for days. It was unsettling, and honestly, I was a little surprised by myself that I felt disappointed. I wondered if she'd come for her daily lesson in martial arts, but when she didn't show up for that either, I got mildly concerned.

It was Ryoko who finally told me she was volunteered by Misao-dono and the other villagers to perform this year's kagura dance—an honor that I was proud of her for receiving. But her lessons to learn the dance took up all of her time in the mornings and we didn't get to see each other.

I was determined to see her tonight.

Not bothering to sheathe my blade this time, or wipe it off, I held it out defensively in front of me and broke out running back toward the well. I had made it as far as the woods near Nachi Falls when I noticed that several demons had either followed me back from the town, lured by my Keeper's Flame, or had been lurking in the woods, waiting to pick off some stray villager.

I had sliced through several more by the time I finally plunged myself into the depths of the well. Only then did my sword find its way back into the scabbard. Climbing hastily out of the next exit to Sosen no Tani, I checked the sun's position in the sky. It was starting to fall closer to the horizon and I knew I only had about an hour before the festival would start. Maintaining a light jog all the way up the mountain, I flew through the interior of the temple and to my sleeping quarters like I was still on the hunt. Several Keepers startled in surprise as I blew past them, a few staring at me like they had just seen a ghost.

Bursting into my small room, I had just enough time to grab a fresh kimono and hakama before flying back out the door and making my way to the sacred pool in back of the temple. A few yards into the forest, an ice-cold pool swirled with foaming water from a small waterfall that trickled down from one of the mountain's streams. I ripped my bloodstained kimono from my body and plunged myself in it with no hesitation. Washing the gore and ichor from my skin, the freezing cold water felt reinvigorating after twenty-four hours of fighting and patrol.

After only a couple of moments, I jumped back out onto the rocks at the water's edge, savoring the sweet feeling of cold water on my skin as the heat of the evening began to re-envelop me. I combed through my hair once with my fingers before fastening it back up into its half knot. Redressing in my fresh set of clothing, I attached my sword at my waist. On the edge of the pool, I peeled some bark from hinoki cypress and sandalwood trees and lit it on fire at the tips of my fingers. Mixing the ash with a little bit of water from the pool, I smeared the paste across my chest and under my armpits just to be safe.

Running back toward the Temple, I found the crowds had already begun to gather, making their way up the long steep steps from the base of the mountain. In the courtyard of the shrine in front of the sacred camphor tree, various festival dances had already started taking place just as the sun was going down. Three Keepers wearing red paraded around in a circle with a faux ox head strapped on top of one man's skull, depicting a story of one of the gods. I breathed a sigh of relief. I hadn't missed it; Kairi's dance would be next.

I relaxed into the crowd, blending into the circle that the mix of villagers and Keepers had formed around the performers. People laughed and cheered at the performance. I smiled to myself, but after finally having a moment to rest, I found my mind and my eyes wandering to gaze out at the mountain range beyond.

The entrance to the shrine was announced by a large red torii gate facing a vast expanse of mountains that spread out over what was known as the Kii Peninsula in the human realm. Yatagarasu's Shrine was positioned so high up on the side of one of these mountains that you could see over the entire town and just about the whole mountain range beyond. The sky had started to bleed a vibrant red color, the same vermillion as the red on the torii gate, when a jingling of bells caught my attention. I refocused my gaze on the performance, just in time to see Kairi take her position in the center of the circle.

Her hair was worn long and straight down her back, falling to the base of her spine and tied back with a single red ribbon. It was the first time I had ever seen makeup covering her face, making her eyes appear deeper and more striking than they already were. She wore bells on both her wrists and her ankles over the tabi socks and sandals strapped to her feet. A black pair of hakama were knotted tightly at her small waist over a bright red kimono with sleeves that nearly brushed the ground.

I felt a strange sensation in my chest as I looked at her. Usually, she wore farm clothes or a simple kimono when we saw each other, but this was something different. The usual playful, soft expression that illustrated her face was replaced by something more calm, focused, and almost reserved. She looked like one of the kami of the forest in the mountains surrounding us.

The audience stilled, a murmur passing over them.

"There's Kairi!"

"Is that the human?"

"She doesn't look like a human! She looks like Amaterasu herself!"

"I thought this was a bad idea, but she just might surprise us!"

Just then, with a single shake of the kagura bells she held in both hands, Kairi began to move. A high-pitched, haunting tune poured out of the flute one of the musicians played at the edge of the circle. I watched as Kairi began turning in slow, rhythmic circles, making soft movements with her wrists and feet. It was immediately clear to me that our brief martial arts lessons had been paying off; the grace and ease with which she commanded her body was no subtle feat. It was hard to believe she only had only learned this kagura in four days. But that was Kairi—an excellent student, albeit a mouthy one.

She kept her eyes downcast as she moved, as if she wasn't ready to yet to connect with the audience. I was almost certain she was nervous, but it didn't show. This calm, poised, mysterious side to Kairi was one I had very quickly forgotten existed. I hadn't seen it since the day she was interrogated by the Elders. I watched as Kairi paused in mid-movement at the center of the clearing. She cast the kagura bells in her right hand in a wide circle around her body, arching up over her head before drawing them back in toward her chest.

Suddenly, as if from nowhere, the beat of the taiko drums interrupted the melodic sounds of flute and Kairi's dance changed from one of slow, trancelike magic to one of high energy. She leapt off the ground, twirling and bounding to the beat of the music. The audience surrounding her let out yelps of surprise and delight. Her feet beat the earth as she stepped and spun, and I could see a smile spread across her face as she began to laugh. The reserved expression she had held onto so dutifully at the beginning of the dance exploded into one of pure joy. Warmth radiated from her smile, from her body, from her movements. I could feel it filling me up, like it did when she first reached out to me in the dream sent by Yatagarasu. She illuminated the village.

Kairi's dance ended in a swell of applause. As soon as it was over, the Elders filled the circle to light the ceremonial Central Flame. Dragging an iron cauldron about the size of a horse to the center of the courtyard, they filled it with wood from the sacred hinoki tree. In unison, the Elders brandished their swords, igniting them with flame, and set the cauldron ablaze.

The flames soared fourteen feet high. The surrounding crowd, in a chorus of oohs and aahs, edged backward some feet to give it space. I pushed my way politely through the crowd, watching Kairi as she stood at the edge of the circle, gazing up at the flames. Her expression of joy just moments prior had melted into one of hesitation and discomfort. It was barely noticeable, but she winced in proximity to the fire. She was close enough that I'm sure she felt the intensity of the heat on her skin and was probably reliving those moments back in the human realm just before she crossed the border into Sosen no Tani. I felt a twinge of guilt as I made my way toward her. That discomfort was my fault.

Moving to stand just behind her on her right side, I leaned over to her and lightly teased, "Kairi, you're not breathing right."

"What?" She turned toward me, startled.

"Inhale deeply through your nose. Feel the warmth from the fire and imagine it spreading through each limb of your body."

I looked at her expectantly. She did as I said.

"Exhale slowly, completely through the nose. As you breathe out, imagine you are breathing air as cold as ice over all of your limbs, extinguishing the flames."

She complied.

"As you breathe in again, feel the fire filling up your lungs. When you exhale, imagine your breath is frosting it over, expelling the flames. Take a few more breaths like this."

She continued to do as I asked. After a couple more breaths, she opened her eyes and looked at me, the look of panic of her face now gone.

"Feeling better?"

She nodded.

"It's a technique the Keepers teach us when we are first starting out. How to withstand the fire—the first step to being able to manipulate it," I explained.

"Thanks. That helps," she said, giving me a soft smile.

"I can see all of that martial arts training is paying off," I added.

"What do you mean?"

"The kagura. You were amazing."

She blushed noticeably before looking away. "You think so? Really, I was just trying not to make a complete ass of myself. Or the people who volunteered me. I just hope I was able to give it some of the spirit Sora-Sensei was talking about. That woman's *tough!*" She was talking quickly, and I got the impression she was flustered by what I had said.

"Oh, you had plenty of spirit," I told her honestly. "It was beautiful."

The flush in her face deepened considerably, but this time, she looked directly at me.

"It's good to see you. It feels like it's been a while, but it's only been a few days."

Around us, the crowd had thinned out as people began making their way to light the torches. Intuitively, we began walk over to the rocks at the edge of the courtyard, taking a seat to talk with one another.

"I know what you mean. I dare say I even *missed* getting verbally accosted while trying to teach you how to be a full-fledged Keeper," I joked.

"Oh really?!" She giggled. I laughed with her. Her laugh had a nice sound to it. Like almost everything about her, it was filled with warmth.

After a moment, her face grew more serious and she said, "How are you? Are you okay? I heard you've been accosted in other ways over the last few days."

I wrinkled my nose at her disgustedly. "Yikes, what are you implying?"

She burst out in giggles again, this time smacking my arm lightly. "Stop it! That's not what I meant. I was trying to be smart with my words, but it came out awkward. Ryoko told me you've been out hunting demons. He filled me in on the assignments Keepers go on when I asked where you'd been. Are you hurt at all? How did it go?"

"Oh, if that's what you were getting at, you should have just said so," I said with a rueful smile.

She rolled her eyes at me.

"I'm fine. But, yes I was out hunting demons. In the human realm, actually. There had been a large influx in numbers of the recent days and the Keepers couldn't figure out why. So they sent us in to do some reconnaissance and to bring the numbers down."

"I see," she said thoughtfully. "So were you successful?"

"In reconnaissance?"

"In bringing the numbers down?"

"Some," I replied, looking at her quizzically.

"I know I've seen you train just about a million times at this point, and I've never seen you get hurt, but I guess I was still worried about you."

"That's kind of you," I said softly. "But there's no need to worry. I've been doing this for years."

"Men are such idiots. What a stupid thing to say! Aren't you supposed to be an all-knowing samurai warrior? It just takes one time to really mess yourself up!" she admonished me. She was right, of course.

I laughed.

"What's it like?" she asked softly after a moment. "Fighting a demon? What do they look like? Are they *stronger* than the Keepers?"

"They look like you and me," I replied. "Most at this point have taken over human bodies and are simply just animating them. Their strengths all differ. Both depending on the host and the evil which that particular demon possesses."

"If they look like you and me, how do you know they're a demon and not human?" she asked.

"It's just a feeling. Something isn't right. The hairs on the back of your neck stand up. And they *smell*. Like rotting flesh, at least to me anyway. You can also tell by the look in their eyes," I tried to explain. "It's a sense the Keepers have been taught to cultivate from a young age. And I think something the Ancestors are born with here, being a part of the spirit realm."

She nodded, mulling over my words. I felt a jolt of surprise run through my body as she gently laid her head on my shoulder. I could smell the scent of vanilla and sage from her hair as it tickled my cheek. A deep feeling of longing stirred in my chest, startling me almost as much as her actions.

When had I become so attached to Kairi?

I like her. The words echoed in my mind.

"Just don't get yourself killed, okay? I know I've only known you a few weeks. But I can't stand to lose another person I care about. First with my mom, and now, potentially with my aunt too. I don't know if I'll ever see her again. Maybe it was even demons who lit that fire in Nachi. I never believed we'd have a wildfire in a climate so humid…" She trailed off.

The ball of guilt I had been feeling resurfaced again as I heard the anguish in her voice.

"Kairi, it wasn't demons. There's something I have to tell you—"

"Mato! It's time! Come light the ceremonial torch!" a fellow

Keeper yelled from the fray, bounding over to where we were sitting.

Kairi hastily straightened, lifting her head from my shoulder.

"I'll be right there!" I responded, exasperated at such horrible timing. "Kairi, I need to—"

"Yes, Mr. Top Tier Keeper, you need to go! Go on; we can talk later. I can't wait to see the torches!" She smiled at me excitedly. I couldn't bear to break the look of childlike joy on her face, so I stood up, conflicted and worried.

"Go on! I'll watch from the sidelines! Let's go; we're going to miss it!" she said, standing up and pulling my hand in the direction of the torches.

I let her lead me to where the crowd had gathered around the twelve supersized bundles of straw and cypress.

"Okay, but please, can we talk after?"

"Sure, I promise," she beamed.

Nodding, I turned away from her and walked into the center of the crowd.

CHAPTER NINETEEN

Kairi

It was time to begin lighting the ceremonial torches for the purification ritual to begin. I waited at the edge of the crowd with anticipation. This had always been my favorite part of the festival as a child. Flame would burst explosively from the straw and the contrast of the balls of fire against the night sky as they dotted the mountainside always looked otherworldly.

I watched as Mato took his position across from the first torch. He would be lighting the first flame, an honor given only to the highest-ranking and most respected warrior of the Keepers, I had learned. Several Keepers in red robes sang a fierce chant as the fire in Mato's hands began to take form. I watched as he used the friction of the energy around him to produce a spark, and in a second, it transformed into a roaring ball of flames he kept contained between his fists. The sight was surprising, although I should have been expecting it. The flames illuminated his near-black eyes, and I could see the fierce expression of the warrior within him as he suddenly exploded with movement. In a deep voice, he sang the Keepers' chant back to them and thrust the ball of flames into the first torch, being held steady by Ryoko.

The crowd erupted into cheers. The remaining twelve Keepers lit their torches from Mato's. Mato then hoisted it up over his shoulder, leading the procession down the mountain toward the waterfall. Ryoko followed suit at his left flank, filling his mouth occasionally with water from a handheld jug and spitting it onto the torch to abate the flames.

The crowd began to move with the Keepers along the sides of the dirt road, making space for the torches in the center. I followed along as we trailed Mato down the mountain. His skin shone with a thin sheen of sweat and his brows remained knitted together as he balanced the monstrous, burning heap of straw on his shoulder.

I felt my heart flutter despite itself.

The dichotomy of Mato's nature had been fascinating to me over these last few weeks. He flowed between his usual easy-going, playful self to a fierce, disciplined samurai as easily as water flowing through a stream. His infectious smile, his lightning-fast speed. The fact that I missed him when I didn't get to see him often. How in only days it felt as natural to hang out with him as it did my own family, as though we had known each other for years. I hadn't realized how attached I had become to him in the short time I had been here. *I like him,* I thought to myself, the sudden realization shocking me. I felt like slapping myself over how oblivious I had been to my own feelings. *I really like him.*

The procession moved down the mountain in a chorus of drums, cheering, and chants. The fire bearers led the way, followed by Elder Ryu and the other priestesses of Yatagarasu's Shrine, the most highly esteemed Keepers of the spiritual sect. Behind them came the palanquin-bearers, the musicians, and townsfolk who filled the streets in eager anticipation.

It was fully dark by the time we reached the great waterfall. As I walked, I noted to myself how the festival differed from what I remembered at home.

Back in Nachi, the festival took place during the day. There was no kagura dance at the beginning, but a dance led by a priest with twelve men and fans at the waterfall's edge to begin the ceremony, called the Nachi no Dengaku. The fire bearers would descend and re-ascend the mountain at least half a dozen times by the time they would finally extinguish their torches in the falls.

At the same time though, there was so much about the festival that had stayed the same. The structure of the torches, the intention of purification and reverence to the fire, the desire to rejuvenate the twelve gods who blessed the shrine throughout the year. The heart and spirit of the festival had not changed after all these years after the ancestors had passed it down to us, even though the human world and the spirit world were now largely divided and the human world was overrun with evil.

A thought occurred to me as I continued my descent. If festivals like Nachi's Fire Festival still existed in our modern world, and the heart and the spirit of these practices largely remained pure, there was hope for the humans and Ancestors. If we could hang on to the values and meanings behind these practices, humans and Ancestors could rekindle their relationship and overcome the demons that now threatened both of our worlds.

The procession halted at the base of the falls, next to what would have been the small Hiro Shrine. The fire bearers filed into lines of six, creating a clearing on either side of the falls where the palanquin bearers lowered the twelve structures to the ground. I watched from the edge of the crowd as Elder Ryu and the priestesses made their way under the torii gate to face the falls.

"Great Spirits of the Falls!" announced Elder Ryu in a voice I never knew her capable of. "We return you home to your ancestral abode! May the waters of the great Hiryu Gongen bring you strength and rejuvenation!"

Together, the priestesses bowed their heads and began a series of chants evoking the kami of the waterfall. Around me, the Keepers and the villagers closed their eyes and began to pray.

It had been hard to hear under the great roaring of the falls, but suddenly, as clear as day, a crow cawed above our heads. Startled, the villagers opened their eyes and looked up from their prayers, the priestesses stopping their chants.

Illuminated by the twelve torches, still blazing, we watched as a large three-legged crow landed deftly on the top of the torii gate in the center of the procession.

"It's Yatagarasu!"

"The gods have a message for us!"

Voices from the crowd spoke up in a mix of excitement and anxiety. Instantly, the entire crowd of villagers and Keepers dropped to their hands and knees in a bow. I followed suit.

"Ancestors of Sosen no Tani." A thunderous voice drowned out the falls.

I spent a wild moment looking around the clearing and up at the sky, trying to locate the sound of the voice. Could it have been the crow that was speaking? I shook my head furiously, trying to convince myself I wasn't hallucinating.

"Yatagarasu is speaking!" Murmurs ran through the crowd.

"I'm the one who is speaking," said a much quieter, steely calm voice this time.

I looked away from the crow at the top of the torii gate in the direction of the man's voice. As if appearing from nowhere, a regal-looking man sat atop the modest roof of Hiro Shrine. He looked no older than thirty, with long black hair trailing down his back, wrapped in a red-clothed ribbon. He wore deep blue robes as if he was a noble from the Heian period. He lounged back on his elbows lazily, eyeing the crowd bowing before him with a sneer of arrogance and thinly veiled anger.

"You stand before the great Twelve Gongen and act as though you have *time* to be revering the kami as you do," he scoffed.

"I, Hiryu Gongen, came on behalf of The Twelve and must share that they, as well as Amaterasu-sama and Inari-sama, are quite displeased with you Ancestors. In a mere two hundred years, a blink of the eye, we have lost more standing in all of the realms than has ever been known in all of time. Not only are we losing our clout, we are losing our homes and even worse, our *lives* and each other. And by we, I mean us kami, the Ancestors, *and* the humans—though they had but little clout to begin with.

The devastation of another ancient rice variety in the human realm has left Inari-sama ill.

"The Ancestors made a solemn promise to the kami that you would right the wrongs of the demons in the human world and save your human brethren. Lest you not forget the promise that breathed you into existence to act as their shepherds. This is *your* responsibility!" Lord Hiryu Gongen hurled the words through the crowd, his scary-calm tone quickly replaced by an enraged outburst.

"Gongen-sama—" Elder Ryu began, but Elder Tadaaki, who had been standing on the far edge of the waterfall, holding a blazing torch, put up one of his hands to silence her.

"Gongen-sama, our deepest apologies. Please continue your message."

Hiryu Gongen's eyes were shooting daggers at the Keepers.

"Your measly attempts to reverse the unmovable wave of destruction that is already full force in the human realm is laughable at best. The fire you lit in that little human town has drawn even more demons to the area. The poison you thought you prevented from spreading has taken an even deeper root on our very own mountainside. Burning that human village to the ground has done *nothing* for us! As if it has been that simple the whole time! Hah! An absolute joke!

"You have let this go on for so long that now, one of our very own, *one of the kami,* may cease to exist in a matter of weeks. You think you have time to be singing our praises? Fix this! *Now.* Or be stripped of your fire! If one of us falls, kami, human, or Ancestor, we fall together!"

In an instant, tumbling water travelling up the falls came crashing over the little shrine and splashing into the clearing. When it receded, the god was gone, the roof of the building completely unharmed, and the torches were extinguished. Yatagarasu stayed on the top of the torii gate, watching us. There was a long silence. Some of the Keepers, now sopping wet, puffed with anger at the scathing criticism. Others looked confused and forlorn. The vacant, disparaging looks in the rest of the Ancestors' eyes told me they were stunned.

And so was I.

Remembering Mato's words to me about an increase of demons in the nearby human realm, remembering the fire, I stepped out into the clearing from where I stood at the edge of the crowd.

"What are they talking about?" I asked.

"Oh, Kairi-san," Elder Tadaaki said, still holding the now sizzling torch. He looked ashamed.

"Burned down the human village… what did he mean? Was he talking about Nachi?"

I watched him debate about answering. Finally he opened his mouth.

"When the Keepers go on assignment, sometimes it's… necessary to take precautions for the greater good. Recently, the demons were spreading a poisonous variety of rice around your town that would wipe out our ancient varieties and would make all people, both yours and ours, sick. So the Keepers set fire to the fields, to be rid of it for sure. Which ultimately led to the fire in Nachi," Elder Tadaaki explained. "As you just heard, though, apparently this didn't work in the way we intended, and now Inari-sama is ill. And we are in great trouble."

"For the greater good… you *burned* down my town?" I repeated their words back to them slowly. "Do you do this often? Creating wildfires?"

He sighed. "Among other things. Floods, and various other disasters. It's the most effective way of combating the demons."

"Really?" I said through gritted teeth, the shock, horror, and anger flooding me to my core.

With growing feeling of dread in my stomach, I asked, "Who lit it?"

"Well, the Elders ordered the Keepers to—" Elder Tadaaki began, but I shook my head, cutting him off.

"Which one of you set the fire?"

After an awkward pause, Mato turned to look at me, taking a step forward. My heart sank.

"It was me," he said.

CHAPTER TWENTY

Kairi

"*What?*"

"Kairi," Mato said. He was looking at me with eyes filled with remorse. But I could no longer see straight. As the truth of the situation began to sink in, Mato's admission had shattered any ounce of self-control I had left.

I whirled on Elder Tadaaki.

"I need someone to explain this to me. So you're telling me, that you, the Ancestors, the *original people,* the great bridge between humans and spirits, our *protectors*, have been lighting wildfires, creating catastrophic floods and various other disasters around the country to kill *demons?*"

There was silence.

"Why, *why* would you ever do that?" I asked.

"Child, please understand," said Elder Tadaaki. "It is simply the most effective way. The demons have taken over human bodies at alarming rates. The systems they have put in place in your world are causing swift and irreversible damage in this one. We often need to act quickly and of large magnitude to wipe out the threats to our village, to our people."

"That's the most idiotic thing I have ever heard," I said matter-of-factly.

A few gasps echoed through the audience.

"The insolence!"

"Just like a human!"

"How could she?"

"Shut up!" I exploded. "Is it? The most effective way? Is that what we just heard from the god who sounded like he just reamed out a bunch of toddlers?"

Silence.

"So you save your own people by killing mine? When your sole purpose for existence is to guide and look out for us humans? Because that's what you're doing. You think when you set off these huge fires and floods that you're only taking out demons? You're killing humans too, probably mostly humans, actually. Most of them are innocents, who know absolutely nothing of your world or this war!"

"Kairi, please just listen. It's the only way to—" Mato started.

"*No!*" I shouted at him. He blinked in surprise. "*You* don't get to talk. *You* destroyed my village, *you* murdered my neighbors. *You* may have killed some of the only family I have left! This is *your* fault! I trusted *you*!"

"Kairi," he said again, his voice breaking.

"The power to manipulate the elements and create disaster is something we Ancestors have possessed for some time, " Elder Tadaaki tried again, his voice growing sterner as his patience gave way to anger. "Just as the gods created torrential rains and thunderous earthquakes when they were displeased with the humans, we have been given similar permissions to this extent. It is a way to make the humans listen. We are trying to send a message, to let them know that something is wrong."

"And how has that been working out for you?" I asked with a sneer. "You're supposed to be these all-knowing beings, but your approach to this is so wildly delusional, I don't even know what to say. This isn't the Heian period! Humans don't even believe in the existence of the Ancestors, or even the gods anymore, for that matter! Almost no one has heard of Sosen no Tani. You said yourselves that the demons have created systems that forced humans to forget and separate themselves from the spirit world, from the gods, from their ancestors. Well, it worked: We *have* forgotten!"

Elder Tadaaki's face remained infuriatingly unreadable as he said, "Gods or no gods, it must be obvious even to the dumbest of humans that something isn't right. What are we to do when the humans aren't even *trying* to stop the destruction?"

"These people are ignorant to all of this! And it isn't their fault! When they see a disaster, they think the cause as climate change—the consequences of the catastrophic systems the demons have put in place—and they don't even know that demons exist! That demons are masking as humans! *We don't know!*

"So what makes you think we are going to see a wildfire and think 'Oh no, the spirits are unhappy! Maybe we need to make offerings and sacrifices.' It's a moot point! You're just causing more destruction and feeding into the chaos the demons want. Why are more demons flocking to Nachi? Because you created a hotbed of death and destruction! The environment they thrive in! This isn't hard to figure out, and my species is supposed to be the dumb one! Why the hell were you doing all of this reconnaissance you ordered? Because clearly, you've learned nothing! What you should be doing is *teaching the humans who are left*—who have yet to be corrupted and controlled by demons. Teach us the old ways of living, help us shift our values back to community and caring for the environment around us. People haven't been acting because they are just trying to survive! They don't know what to do! *Remind them!* And then strategically use your military power to seek out and destroy the demons who are at the highest point of influence in these systems, who are leading them, perpetuating them, creating them. Kill those bastards, not my family!"

A sea of over a hundred faces just stared back at me, not speaking, mouths gaping.

"Is what I'm saying making *any* impression on you? I'm starting to think the demons aren't out there, in my world, but right here in front of me. I've wasted way too much of my time here. My family needs me."

I threw the kagura bells I still carried to the ground. Without looking back, I turned and began running for the well.

"Kairi!" I could hear Mato calling out to me, but I didn't slow my pace in the slightest.

Above me, a crow cawed, and the three-legged creature swooped into my vision as it flew in front of me. Yatagarasu was guiding me.

I'd be going home.

***

I ran as fast as I could without looking back. Luckily, it wouldn't take me long to find the well. With Yatagarasu's black form silently guiding me through the forest, I knew it'd only be a matter of minutes before I was on my way home. Tripping on the occasional tree root or bush, all of the hurt and anger I had been feeling just moments beforehand was replaced with a feverish determination, propelling me forward as if by some unseen force.

Within minutes, I reached the lip of Sosen no Tani's well, and Yatagarasu above me departed off into the trees. Just like I had that first night in Nachi, I dove into the opening full force, not bothering to descend the ladder and plunging into the pool of black water below me. Resurfacing in the tunnels, I swam to the edge of the underground stream and pulled myself onto the footpath. Not wasting a single second, I took off, sprinting upstream, and didn't stop until I saw the faintest hint of light from the nighttime stars above. Climbing the ladder to the exit, I dismounted over the side of the well. I didn't need to create a marker for myself this time to know I was no longer in Sosen no Tani. It was as black as night, but the stars were all too visible from where I stood at the edge of the well, illuminating the dead, leafless branches of trees that had been singed to a crisp from the fire.

"It was me."

The memory of Mato stepping forward and claiming

responsibility for the horrific damage playing out before me flashed across my mind. I shoved it aside and got moving. Running almost as blindly as I had when attempting to escape the fire that night, I now retraced my steps and made my way back to Nachi. It was hard at this hour in the night to tell just how much damage the fire had caused in town. It looked like most of the power on the mountain side had not yet been restored, as I didn't see a single house or streetlight as I ran, except at the base of the mountain, where I assumed most of the shelters were being run. But I wasn't going there.

Logically, I knew Auntie Mie would most likely be staying in one of those shelters too, especially after witnessing firsthand how the fire had engulfed our neighbor's home just a few houses away. But I needed to see what had happened to the house, to the childhood home she and my mother had shared. Besides, Auntie Mie was stubborn and valued her family legacy more than anything. She'd want to be back in her house, and I had a feeling she would be waiting there for me.

By the time I arrived in front of Auntie Mie's, my heart sank. I didn't see a single light on. I was out of breath and dripping in sweat. Still wearing the ceremonial clothes lent to me for the kagura dance, now damp from my dip in the well, the bells on my wrists and ankles had jingled with every step I took, announcing my presence long before I actually arrived.

From what I could see in the pale moonlight, the house appeared to be in pretty good shape, almost untouched compared to those around it, which lay half crumpled in ruins. I couldn't see any signs of smoke damage from the exterior, but I was sure they were there. Slightly behind the main house to the right sat the kura storage building. I could see some damage on the roofline.

Making my way to the front door of the main house, I rapped on it hesitantly. Gently sliding open the heavy wood, I stepped inside.

"Auntie Mie?" I called softly, my heart in my throat. "It's me, Kairi. I'm home."

I prayed to myself silently, with all of my being, that she was alive. And if I was lucky, that she was here. In the few weeks I had spent in the spirit realm, I hadn't prepared myself for what I would do if she wasn't. I had hoped desperately that I wouldn't have to. As I made my way deeper into the house, moving past the front entry way and stepping up onto the tatami mats, I could see a soft glow emanating from the kitchen.

"Kairi? Is that you?" I heard my aunt's voice, followed by a clanging noise as she got up to move toward me.

Relief flooded through me and I nearly collapsed where I stood. She was alive, she was safe, she was *here.*

Peeking my head through the archway into the kitchen, we met each other in mid-run.

"Auntie Mie!" I said, tears fully taking hold over my throat.

"Oh, thank goodness," she breathed. "You scared the shit out of me!"

Without another word, we hugged one another so tightly, it hurt. So grateful to see one another, alive, it barely registered to me that my uber traditional aunt had just swore, nor that her left arm was in a sling.

Finally pulling back and noticing the wrap, I said, "Are you hurt? I hope I didn't just make it worse for you."

But she just continued to run her hand over my hair and shoulders and asked, "Kairi, is that really you? I can't believe you're here. *What happened to you?!*"

"It's me, it's me. I'm home."

Before I could answer her question, another voice came from the back of the house.

"Kairi? Is that Kairi?"

"Dad?!" I called.

My father stepped into the kitchen, ducking under the archway.

"Dad!" I screamed, running to him and slamming into his chest almost immediately.

He gave me one of his huge, familiar bear hugs, and although I had already been crying, he now joined me.

"What are you doing here? When did you get here?"

"He flew in about two weeks ago, a few days after the fire, after I told him you were missing," Auntie Mie replied, saving my father from having to talk.

Fully bawling now, I looked between the two of them. How much pain and worry this must have caused them. "I'm so sorry," I blubbered through my tears. "I'm so sorry to have made you worry so much."

"We're just happy you're *alive*." My dad finally spoke. "I don't know what I would have done if I would have lost you too…" he trailed off.

"So am I–Auntie Mie, I had no idea if you made it out of that explosion. This whole time I've been worrying…" I tried to speak, but the tears overcame me and I gave in to all of the emotions of fear, pain, and worry I had been feeling over the last few weeks. And all of the new emotions of betrayal and anger of the last few hours I had yet to process.

"Shh. Calm down. It's alright. Come; I'll make us some tea. Dan, you make us a fire in the woodstove," Auntie Mie instructed my father and me, sitting me down in a chair at the kitchen table.

I nodded numbly.

"Now, we have lots to catch up on."

***

In a few minutes, my father had gotten a fire started in the woodstove, and Auntie Mie had heated up a pot of bancha tea, placing a cup in my hands while I processed my emotions. I watched as they fussed over me, making sure the temperature in the room was perfect and giving me a warm towel to wipe my hands. I was still amazed that both of them were even here, that Auntie Mie, aside from her injured arm, was unharmed.

When a majority of our tears had subsided, the three of us sat down around Auntie Mie's kitchen table and began to retrace our steps from the explosion.

"I suppose I'll begin," Auntie Mie offered. "We got separated after Hiroko-san's house blew up. The blast knocked me out, but when I came to, I was buried in rubble, and I knew my left arm had been broken. It was being held down by Hiroko-san's heavy old armoire and when I finally pulled it free, it felt like my elbow all but shattered, which it practically did, of course. Anyway, the flames were basically fully engulfing the area at that point, and I looked frantically for you and Hiroko-san in the debris. I thought I was going to die then and there.

"I searched under everything, but you were nowhere to be found. I eventually found Hiroko-san, whose fall had been cushioned by her futon and miraculously seemed completely unharmed. Her wheelchair had landed not too far away from her. I don't know what came over me, maybe some sort of superhuman adrenaline, but I hoisted her into the chair myself and took off running before the fire surrounded us completely. I figured you had somehow got away. At least, that's what I told myself."

I nodded to myself, feeling reassured that we had taken the same course of action during the moment I had felt most guilty for. I was in awe of my aunt's strength and lack of selfishness to continue rescuing Hiroko-san, and marveled that the tiny woman had hoisted her neighbor into a wheelchair with a broken arm.

"We eventually made it down the hill and to the base of the mountain, where everyone was evacuating. We were picked up by fire rescue and some other first responders and taken to a shelter on the other side of the river. Nachi being so small, this was the only shelter they had available for those who made it out. I looked for you all over that place. For days, I kept expecting you to show up; I figured you had run off and spent the night somewhere to survive. When it didn't happen, I really began to worry. The thought of me leaving you in that pile of debris and taking off without looking back would have haunted me until the day I died. Your mother's ghost would have haunted me until the day I died."

I reached out and put my hand over hers, squeezing it to still the small tremble it had taken on.

"But she hadn't shown up yet, so that's what was making me think you must have still been alive. Well, anyway, after only a couple of days, I called your father and told him what had happened and that you were missing. He flew in the next morning. We told the first responders, who worked with the police force, and eventually the Japan Disaster Relief and Self-Defense teams took up the search for you. Every day, they've been combing the woods for a sign of you and checking the rubble. Until just an hour ago, you came walking through that door," Auntie Mie concluded.

"I'm so sorry to have worried you. I don't want to cause you that stress ever again," I said, shaking my head. "And Dad, you said you didn't know if you could ever step back in Japan after Mom…"

"Kairi, you know me well enough that if my daughter is in danger, I'd go anywhere."

I reached out with my opposite hand and grabbed his across the table.

"So, Hiroko-san is doing well, then?" I asked Auntie Mie.

I watched her eyes fall, somberly staring into her tea cup. "Unfortunately, no." Her mouth pressed into a thin line as she struggled to control her voice. "She had *seemed* unharmed when I saved her from the rubble, but it turns out an impact to her head during the explosion left her with internal bleeding we were unaware of. She had an aneurism and passed away the following day."

A heavy silence filled the space between us. I fought hard to bite back the bile rising in my throat.

She had died.

My sweet, helpless neighbor who whispered *Thank you, thank you thank you,* to us as we attempted to hoist her out of her bed that evening had died because of the fire that Mato set. Mato had killed her.

He killed her. He killed her. He killed her. He-

I cleared my throat.

"Your house looks to be in pretty good condition. Did the fire damage it at all? And how's the antique store? How badly was the village damaged? How many people died?"

Mato's face was lingering behind each of my questions. Just how much damage did he do? What exactly was he responsible for?

"That's enough for now, child. We can talk about such things later. It's getting late and we all need rest. What I'm interested in is where have *you* been these last few weeks? What happened to you on that night? And just *what* are you wearing? You look like a shrine maiden." Auntie Mie said.

I took a breath and tried to push Hiroko-san's face out of my mind. I tried to think of the best way to explain everything that had happened to me over the last two and a half weeks in a way that might actually be believable. Finding absolutely none, I decided to just dive in full force.

Taking a sip of my tea, I began. "Okay, so, you should know that if I was able, I would have absolutely contacted you as soon as possible, and I would have come home a lot sooner than this. I guess I should start by explaining what had happened earlier that morning, when Auntie Mie and I went to Hiro Shrine."

Noting the questioning looks in their eyes, I continued to tell them how I was led by a three-legged crow to an ancient well on my way home from our offering at Hiro Shrine. I explained how I became separated from Auntie Mie the night of the fire, how I too had searched all over for her in the rubble, but ultimately found myself fleeing as if taken over by instinct after hearing my mother's voice. I told them about my desperate jump into the well, thinking I was going to die, and instead waking up in Sosen no Tani. Finally, I told them all I had learned over the last two and a half weeks about the Ancestors, their separation from the humans, the village that looked like Japan in the Edo period, the waterfall that traveled backward, and the Fire Keepers. I explained my attempt to return to the human world, how Yatagarasu had not allowed it, and my eventual success during the Fire Festival that had led me back home tonight.

What I failed to tell them, though, was the event that motivated me to try the well for a second time and the fact that the human race and its systems had become overrun by demons. I wasn't sure why I was refraining from sharing this information, or why I felt a weird need to protect Sosen no Tani or the Fire Keepers' image. Especially after what the Keepers and Mato had done to me, to all three of us, to Hiroko-san, and to my town. But I did. And for the time being, I left that part out. At least until maybe I could accept it myself.

When I finished my story, I took a deep breath and another sip of tea. At the first mention of the three-legged crow and then Sosen no Tani, Auntie Mie's eyes had grown wide, but she had stayed silent. The whole time while I talked, she sipped her tea thoughtfully, her face taking on a serious expression. It was hard to tell what she was thinking, but every so often, she would nod encouragingly, or mumble a few noises of understanding. My father, on the other hand, looked at me as though I had lost my mind.

Reaching out over the table, he gently smoothed my hair and asked, "Kairi, did you hit your head at all during the explosion?"

"Well, yeah. That was the injury I was resting from at Misao-dono's house."

He looked nervously over at Auntie Mie.

"You had just told her the story earlier that day and she hit her head when Hiroko-san's house exploded. This probably is one very elaborate dream from the trauma and her head injury."

"That would be one very long, two-and-a-half-week dream," Auntie Mie replied to him frankly.

"I promise you it was not a dream. It took me several days to convince myself of that," I replied, realizing too late that there wasn't much I could say without proof to sway his opinion. Any new detail just seemed to add to the case of my delusion further.

"How would one survive in a dream for two weeks?" Auntie Mie asked again.

"Probably a trauma response," my dad started to say, but Auntie Mie cut him off.

"Besides, my last question hasn't been answered. Just *what* are you wearing? You certainly weren't wearing that when we left the house the night of the fire. You look clean enough, and not as though you've been roughing it in the woods for weeks. Your hair is neat and brushed, albeit a bit wet. You have bells around your wrists and ankles; I'm positive you didn't find those in the woods."

"I performed the kagura dance for Sosen no Tani's Fire Festival," I replied. When no one immediately responded, I added, "It was a show of a good faith between the humans and Ancestors—I was helping to bridge the centuries-wide gap between us."

I couldn't tell if they believed a word I said.

"Well, you don't appear to be injured. We're just so happy you are home. I can't believe it, after all of these weeks," my dad finally said, swallowing his questions and disbelief for later.

"You must be exhausted. It's getting late. I know I'm tired. How about you get cleaned up and let's all go to bed?" Auntie Mie proposed. "We have plenty of time to catch up tomorrow."

Each of them squeezing me tightly, we readied ourselves for bed. None of us feeling the desire to be separated by even a door after the circumstances of the last few weeks, I offered we all pull our futons in the living room. My dad and Auntie Mie readily agreed. When my head finally hit the pillow, I closed my eyes in utter exhaustion from the emotional overwhelm of the day. I tried to refrain from fidgeting too much as I fussed with the t-shirt I had put on to sleep in. I had unintentionally become accustomed to sleeping in soft, thin, cotton kimonos. It was hard to believe I was finally home, with Sosen no Tani starting to feel like a distant dream.

"Are you comfortable?" Auntie Mie asked. She and my father were still up and milling about in the kitchen as I lay down to get some rest. Blinking my eyes open briefly, I reassured her that I was.

She went back to her work closing down the house and I felt myself beginning to drift off. Somewhere between sleeping and consciousness, Mato's face swirled in and out of my mind's eye. I realized at one point that I had forgotten to say goodbye to Misao-dono. The heat of tears escaping the corners of my eyes, trailing hotly down my cheeks, woke me briefly from my dazed sleep. In my short bout of consciousness, I could overhear my aunt and father murmuring to one another in the kitchen.

"Come on, Mie. Can't that wait until morning?" my dad's voice was saying. "Give the girl a few hours of peace before the town descends on her."

"You've always been so resistant to consider your community, Dan. The sooner I tell the captain that Kairi has returned safely, the sooner they can use their resources to help other folks. It's a matter of consideration."

"I'm trying to consider how Kairi would feel being swarmed by news cameras tomorrow morning."

"I'll tell him to hold off from alerting the media, so that she can rest."

"Thank you. Besides, we might want to have a doctor see her tomorrow anyway…"

The rest of his words faded away as I fell back into a listless, dreamless sleep.

CHAPTER
TWENTY-ONE

Kairi

I woke up in the morning to a crow calling. Being sufficiently conditioned to waking up early at this point, I found myself padding to the window of the living room. Careful not to step on my dad or Auntie Mie's beds, I pulled the curtain aside, eager to confirm if the crow in question had three legs. Dawn was just beginning to break over the Kii mountain range, telling me the hour was somewhere close to five in the morning. Hearing the sharp cawing sound once again, I located the bird as it perched across the street from me, balancing on the decrepit remnants of a neighbor's house. I felt my heart drop in disappointment when I saw it only had two legs.

Did Yatagarasu really take me all the way to Sosen no Tani only to discover it was the Keepers who lit the fire in Nachi?

It didn't seem much like a god to want to throw its subjects under the bus. I thought of the argument I'd had with Elder Tadaaki and the other Keepers in front of the waterfall. Maybe my presence in Sosen no Tani was to help the Ancestors recognize how deranged their fighting strategies had become.

"Kairi, dear. Are you awake already?" Auntie Mie asked, gingerly rolling over and propping herself up on her good elbow.

"Oh, I'm sorry to wake you," I replied.

She looked at me bleary-eyed for a second before responding, "Hold on. Let me put some tea on the stove."

190

As Auntie Mie made me tea, I yearned to do something normal. So much had changed in the last few weeks, I wanted some sense of routine to kick me back into gear, back into feeling like my normal self. Honestly, I was feeling significantly despondent upon waking up back in Nachi. I had been so relieved to see Auntie Mie and my father the night prior, having been so concerned for their safety and having no way to reach them. But now, I was feeling anxious, jittery, and like there was something I needed to be doing. Like I was being too idle. I also felt an aching, gnawing sadness that I suspected had to do with Mato and the Keepers' apparent betrayal.

They had regarded me as the enemy since the moment I arrived. I guess I shouldn't have been so surprised at the way things turned out, seeing as even Mato clearly had been keeping things from me, like the details of his assignments. But I still felt the bitter shock and denial that comes when the people you trust and admire let you down.

Waking up to join us for morning tea, my father, Auntie Mie, and I sat around the kitchen table just as we had the night before. Feeling a mild headache coming on from all of the crying I had done the night prior, I looked at Auntie Mie with newfound restlessness and a burning desire to push all uncomfortable thoughts from my mind.

"Auntie Mie, how did the shop and farm fare after the fire? Is there anything I can help with this morning to clean up? Please, I absolutely have to make myself useful today."

Both she and my father looked at me with expressions of surprise and mild concern.

"Shouldn't you be resting, Kairi? You've had quite the few weeks. And you were injured. You should take the time to get used to being home," my dad attempted to advise me.

"No, no. I have to see how the town is. How bad was the damage? How can I help? Please, I'll feel the best if I can help restore things back to normal as much as possible."

Sensing this was a battle that neither of them were

going to win with me, Auntie Mie said, "Alright, if you insist. Let's get cleaned up, and we can go on a walk around town and to the antique store. Most of the building faired okay. But unfortunately, the backmost room was burnt to a crisp. We lost a lot of the tansu I had stored back there."

Not the tansu, I thought, feeling another wave of anger at the single-mindedness of the Keepers.

After brushing my teeth and hair and dressing in a simple shirt and cargo pants for the day, I walked solemnly alongside Auntie Mie and my dad down the road from her house. It was hard to believe I was seeing the same town I had lived in for the past three months, the town I had visited since I was a child. The houses surrounding Auntie Mie's were all in various stages of disintegration. Kei cars still sat in my neighbors' driveways, now looking like part of an apocalyptic movie set. Wooden beams lay charred in heaps next to singed tile and concrete. If I looked closely enough, signs of previous life still clung to the piles of ash.

A dented refrigerator.

Parts of bedframe.

Broken dishes and glassware.

At one of my neighbors' houses, a tattered teddy bear was a brown splotch of fuzz against the ruins. I thought of the lives people lived here; houses that had been passed down through generations. The meals that were shared between family and friends. I thought of the memories I had with my mother here, the memories the land held of her childhood and adolescence. I could no longer see the high school she would have attended, or imagine her anxiously entering the local ramen shop for her first date. It was like the fire had wiped away this remaining part of her too. My heart leapt in my throat. I forced myself to look away before emotion could overtake me and I lost myself in thought.

I didn't actually think the Keepers were malicious enough to purposefully be murdering humans in their attacks against the demons—it would go against the entire reason they were fighting in the first place and was the reason they were created by the gods. Didn't the kami that appeared during the Fire Festival—Hiryu Gongen—condemn them for that kind of destruction anyway? For their failure to protect humans and the environment? And threaten to strip them of their fire if it continued?

It seemed to me that the Keepers were just acting with blinders on. Thinking in archaic ways without fully understanding how much the world had changed in the two centuries of their absence. But, then again, maybe the whole story of the Keepers wanting to guide the humans was some sort of lie they told me. But wouldn't they have just killed me outright when they first saw me? I didn't know what to think.

"What are you thinking about, Kairi?" my dad asked nervously. "You seem deep in thought."

"I hope this isn't too much for you to process right now. I know you said you needed to see the state of the town, but please let us know if it gets overbearing," Auntie Mie chimed in.

Before I could respond, a voice called out to us down the road.

"Is that Kairi? Kairi Raynott?"

All three of us stopped walking and looked behind us in the direction of the voice. Running furiously up the road was a group of people carrying various camera equipment and microphones. A news crew. Beside them walked a group of five men, all wearing suits. One man, clearly the most important, walked ahead of the others, who kept at a close distance behind him on either of his flanks. He appeared to be in conversation with one of the team members from the news crew. A chill ran up my spine instantaneously.

"Ah Jesus, Mie, this is what I was afraid of," my dad muttered under his breath. "I thought you told the town not to alert the media?"

"I did," replied Auntie Mie, equally as displeased to see the crowd as my father was. "I told the captain of the Japanese Disaster Relief brigade in charge of Kairi's search. But maybe one of the calls he had to make to his inferiors didn't pass on the message," she said with clear annoyance in her voice.

My eyes remained fixed on the frontmost man in the suit. Something wasn't right about him. He was a lean man, likely in his mid-forties, slightly taller than average in height. The suit he wore clearly distinguished him as some high-ranking salary man from Tokyo, likely designer brand. But the expression he wore on his face concerned me most. He exuded an air of arrogance and self-importance and he appeared to be chatting amiably with the man on the news crew. However, his eyes slowly scanned the environment around him, and when they flitted toward me, the cold, calculating, and menacing stare felt like I had just looked evil in the face.

He was a demon.

The realization seemed to click within me at once. Suddenly, Mato's words came flooding back to me. "It's just a feeling. Something isn't right. The hairs on the back of your neck stand up. And they smell. Like rotting flesh, at least to me anyway. You can also tell by the look in their eyes," he had said.

The news crew was almost on us now, as we stood waiting. I felt an instinctual understanding come over me that I couldn't give any indication that I knew the man with them was a demon. I had a feeling that if I let on even in the slightest that I was afraid of him, it would be trouble for me and my family later.

"Kairi," the woman leading the crew gasped as she slowed her run to catch up with us. She held a microphone in her hand and was probably in her mid-thirties. Her hair was cut in a short bob style with not a strand out of place and she looked incongruous against the disheveled wreckage of the country town surrounding us.

"We're sorry to interrupt your walk," she addressed my family. "We're with the Fuji News Network, and had come to the area to film with executives from Monsoko Corporation to discuss their disaster recovery efforts for farmers in Nachi. We heard your story, Kairi, just this morning and couldn't believe our luck when we saw you walking down the road just now. The Japanese who has been living in America for a decade, who gets caught in this unprecedented wildfire and goes missing for weeks just after finally returning to Japan again. What an incredible story. We are so happy you have returned home safely."

"Uh-huh," Auntie Mie muttered, not sounding even slightly convinced.

"You were filming Monsoko's disaster recovery efforts?" I asked her, eyeing the man behind her who I suspected to be a demon. He was smiling at us with masked politeness but was clearly displeased to be taking this detour.

"Yes! But after running into you like this, we'd love to be able to interview you too, if it's okay?"

So they're from Monsoko, I thought. Remembering the highly capitalistic, industrial agriculture company that my aunt so detested for eroding resilient seed saving across Japan and creating farmer dependency on their genetically modified products. I could easily guess what they were doing in Nachi in the immediate weeks after a disaster. *And she said executives.*

I looked closer at the man and his entourage, the whole group seemingly making the hair on the back of my neck stand up. Looking at the eyes of the men surrounding him, the feeling of dread that had come over me increased. They were all demons. And I could bet, the man in the middle, the one who I had first sensed was the strongest of them all, by no doubt was the leader.

"How'd you hear about Kairi's story?" Auntie Mie asked her.

"Well I overheard the captain of Japan's Self Defense force this morning on a phone call, you see. Rather rude of me, but of course I had seen articles spreading as far as Tokyo of the girl who had gone missing in Nachi's fire," she added.

"How'd you know it was us walking just now?" My dad asked her.

"Oh! Well, a young girl who looked *hafu* walking with a

foreigner and Japanese woman in the middle of a country town being just wrecked by a disaster? It must be Kairi!" she said joyfully, oblivious to my father's insinuation.

He just nodded expectantly.

"So Kairi, are you willing to be interviewed?" the news reporter asked. Next to me, my dad began to decline on my behalf, but I interrupted him, an insane courage, and rage, welling up inside of me.

"I'll do it," I replied. Out of the corner of my eyes, I watched my dad and aunt gape at me in surprise.

"Excellent! Thank you so much!" squealed the news reporter. "Just one second and we will get started!"

Running back to the man who was talking to the Monsoko executives, I watched as she eagerly told him I had accepted an interview. "Just one moment, Hyuga-san," the man said apologetically to the head executive. "Surely you understand this is quite the exciting day for our small department on Fuji News. Sakura-san will only do a quick interview and then we will be back to programming Monsoko's outstanding work. We can even ask the girl to endorse it if you like." The head Monsoko demon scowled but gave a curt nod.

In a moment, the news reporter, Sakura-san, was bounding back over to where my family and I were standing. "Sorry for the wait," she said to me. "That's Gento Hyuga, the CEO of Monsoko. He requires a bit of indulging," she replied. *Gento Hyuga,* I thought, remembering the name. I thought he looked familiar. If I remembered correctly, Hyuga had been the CEO of Monsoko for almost twenty years. And therefore, he had been one of the most influential contributors to the international industrialization—and destruction—of agriculture in the twenty-first century. And he was a demon, a powerful one at that. For all I knew, he could have been the CEO of Monsoko since its inception in the early 1900s, changing bodies every time the one he occupied weakened. I didn't fully understand how the rules worked, but I wouldn't put it past them.

My words, hurled at Elder Tadaaki, Mato, and the rest of the Keepers in Sosen no Tani came back to me. "...Use your military power to seek out and destroy the demons who are at the highest point of influence in these systems, who are leading them, perpetuating them, creating them. Kill those bastards, not my family!" I had screamed.

I need to tell the Keepers.

It took the news crew several moments to set up their equipment and choose a background to shoot. They decided on the rubble of one of my neighbor's charred houses, deciding the drama of the scene would draw the most attention and views. It took immense effort for me not to wrinkle my nose in disgust. The Monsoko demons were still watching me, and I did everything I could to appear an innocent young girl who was just happy to be home with her family. The news crew decided to film the interview live, wanting to be the first network to have located the Japanese American lost in the Nachi Fire. I had no idea I had grown so famous in such a short amount of time. The thought made my stomach flip, but I tried not to think about it. It didn't matter right now.

When the news crew was finally ready, Sakura-san began the interview by welcoming me home, asking me about myself, and asking me to recount the night of the fire. I obliged, telling a perfectly concise rendition of becoming separated from my aunt and making a break as best as I could for the Nachi River (all true). What I left out, however, was my discovery of the ancient well and impromptu journey to Sosen no Tani.

"And just *where* have you been over these last two weeks?" Sakura-san asked me, full of probing curiosity.

"Well, you see, Sakura-san, it's been nearly a decade since I moved overseas, only growing up in Japan as a little girl. And I was living in Tokyo at that time, only visiting Nachi to see family occasionally. So, although I had been back for almost three months, I still really wasn't familiar with the forest surrounding our little town. I'm afraid I thought I was running in the direction of the river, but I actually got lost. I've spent the last two and a half weeks surviving on my own in the Kii Mountain range," I lied. "Luckily, I seemed to have outrun the area that caught fire and didn't have any extensive injuries."

Her eyes widened. "You survived in the wilderness alone for *two and a half weeks?*" she repeated. "But how? You must have had prior experience in the wilderness."

I laughed politely. "Not at all. My father is something of a survivalist and taught me some simple knowledge since I was little, like how to build shelter and find water. And my aunt, accustomed to satoyama-living, taught me how to identify many herbs in the forest. There's a whole pantry there, if you know how to look. I also made sure I kept a faithful practice of worshipping the kami to help guide me home safely," I added on thickly. "I made a makeshift shrine and offerings to a rock in a cave that helped shield me from a majority of smoke the first few days. And the small stream I found to drink water. I really drew upon the knowledge passed down to me from my ancestors. And this, I believe, is how I was able to survive," I said, staring directly at Hyuga. He looked back at me evenly, with eyes as cold as ice.

"That's amazing," Sakura-san murmured. "How is it you eventually found your way back to the village after search crews had been looking for you for so long?"

"Honestly, Sakura—can I call you Sakura? It was the strangest thing. I had been staying put, hoping the search and rescue teams would find me. But one day, during my second week in the woods, a three-legged crow appeared outside of my shelter and almost seemed as though it wanted me to follow it. So I did, and it led me right back to Nachi, to my aunt's house."

It was the partial truth. I wanted to give them just enough mystique to make viewers interested in the old legends.

"A three-legged crow? Like Yatagarasu? The mythical bird the Kumano region is so famously known for?"

"I believe so, Sakura. Just like Emperor Jimmu thousands of years ago, I believe Yatagarasu guided me home last night. But you know, my aunt, father, and I were all just taking a walk this morning to show me the impacts of the fire on the village. I am so devastated by what happened to our precious community, and so eager to know how my neighbors and supportive groups around Japan have been helping us to respond and recover. I know the fire directly destroyed so many rice fields. Most of us in this town are farmers, my aunt and me included. Would you actually mind sharing with me what has been happening to restore Nachi these last few weeks?"

Sakura-san had glanced over her shoulder briefly at her boss behind the camera. I had given her an opening. Her boss nodded.

"Well, as our viewers may already know, we have been touring the town with representatives from the Monsoko Corporation this morning, as they have been some of the biggest supporters of Nachi's recovery. Just as you mentioned, the farmers in this region have been so negatively impacted by the fire. Almost all of their rice crop and seed was destroyed by the flames. Monsoko has been generous enough to donate hundreds of packages of their newest developed variety of rice, modified in their very own labs to increase yields *and* resist dry conditions! They even will be partnering with Tagama Tech Company to donate free, new rice planting machines and greenhouse technology to get the rice planted next season. How does this sound to you, Kairi? Hopefully, this gives you some relief after coming home to see the destruction that's occurred here," Sakura-san said, moving the microphone back to my mouth so that I could speak.

"Actually, Sakura, that doesn't relieve me at all. I find this information quite concerning. Terrifying, even."

A puzzled look came over her face. I had not given the reply she was banking on.

"I'm assuming this new variety of rice is genetically modified or at least a hybrid variety?" I asked.

She nodded.

"Then I'm afraid Monsoko Corporation is not helping my village to recover at all, but is actually taking advantage of us. The rice that is grown in their labs does not have the ability to be saved from whatever new seed it produces. Nachi farmers have been successful since ancient times by saving the seeds produced by their rice, their vegetables, their mikan trees, each harvest, season after season. My aunt even taught me this sacred practice as soon as I arrived back in Japan. She taught me these plants have adapted to both the subtle and sudden changes in our environment through each generation. There is enough diversity amongst the saved seeds to always allow for some of the crop to survive even if the climate changes that year unexpectedly. It does not matter if you modify a seed in a lab to be able to withstand drought—all of those seeds will genetically be clones of one another; there's no diversity. In this age of unpredictable climate change, what if next year it's not a fire caused by drought, but heavy rains and floods? None of those crops will survive.

"And even if they did, they can't be saved for the next season by our farmers. Our farmers will have to buy their seeds year after year from Monsoko, spending more money than they would ever need to if they were saving their own seeds. What a convenient way to build a consistent stream of revenue for a corporation. All the while creating a consistent stream of dependency from our farmers, robbing them of their autonomy and self-reliance. Robbing our community of its resilience. Not to mention, none of them can afford to maintain these expensive, overly complicated harvesting machines and planting technology. People have been doing it here by hand for centuries, just like my aunt and I are now. There is no consideration for the farmers or my community here. Monsoko is solely trying to make a profit," I spat.

"Corporations and wealthy investors are swooping in after my community has been devastated and is still in shock from the disaster. They are making a bunch of decisions in the blink of an eye, instilling new systems, like giving the farmers hybrid or GMO seeds, under the guise of helping or saving the community. And probably even trying to buy land for all I know. All while our community members are all too shell-shocked or frazzled to resist. Or even *know* it's happening. And then, once we have some semblance of an idea of what's going on, we'll realize it's too late and we've been taken advantage of. Monsoko is taking advantage of my community's trauma to exploit them for their own financial gain."

While I talked, Sakura-san squirmed uncomfortably, eyeing her boss every now and then in a desperate attempt to bring this interview to a close. I'm sure she was regretting her decision to broadcast this live. There was nothing she could do.

The whole time, I had kept my eyes on Gento Hyuga, all the while knowing I was painting a significant target on my back and the backs of my family. He stared back at me evenly, a smirk on his face. His eyes were filled with steely contempt.

"They should be supporting our farmers in salvaging the heirloom seed varieties they have been saving, and working to restore the soil that has now become polluted from the fire. They should be helping restore our farmland and our farmers' autonomy. So no, this information doesn't relieve me at all," I finished.

Suddenly, Auntie Mie swooped into the frame, putting her hands on my shoulders.

"Okay! Well, Kairi actually really should get some rest today. She has only been home for a few hours now, and as you can see, the emotions are still very raw. Thank you for your time!" she said, steering me out of the frame.

Sakura-san and her crew thanked me awkwardly and continued on their way down the road. All the while, the Monsoko CEO watched me from over his shoulder. As soon as they disappeared from our line of sight, I yanked Auntie Mie and my father back into Auntie Mie's house and pulled the blinds.

"What was that?!" she howled at me, clearly stunned by my rudeness and probably my desire to even be interviewed in the first place. Behind her accusatory tone though, I could tell a part of her was also mildly impressed with how much I had been paying attention to her global political rants and absorbing her agricultural wisdom over the last three months.

"There's more I haven't told you about Sosen no Tani," I told them hurriedly.

"Sosen no Tani? That again? I thought what you told the news people about being lost in the woods was the real story," my dad said.

"No! Dad, obviously not. That was a lie for the interview. My story is the same one I told you last night. I went to Sosen no Tani, but there was more going on that I left out."

"Kairi, *what* is happening? And why are we hiding?"

As quickly as I could, I filled them in on the war between the Ancestors, kami, and demons and why the spirit world separated from the human world two centuries ago. I told them how the majority of humans had been taken over by demons, and how demons were leading some of the most oppressive and exploitative systems in our societies today. And finally, I told them what really happened the night of the Fire Festival, and why I left. Sharing that the Keepers and other Ancestors had been the causes of strange climate-related disasters around the country in an effort to fight the demons, but their methods had been skewed. I didn't mention anything about Mato.

"Because of what I said in that interview, I now have a target on my back. That man, the Monsoko CEO, was not human. He was a demon, an oni. And a *strong* one. I could feel it. And I know it wasn't the smartest move, but I had to fight back in my own way. I couldn't let him poison our town like that. But now I've surely put a target on your backs as well."

"How would you know if that man was a demon, Kairi?" Auntie Mie asked me. She appeared to be taking in my story and giving it serious thought.

"I don't know; it's just a feeling. I never noticed anything like it before I got back from Sosen no Tani, but you could just see it in his *eyes*. He gave off this horrible feeling of dread, like I was close to death. But I can answer questions later. For now, I need you to trust me, and I need you to do me a favor," I instructed.

"Go into town right away and get to the nearest shelter.

Round up everyone you can and make sure they stay inside. I don't want anyone to be involved unnecessarily, and the more people surrounding you, the less likely any demons are to make any moves. They are still trying to maintain their human appearance—until they get you alone, that is."

"How are we supposed to trap people in a building?" Auntie Mie asked.

"Make up some sort of excuse. Literally anything; I don't know, but you'll figure it out. For now, I need to go and warn the Keepers."

"You're *going?!*" my father asked.

The whole time I had been talking, I was flying about the living room, putting on proper running shoes and trying to prepare while realizing there were no preparations to make. Now, as I moved toward the door, my father stood up and caught my arm around the wrist.

"No! Kairi, this is *ridiculous.* You cannot go. We thought you were dead for the past two weeks! I am not letting you go!"

I could feel the pain in his voice. As I stared at his face full of terror and anxiety, I felt some of my resolve soften, a lump rising in my throat.

"Dan," Auntie Mie said, gently placing a hand on his tall shoulder. For a moment, they exchanged a long glance. "I trust Kairi. I believe she has our best interest at heart right now. And I believe she's capable of what she is planning to do. She survived the last two and half weeks on her own. She will come back as soon as she is able."

I watched a million *buts* flash across my father's face as he fought with reason and paternal instinct. Finally, he set his jaw and I watched his eyes harden as he gave Auntie Mie a final nod. Pulling away from her touch and his grasp on my wrist, he ordered, "Wait" before disappearing from the room.

When he reappeared, he was holding a foldable multipurpose knife in his hand. Holding it out to me, he motioned for me to take it. I recognized it as the knife he kept with him at all times back in Vermont. "You never know when you will need something sharp," he used to tell me.

"Dad!" I exclaimed. "How did you even get that through TSA?"

He smirked at me. "I'll answer questions later. Now you, *go.*"

Hugging them both tightly and promising I'd return as soon as possible, I wished them luck before sprinting out the door. I made my way through town as calmly and quickly as possible, trying not to draw attention to myself by making a mad dash down the street. Every new street corner I turned, I kept a watchful eye for my friends on the news crew, hoping they had made their way well down the mountain by now.

By the time I had reached the turnoff point for the trail to the well, I quickened my pace, feeling both grateful and reassured by the tree cover. But the feeling was premature.

Brushing a tree limb aside, I strode into the clearing where the well was located, coming to an abrupt halt when I saw what was there waiting for me.

Sitting cross-legged on the lip of the well was a man, dressed in dark work clothing. The collar on his navy blue uniform read *Monsoko*. He had been lounging, lazily inspecting his fingernails. When I came crashing through the woods, he looked up at me with frigid eyes and a snide smile. A chill ran up my spine.

"I was betting I'd find you here. And it looks like I was right."

CHAPTER TWENTY-TWO

Kairi

I had miscalculated.

Shit, I thought.

I had let my guard down the moment I entered the woods, thinking that the cover from the foliage would be enough to shield me from the eyes of demons. But that was a very naïve and ill-timed assumption, as I stared into the inky-black pits of the one sitting before me.

The demon had inhabited a body of a young man no older than twenty-five. He leaned back on the palms of his hands with a youth-like arrogance, like a boy who still hadn't fully matured yet.

I felt my body stiffen as I watched him on high alert. His eyes raked my body lazily, like the gaze of a predator who barely has to try to make his kill.

Clearly reading the surprise on my face, he said, "You gave yourself away when you mentioned the bird. Back in your little demonstration on live TV. If you hadn't mentioned that three-legged monstrosity, the boss wouldn't have thought to look for a portal around here. I caught your scent in town and followed it all the way back here. Figured you'd show up on your own eventually, seeing as you didn't hide your Sight very well. And here you are, coming to me on a silver platter."

The demon stood and walked closer to me. I felt my

breathing quicken, my body going rigid. *"You're not breathing right, Kairi."* Mato's voice came back to me. I forced myself to slow my breathing, relaxing my muscles one by one as I kept my eyes on the demon.

"You caused a bit of an annoyance for the boss, you know. But an annoyance is all it is. He wants me to dispatch you quickly, but you're so pretty. So full of life. It'd be a shame not to enjoy our time together a little before we end things." The demon lifted a strand of my hair and twirled it around his finger. His cold eyes flashed.

I felt a new wave of fear flood down my spine, the kind of fear most women in the world are used to experiencing at least once in their lives. This was bad. I had underestimated demons right out of the gate and now I was quite literally staring death in the face. I hadn't expected their ability to use scent to track me and now it was safe to assume that they were capable of quite literally anything. I assumed the one standing before me would be faster, stronger, and have sharper instincts, if not some additional supernatural abilities. It was worse that I didn't know how the freaking rules of this supernatural world worked. I cursed myself silently for not asking Mato more about them when I had the chance.

While the demon trailed his ice-cold fingers down my collarbone, where he had dropped the strand of my hair, I raced to try and come up with a realistic plan for surviving this. I couldn't win by sheer force. I would need to find a way to outsmart him.

Just as the demon's hand trailed dangerously low on my chest, an idea flashed across my mind. In an instant, I turned until my body aligned with his, facing the same way, my left hand on his right elbow, my right hand on his wrist. Then, I simply turned in place, right foot sweeping behind me, hips lowering my center of gravity. My arms locked his elbow joint, his own body weight driving him down and falling forward to the ground. It was a move Mato had taught me a week prior. The moment his face slammed against the ground, I wasted no time in a futile attempt to get the better of him, dashing over his body and into the well instead.

He would follow me any second now. I knew this and was betting on it in the few seconds' head start I was given. Landing gracefully on the footpath on the edge of the well, I took off full sprint downstream. The goal, for now, was to prevent him from throwing me into the stream of moving water. And to make it up the ladder when I reached Sosen no Tani's exit. Actually, scratch that. The goal was to *make it* to Sosen no Tani's exit.

"How interesting," I heard the demon's voice call as he landed in the well behind me. "I expected you to put up a fight, but I didn't expect to enjoy it this much. Let's take our time," he growled.

From the sound of his voice, I could tell he was walking slowly behind me, his ego still filling him with the arrogance that he'd be able to catch and kill me in a mere second. Which, I'm sure he could, but this assuredness was what I was banking on. He was intentionally playing a game of cat and mouse with me, likely to fill his own boredom or some twisted desire to enjoy the suffering of his prey before he killed it. And it was that tendency that gave me an opportunity for survival.

I felt ill at ease though, when I reached the exit for Sosen no Tani with no sign of him attempting to catch up with me. There was no way he would have gotten bored and turned around. There was no time to think about it, though; I needed to climb the ladder and get out of the well as fast as possible. Remembering the knife my father had given me, I slid it out of my belt loop as quickly as I could, holding it in the palm of my left hand as I began to climb. By the time my feet hit the third rung, I felt something cold as ice grasp my ankle. There was no sound to warn me, no indication that the demon had been anywhere near me when he yanked hard on my leg, wrenching me off of the ladder and slamming my back into the ground.

I felt my breath leave me. It was as if every one of my ribs shattered at once. My mind reeled from the pain; the demon's heavy body straddled mine. I struggled under the oppressive force of his weight, wriggling side to side as his knees braced either side of my torso, pinning my arms to my sides.

"Stop moving! I appreciate you making this more private for us," he said, trailing his disgusting tongue along the edge of my ear. It was everything I could do not to scream.

"But I've had enough now. It's time to get on with it."

"Who are you? You work for Gento Hyuga?" I asked him through gritted teeth.

"Ah, so you know the boss's name. I suppose that makes sense; he is quite famous. Yeah, I work for him. I'm Kenzo. I suppose it's right you know who you're spending time with."

He righted himself for only a second, tearing at his belt. It was all the time I needed. The demon hadn't realized that in all of my wriggling and talking, I had freed my right hand.

In a quick motion, I flipped the knife open and jammed it into his inner thigh, using all of my strength against his body weight to carve it in an upward motion toward his groin. Once again taking advantage of his surprise, I remembered a jujitsu roll that Mato had taught me for self-defense that worked well if the enemy ever had you pinned to the ground in a straddle. I had blushed significantly when Mato demo'd the move with me, but I was thankful I wasn't too distracted to forget the technique.

I definitely wasn't blushing now as I bent my left knee and lifted my hips, using enough momentum to roll the demon off of me, so that we had switched places and I was now pinning him to the ground. I knew of course that this would last only a matter of seconds, and I intended to use every one of them. The sick bastard looked at me with a flash of surprise and rage for a moment before his face showed real pleasure.

"That was quite unexpected, human girl, but I have to say I'm into it."

I nearly vomited.

Refusing to lose my opportunity, I took the knife that was still in my hand and drove it straight into his throat.

"That should keep you from talking," I said.

"You bitch!" he howled, the blood gurgling where my knife

made impact. His hand swung up from underneath me and seized me around the throat, squeezing hard. I slit his wrist where his hand held me and drove the knife down over and over again into his throat, my animal brain taking over.

"You fire till the foe falls," my father had always told me when we lived in Vermont. America had been a much different transition from the seemingly safe Japan, and my dad had taken me to a few self-defense courses when I was a young girl. "Fire till the foe falls" was shooting lingo for *make sure the enemy is dead before you try to run away*. Or at least severely incapacitated.

When his grip loosened on me and he seemed to have lost consciousness, I disentangled myself from him and made a break for the ladder. Reaching the lip of the well, I searched the ground frantically.

Suddenly, the ice cold grip slapped itself back around my ankle. Without thinking, I kicked hard in a downward motion, connecting with what felt like the demon's head. He dug his fingernails, which now felt a lot more like claws, into the skin on my calf, and twisted hard. I heard a snap and nearly saw stars as my leg broke.

It was everything I could do to keep pulling myself out of the well, proceeding to try and kick myself free the whole time. The demon Kenzo's hands tore up my thigh. I could see his face now as he clawed up at me, his eyes, once impenetrably cold, now burning with pure rage, hatred, and hunger. With my torso finally over the ridge of the well, I twisted in his grasp onto my back just as he reached to plunge his hand into my chest.

Utilizing his balance against him one final time, I grabbed his arm and pulled him up over me, all while rolling to my right side. Kenzo came toppling over me with enough force that the iron rod I had stuck in the ground outside the well weeks ago now impaled him through the stomach, trapping him where he landed.

I crawled as fast as I could away from him, breathing heavily as I watched him thrash. He tried to pull the rod out of the ground, but ultimately couldn't free himself.

"You vile bitch!" he shouted at me over and over.

Eventually, after a minute or so of this, Kenzo appeared to finally succumb to his injuries, falling silent, his body going limp.

I sat back and stared at his body in shock. As my adrenaline began to wear off, the pain in my leg was starting to become noticeable and I groaned out loud. The gravity of the situation began to sink in. Once again, I had narrowly avoided death.

For several minutes, I just sat there, trying to catch my breath and breathing heavily. *He's dead, he's dead, he's dead,* I told myself over and over again. Logically, I knew I had killed a demon who was going to kill me, among other things, but my mind was playing tricks on me. He looked so *human* now that the life had left his body. He was so still.

As if reading my thoughts, Kenzo's body jerked violently, his head snapping to the side to face me. "You won't get away with this. I'm going to tear your body limb from limb!" he screamed at me as he resumed his struggle again. His jaw had become dislocated from his skull and his eyes had turned bloodshot. I stared in horror as I realized he hadn't died yet, but had only appeared to be unconscious from his wounds.

I winced at the grotesqueness of his face, closing my eyes in a brief moment of weakness. I heard a sickening thudding sound and an awful, low-pitched gurgling scream.

I snapped my eyes open, expecting Kenzo to have removed himself from the rod where I had trapped him. Instead, Gento Hyuga had stepped out from the well and sunk a long-bladed katana into Kenzo's skull.

I became very aware that I, a mere human, had gotten very lucky in my brawl with Kenzo, and was now lying injured with a broken leg only a few feet away. And I was alone.

"How foolish," Gento muttered to himself. "This is what you get for disobeying my orders and letting your lower instincts run wild." He spoke to Kenzo matter-of-factly, as if he could still hear him. "The idiot could have just removed his human shell at any time to free himself from such a pitiful trap."

I felt genuine fear race up my spine when he turned his unfeeling gaze onto me.

"I've got to hand it to you, human girl. Although you are a nuisance, you are smarter than I had expected. Demons can only die by slicing their heads off. Whether that's decapitating them or slicing the head in two, same difference," he shrugged. "But only a sword brandished by special beings can kill us. Only another demon, kami, or Ancestor could do it. Not the likes of you." He smiled at me menacingly.

Walking toward me, he raised his right arm as if he was reaching for me. Despite myself, I shrank back from his hand, not sure if he was planning to taunt me, hurt me, or kill me in that very moment. He had taken a step closer to me when unexpectedly, the whistle of a sword, wrapped in a swath of fire, sailed through the air and cut his raised arm clean off. The tip of the sword buried itself in the ground directly in front of me, the fire spreading to form a shield between Gento and me.

"You don't touch her."

Gento looked at his arm curiously and turned slowly in the direction of the voice.

Standing at the edge of the clearing was Mato.

"Now, *he* could," Gento said, smiling cordially.

"Mato," I said. "You came for me."

"Kairi!" Mato shouted as he ran to my side.

I felt my whole body flood with relief to see him and I realized somewhere within that I had missed him too. But at the same time, frustration and anger welled up within me once again and I found myself lying through my teeth "No one asked you to come! I've got it handled."

I expected some snarky comment, or for him to at least raise his eyebrows at me. But instead, I only saw his face melt in pain and understanding. Behind him, I could see Gento looking on in mild amusement.

Mato looked at me softly, now standing in between me and the demon and said, "I'm sorry."

CHAPTER TWENTY-THREE

Mato

"Mato, you came for me." Kairi's words, spoken out loud now, echoed those from my first dream of her two and a half weeks ago.

"We waited for you. You never came."

I thought of the voices of my parents.

I looked at Kairi, and with the entirety of my heart I said to her, "I'm sorry."

I shifted my gaze before I could watch her expression change.

I stared levelly at the demon in front of me, putting myself between him and Kairi, who was lying behind the wall of fire I had erected to prevent the creature from getting any closer to her. I had no idea what she was doing here, or what had happened, but she had at the very least broken her leg and wouldn't be moving anytime soon.

The demon in front of me was no ordinary demon either. On the surface, he looked to be a man in his mid-forties, dressed in something Kairi had explained to me was called a suit. He mildly eyed the stub where his arm had just been. And in an instant, he shed the human body he was animating like a second skin, the corpse collapsing to the ground. His true form appeared only a few feet away, brushing off his arms and drawing a katana from its sheath at his waist.

Elder Tadaaki had told me in my first few years training as a Keeper that the most powerful demons were the ones whose true forms mirrored that of humans. I was used to a demon shedding the human body it had occupied, but their true forms took on some grotesque, vile-looking creature that easily distinguished them as what they were. This demon's true form, however, took the shape of a serene young man, dressed as though he was a monk from the Nara period. His long black hair that flowed down his back was hidden under a straw *tengai* hat and he wore a black kimono beneath his Buddhist, saffron *kasaya* robe. He easily looked about twenty years younger and had a calm, gentle expression on his face. If it wasn't for his aura radiating ungodly, wicked energy, you would have never taken him for what he was. A demon, and one of the strongest ones I had ever seen.

The demon studied me carefully. He turned back in Kairi's direction. "Interesting. You, girl, started out as a mere nuisance to my plan, just a small irritation in the scope of things, but it seems you've become a lot more useful to me than you could imagine. Leading me into a nest of Ancestors. You have no idea how much easier this makes things for me," he drawled.

The words were meant to provoke her. Sosen no Tani was no secret to any demon, especially not to one as powerful as him.

"You must think highly of me," I replied, "if you think just one of me is considered a nest."

He nodded appreciatively. "And one of the finer Ancestors you are at that."

"You're pretty old, aren't you? When were you born? The Heian period?" I asked him seriously.

"And you're not quite as dense as you look," he replied. "Older. I was born in early Japan. Even I am not sure of the exact date myself. Sometime before the Nara period. I am as old as the land here itself."

"That's quite a lot to brag about," I replied, but I knew he was telling the truth. "So tell me, what is a demon as old as Japan itself doing wasting time on a human girl?"

"I'm ancient, but that doesn't mean I've become any less petty than I was. I'm self-aware enough to admit that. She hurt my pride quite a bit earlier this morning. Made some of my work a little bit more complicated for me, and I couldn't let that go unpunished," he said calmly.

I stole a quick glance at Kairi, who was breathing heavily in pain behind me. She needed to get medical attention soon.

"He was masking as the head of one of the world's leading companies in agriculture," she said weakly, noticing my glance. "Called Monsoko. He was the one who invented the poisonous rice varieties. He's still trying to spread those seeds across Nachi —and probably the rest of the world too."

"Which begs the question," I continued, "of why an ancient demon, who already has apparently such worldwide influence, is wasting his time on a small town in the countryside?"

He looked at me quizzically for a moment before replying. "Why, to keep things moving, of course. I suppose there's no reason to keep it from you. Seeing as you both will be dead soon anyway. Nachi, in the human realm, is a unique town. One where the humans have held on longer than other rural villages and resisted the new ways of society the demons have been seeding for centuries. Our influence, young Ancestor, as I am sure you are quite sheltered and do not know, is felt by every country and every person around the world. However, Nachi continues to be one of the communities with the highest level of heirloom seed varieties saved each year. It's patches of resilience such as these that keep those gods, such as Inari, alive. So we try to snuff them out. It's as simple as that. We try to move with precision, and intent. We recognize great things take time. Small, insignificant town by insignificant town, our influence spreads. And you, fine Ancestors, made it that much easier for us to accomplish this goal by laying waste to the whole town. So brash and extreme in your thinking. I thank you for that. Now, all of the farmers will need to rely on Monsoko's seeds to make a living year after year. And Inari will fall ill and perish. And we will swallow up

THE LEGEND OF SOSEN NO TANI

The weight of his words sunk in. Echoes of both Hiryu Gongen and Kairi's admonishment came back to me. It's true. The fire that the Keepers lit—that I lit—in Nachi caused more harm than good. It was clearer now than ever that we'd need to change how we fought this war.

"I thought as much," Kairi muttered disgustedly from where she lay.

The demon turned on her, "Aw, don't act so high and mighty, young human. You've brought this on your village just as much as that young Ancestor here did."

Kairi just glared at him.

"How kind it was of you to have your little family round up all the humans for me in that shelter. Even I don't think I could have convinced every one of them to stay in the same place at once. But that aunt of yours has quite the influence, doesn't she? You made it so very easy for my men to surround them and contain them there. They're waiting patiently any minute now to exterminate them. Once I'm finished enjoying myself here, of course."

I could feel Kairi freeze in horror behind me. Her eyes widened in realization.

"Demon," I asked, "What's your name?"

He smiled at me, a slow, wicked smile that would make any living creature freeze to their core.

"It's Gento Hyuga," he replied, smirking at me.

"No, not your human name. Your original name."

His smile broadened.

"Shuten doji."

In an instant, I lit a ring of fire around him and me, enclosing the two of us only, so that Shuten doji would have no way to escape toward Sosen no Tani or back through the well. Normal fire does nothing to demons, but a Keepers' sacred fire can reduce one to ash in a second. In his case, it definitely wouldn't have that effect, but it could likely still injure him.

In the beginning years of my training, Elder Ryu warned us of the Circle of Three. The three most evil demons that were said to have been created alongside the kami to keep the world in balance and held the most power of all that came after them. They were called Shuten doji, Tamamo no Mae, and Sutoku Tenno.

Before me stood Shuten doji, one of the ancient Circle, as I had suspected. He was known in the old days as an incredibly strong and cunning demon who often disguised himself as a monk and studied the art of black magic. I had never seen a demon that exuded as much strength and menace as he did. I had definitely never seen a demon whose true form looked human. And I knew that I was now in what would be one of the most difficult fights of my life yet.

In the distance, I could hear the calls of the Keepers as they made their way toward us. Bursting through the clearing, Ryoko called out to me, reading the situation.

"Don't interfere!" I called. "Take Kairi and get her to Misao-dono's! Make sure none of the villagers leave town!" I barked orders out quickly while keeping my eyes locked on Shuten doji.

"No! Mato, you can't do this alone!" I heard Kairi yelling in protest behind me.

"The rest of you, go through the tunnels to Nachi. Clear the town of any and all demons—kill every one that you see. They will be holding humans hostage in a shelter somewhere at the base of the mountain. No human is to die at any cost. Now go!"

A few of the Keepers paused momentarily, looking between Shuten doji and me, but didn't break my command. I wasn't as cocky in my abilities to think I could finish him off alone, but had wanted to take advantage of my position enclosed with him to make sure the humans would be saved first. I could likely stay alive long enough to last until the Keepers came back, but didn't want to break the circle I had formed around the two of us. Any chance for an opening, and I knew this demon would take it.

I readied myself to fight.

With a smirk, Shuten doji watched them begin to scurry away. At lightning speed, he flew across the circle at me, pulling his sword in a batto-style draw from its sheath and attempting to slash my torso in half horizontally. I dodged his attack in a mere matter of microseconds, stumbling backward a few steps to regain my footing. But Shuten doji was still moving, coming toward me with a brute strength I had yet to experience even against Yoshizo-san. He repositioned his blade and attempted to bring it down on my chest diagonally, but this time I parried, matching his force.

"Not bad, little Ancestor." The demon smiled a set of pointed teeth at me, the first indicator that even his true form didn't look entirely human.

I didn't bother to respond. By this point, I could feel my mind slipping back into a state of unconscious battle, moving on pure muscle memory and instinct that absorbed me every time I fought. My breathing evened; my senses became animalistic. Everything around me began to slow.

To my eyes, the exchange of blows that followed between the two of us felt as though it took hours, but in reality, it likely all happened in matter of minutes or less. I was fighting with every ounce of training I had gleaned from Elder Tadaaki, the other Elders, Yoshizo-san, and the rest of my ten years as a Fire Keeper, destroying demons since I had arrived at Sosen no Tani. Every instinct I possessed and had honed was guiding me in full force as I dodged, kicked, blocked, and slashed my sword for my life. I was fighting at the peak of my strength, but I knew I had to keep it up, to keep Shuten doji distracted long enough, for the rest of the Keepers to return. And who knew how long that would be.

I didn't think I could kill him, but my goal was to injure

him by the time my comrades returned. Twice, I was able to land a blow on him. Once, I slashed my sword across his chest, opening up a long, thin wound that bled black ink. The second time, I brought my katana up above me, aiming to bring it down on his skull, but he knocked my sword aside at the last moment so that the blow landed on his shoulder. It should have severed the muscle and shattered his collarbone, but he kept moving, completely unphased and laughing the entire time.

Shuten doji, on the other hand, was landing his fair share of blows on me. Each time, I was able to block his strikes from inflicting any major injury, but my legs and forearms at this point had been sliced to bits. At one point, the demon struck me with the hilt of his sword so squarely in my diaphragm that I had to leap away to avoid him taking advantage of my momentary weakness. I coughed up blood.

I couldn't see anything aside from Shuten doji's form, moving in streaks of light from side to side as we dueled. Behind him was nothing but the swirling colors of burning flame. I heard nothing but my own breath. I had no idea if Ryoko had taken Kairi to safety successfully; I had no idea if the Keepers were back yet. But I knew I was running out of energy and therefore, I was running out of time. I needed to maintain my laser focus as long as I could if I wanted to survive.

Suddenly, above the roar of my own blood pumping in my ears, I thought I heard a voice yell, "Mato!" In that single moment of distraction, Shuten doji, taking advantage of the opening, beat my blade out of my hands. Immediately, the demon brought his sword back in an effort to maim my hands and neutralize my ability to use a sword. The thought did not even occur to me that I was about to die. Without thinking, my hands grasped the sharp steel, halting his strike where he swung. I could feel the bite of the metal as it split open my palms. Shuten doji's pointed smile widened into a sneer as he assumed he had won, my swordfighting hand now likely destroyed.

Just as it had a week ago with Yoshizo-san, I felt the pooling of energy in my palms. I watched Shuten doji's triumphant grin twist in confusion as the blast of my fire sent him flying backward. His expression hadn't changed by the time I recovered my burning sword and severed his head.

The instant I watched his body burst into flames, I collapsed on the forest floor. The circle of sacred fire I had erected around us fell with me. I was conscious of the voices of the Keepers rushing toward me as the world slipped into blackness.

CHAPTER TWENTY-FOUR

Tokyo, Japan

"I stand in the center of Nachi Falls, a little town in Wakayama Prefecture best known as a key pilgrimage point on the famous Kumano Kodo pilgrimage trail. Only a week ago, we stood in this very spot assessing the devastating damage that had impacted this humble and quiet town. Now, as you can see behind me"—the young reporter motioned to the throngs of townspeople milling about behind her, hard at work on debris removal—"Nachi has come a long way in the last week alone, taking recovery into its own hands.

"The local mayor has made an official announcement that the town will not be accepting any form of donations aside from cash, nor will it be externally contracting out reconstruction of damaged infrastructure. The town urges any volunteers deploying to the area to assist in recovery efforts, not to act on their own accord, and to adhere to the wishes of the community.

"It's a far cry from the initial thinking we heard from local community leaders just last week, as we walked the town with representatives from Monsoko, who planned to donate rice seeds and planting equipment in partnership with Tagama Tech Company. Now, after the mysterious car accident that killed Monsoko CEO Gento Hyuga and other executives of the company after our visit, Monsoko has since rescinded its donation, as its corporate structure and market shares have crumbled in one of the quickest down-spirals the world has ever seen. And the town has rejected any corporate assistance."

The reporter paused as a petite older woman walked by her on camera.

"Mie-san!" she called to the woman, gently getting her attention. "We're live on Fuji News Network, speaking on Nachi's recovery. Since you've been a key community leader in the town's recovery, would you care to say a few words?"

"Sure, Sakura-san," the woman replied amicably. "The town of Nachi has taken the incident of the wildfire very seriously. It has been made unbearably clear to us through this tragedy that we humans are to blame for the worsening climate conditions leading to unusual and more extreme disasters. We intend to recover from this calamity in a way that will hopefully prevent similar events from occurring in the future—and if they do, to build our community's resilience to them. Now more than ever, we are looking to the guidance and ways of the ancestors that came before us to teach us how to be a true satoyama community and live in harmony with the forest and living beings around us. By attempting to salvage the ancient ways of living, and respecting our relationship to each other, our food, our resources, and our environment, can we then ensure that we have truly recovered. We invite those who are interested in learning these ways to come assist us, but kindly ask that you do not interfere with the community's endeavors down this path. Thank you, Sakura-san." The woman bowed.

"You sound so much like your niece, Kairi, who I interviewed here just a week prior and had been missing for two and a half weeks after the fires. She condemned the use of industrial agriculture to rebuild the town within hours after arriving home," the news reporter commented.

"Well, she didn't get her ideas from nowhere! Besides, as she said herself, she was able to survive through the use of ancestral knowledge and praying to the gods daily. We truly believe she was guided home by Yatagarasu himself. Therefore, this will serve as a model for us as we rebuild." The woman smiled before shuffling off to command a group of younger men behind her.

"There you heard it, ladies and gentlemen. If you are looking to support Nachi on its path to recovery, please reach out to the numbers we have listed on the screen. May we all support this little town that appears to be strengthened by the kami themselves. This is Sakura Morai, signing off."

Mizukume Zukeran switched off the television that hung on the wall of her office. Rising from her chair, she walked over to the large glass window that overlooked the city of Tokyo. *The bastard,* she thought, crossing her arms. *He was always known as a drunk. Become too drunk off one's own power and find yourself killed.* Within moments, a knock rapped on her door.

"Ma'am." Kenji said.

He was a young demon, but had risen through the ranks due to his sheer ambition and cold-blooded nature alone. Mizukume trusted him more than some of her oldest advisors—but she knew Kenji would betray her eventually if she gave him too much importance. However, the young demon was a master of human manipulation, and she needed him in her ear for just a bit longer. They were so close, she and her underlings, to making the breakthrough they needed. Mere steps away from hooking the humans on a technology they could never escape.

"Have you seen the news, Kenji?" Mizukume asked.

"Yes, ma'am. Shuten doji has been killed, ma'am."

"So it seems he has. For now. I have a job for you."

CHAPTER TWENTY-FIVE

Kairi

"We should really get going," I said to Mato, edging toward the door of Auntie Mie's farmhouse.

He casually rose from the floor cushion he was sitting on. "Okay."

"Is Auntie Mie back yet from town?" I asked my dad, who also was attempting to stand up with grace.

"I'm here! I'm here! Don't go anywhere without me!" Auntie Mie called, bursting through the front door in a flurry.

It had been seven days since Mato and the Keepers killed the leader of Monsoko Corporation, Gento Hyuga—or I guess I should refer to him by his real name, Shuten doji—and the other demons he sent to threaten Nachi Falls. In that short time, a lot had shifted for both the Ancestors and humans, mentally and physically. For one thing, my leg had already healed just by staying a few nights in the spirit realm. But more importantly, the whole incident, coupled with being publicly ridiculed by Hiryu Gongen, finally convinced the Fire Keepers to change their strategy in their war against the demons.

Following the advice I had admonished them with in a moment of rage, Nachi had been the first town the Ancestors decided to reeducate and remind of the ancient ways. I had volunteered Auntie Mie to lead the charge as a beloved and trusted member of her community, as well as one of the few people left who remembered the legend of Sosen no Tani. She had been hard at work in the village every day since, working closely with Fire Keepers who had crossed through the well (and who we had dressed as volunteers) to learn the traditional methods of agriculture, land management, Shinto and Buddhist ceremony, medicine, cooking, and even housing construction to apply to life in modern Nachi. She and a handful of other local leaders passed these methods on to the townspeople as they cleared debris, worked to restore their polluted fields, and started rebuilding homes.

When I had first told Auntie Mie and my father about Sosen no Tani and the Ancestors, the day I had seen Monsoko demons in the village, I wasn't sure if either of them had fully believed me. Even though they had enough faith in me to still do as I had asked and rounded up all of Nachi's community members in the makeshift shelter, I don't think it was truly until the arrival of the Keepers, dressed as old samurai and brandishing fire in the palms of their hands, that they were convinced my story had been real.

The town had agreed to keep the existence of Sosen no Tani and its Ancestors a secret, in an effort to keep the Fire Keepers' new strategic advantage and to refrain from drawing excessive attention to itself in a world full of demons, so that it could develop and protect the skills they were relearning.

When the fighting had ended, Mato brought the information back to Ryu and the other Elders that Monsoko's CEO had been an ancient demon of the Circle of Three and explained how he had garnered his position over the last hundred years basically controlling the course of the world's food systems. With the trial of re-educating Nachi going as successfully as it was, and the realization that the remaining members of the Circle were likely behind some of the biggest systems of destruction threatening the world today, the Keepers ordered Mato and me to lead the new movement to partner with the humans and target the most powerful demons perpetuating destruction. There was to be a ceremony to initiate and bless us in this effort tonight, before we were to travel north to gain support from other members of the spirit world and provide aid to the kami. In the human realm, the other Keepers would begin educating new human towns throughout Japan's countryside, clearing them of demons along the way.

After Ryoko had carried me back to Misao-dono's house, I made the Keepers help me get home to Nachi as soon as the fighting ended. I had refused to worry my family any more than I already had in the weeks prior. Mato had volunteered to take me, and he carried me through the well and back to Auntie Mie's house so that I could explain to my family that I was all right. We decided it was best for me to stay in Sosen no Tani for a few days to let my leg heal, knowing that the spirit world had strong herbs, or some sort of magic about it, that allowed for faster recovery than in the human realm.

After embracing me, my father had given Mato a stern handshake, thanking him for protecting his daughter. However, when I returned to Nachi today, wanting to say goodbye to my family before departing on the long journey ahead, he had sat and stared at Mato awkwardly for the first hour of our visit. Auntie Mie hadn't been home, working on reconstruction efforts downtown, so we had to wait for some time for her return before I could say goodbye. Mato had sat on the floor and if I hadn't known better, seemed oblivious to my father's stare. He looked around, fascinated at the modernity of my aunt's house, and politely acknowledged my father as he spoke.

Eventually, my dad's curiosity got the better of him and he asked to look at Mato's katana. For the last hour, the two had been poring over it at the living room table, while Mato described how to wield it and told my father stories of all the action it had seen.

Now that it was finally time for us to go, my dad pulled Mato in for a bear hug, clearly indicating Mato had won him over. But even as he pulled back, he looked at Mato with a stern expression and said gravely, "I don't care how extraordinary of a warrior you are, or if you can shoot fire from your hands. If you hurt my daughter, I will not hesitate to find a way to murder you where you stand."

"Jesus, Dad," I said in English.

"Sir, I would completely agree to that course of action. You have my word." Mato bowed formally.

A little too late for that, I heard a voice echo in the back of my head. I had yet to fully sort out my feelings for Mato after learning about the fires and I still hadn't told my family that he had lit them directly. I still hadn't forgiven him for lighting the fires that burned Nachi, but I couldn't help but relax into a familiar routine with him when so much had been going on. I knew Nachi was not the first fire he had lit. He had *killed* people. *Killed* Hiroko-san. But once again, I found myself pushing this knowledge off in the moment.

"Do you have your survival kit?" my father asked pointedly as he looked at the bag slung over my shoulder.

He was having a hard time letting me go to the spirit realm after all that had happened, which was massively understandable. But even he knew the journey Mato and I were to embark on was bigger than the two of us. After all we had been through together as a family, he had a propensity to understand the importance of taking action on large-scale issues.

When I asked him what he would be doing while I was gone, he had said he planned to hang out a bit longer with Auntie Mie, who had graciously offered to host him, recognizing she would need a new set of hands to help in the garden and around town with her new position leading the cultural recovery of Nachi. My father had accepted, wanting to be as close to me and the portal to Sosen no Tani as possible. I had promised to write them both regular letters, seeing as cell phone service definitely did not exist in the spirit realm. I would have one of the Keepers meet Mato and me wherever we were to deliver the letter personally to them in Nachi.

"You bet," I replied to my dad. "A fire striker, compressible bottle to hold water, a first aid kit that I'm going to further outfit with herbs from Sosen no Tani, some paracord, a couple of knives, soap, containers to make food if we need to, heating pads, and also an extra hat and mittens even though it's still summer..." I trailed off, listing the items.

I kept expecting Mato to say I wouldn't need nearly as much as my father had insisted I bring, but instead he was staring fascinatedly at the pack.

"Hey, who knows how long you will be gone for, and you will be headed through the Alps! You need to be prepared!" my father protested.

"I know, Dad, and I am, thanks to your survival kits." I gave him a kiss on the cheek.

"I want to hear all of the amazing stories you bring back, all of the knowledge you learn, and all about the incredible things you see. Don't worry; I'll set some antiques aside for you while you are gone," Mie said, winking at me and giving me a squeeze on the shoulders.

"Take care of this place, Auntie Mie," I replied. "I can't wait to see what it's like when I get back. If there's anyone that can restore Nachi, it's you. And please, the both of you, stay safe."

With some final hugs and farewells, and multiple assurances from Mato that he would take care of me, we were off and headed back on our way to Sosen no Tani. We arrived just in time for the sun to be going down, and it wasn't long before we had to make our way to the Fire Keepers' Temple, where the final ceremony would commence. Mato and I would be setting out from Sosen no Tani the following morning, as soon as the sun came up, with the goal of making it to the Kyoto of the spirit realm as quickly as possible. There were a few allies there that Elder Tadaaki had instructed us needed to join our forces. He had also told Mato rather seriously that he needed to seek out *The Door* in the Alps, whatever that meant. He wouldn't explain why, but it was clear that we had a long journey ahead.

The ceremony seemed to be more for Mato than it was for

me. After he single-handedly managed to slay one of the most evil and ancient demons in Japan's history, it was clear that his role as a Fire Keeper had ascended to the most valuable warrior and member outside of the Elders. The ceremony tonight was meant to bless the both of us for the journey starting the following morning, but it was more to initiate Mato into the status of the highest-ranking Keepers.

The Elders had made it clear that I played an important role. Being the first human to successfully be reintroduced to Sosen no Tani, and also being the first human to change the entire military strategy and perspectives of the Fire Keepers, I was to act as the bridge between the humans and the Ancestors. But I mostly sat on the side of the tatami-floored room while the Elders and various important members of the Keepers swirled around Mato, who sat at the edge of the sunken hearth in the center of everything.

Elder Ryu, Sora-Sensei, and various other Keepers in red robes burned incense and chanted benedictions to Mato as he sat cross-legged, as still as the Buddha himself, next to the fire. The flames rose and fell with his breath. They had stripped him down to his waist, and he sat waiting to receive a script of ceremonial tattoos along his back. The tattoos were given only to the most enlightened and powerful Keepers among their ranks; to those said to be touched by the gods. I was told they had only been administered thrice in all of Fire Keeper history. Not even Elder Tadaaki had acquired them. The tattoos were said to give those who were gifted them additional power, bringing more clarity, strength, and understanding needed to further protect the Ancestors and their people.

I watched as the sage who stood behind Mato dipped a needle into a jar of ink and began writing lines of cursive script down Mato's right shoulder blade. I watched as Mato's thick black eyebrows furrowed and his jaw tensed in concentration, breathing through the pain of the needle. But I quickly became absorbed with watching the swirling patterns of the needle on his tanned skin. A thin layer of sweat had broken out in a sheen on his back, accentuating the well-defined muscles that coiled there. The soft thrumming of drums and the Keepers' chants filled my ears. The room smelled like sandalwood. I could almost forget the horrible things Mato had done with a swing of his sword.

The night passed like any other, quiet and filled with stars. In the morning, I awoke to Misao-dono shaking me gently. I dressed in functional farmer's clothes and packed a thick silk kimono into my bag in case the situation called for it. At the stroke of dawn, Misao-dono and I met up with Mato, the Keepers, and other villagers waiting to see us off at the entrance to the Kumano Kodo pilgrimage trail on the side of the Keeper's Temple. In the distance, I could hear the roar of Sosen no Tani's falls. Around us, mist rolled in between the mountains. It was so quiet, so early, that not even the uguisu bird had awoken from its slumber.

Mato and I stood facing the torii gate at the entrance of the trail that would welcome us into our journey ahead. Around us, the villagers looked on with hopeful eyes, while Elder Ryu and other Keepers began their chants. Taking out a large conch shell slung on her back, Elder Ryu held the thing to her lips and took a deep breath before blowing her breath out forcefully. The shell sent out a deep noise that reverberated across the valley. I recognized it as the practice of Shingon, the blowing of the conch shell to ask the kami of the mountains for safe passage as a pilgrim was about to head out on a dangerous or arduous journey.

Unexpectedly, I felt tears spring to the corners of my eyes as the realization of what we were doing hit me. The sound of the conch shell echoing out over the mist of the early morning filled me with a sense of knowing that was so innately human, so instinctual, I felt like it took me back to the very core of what it meant to be aligned with the Earth, with my ancestors, with the Universe of energy swirling around me. I took a deep breath and closed my eyes, letting the sound of the conch fill my ears.

Please watch over us and grant us the tenacity and willpower to be successful, I thought to the kami in the mountains surrounding me.

The conch sounded a total of three times before Elder Ryu lowered it from her lips. I looked over at Mato and he stared back at me.

"Are you ready?" he asked.

"Let's get going," I replied.

ACKNOWLEDGEMENTS

I want to first begin by giving a hearty thank you to the Japanese culture, from which many legends, folklore, practices, and beings are inspired from in The Legend of Sosen no Tani. While centuries old Japanese myths, religions, stories, and methodologies have served as a foundation to this storyline, I want to make it clear that I have taken fictious liberties and woven in some of my own derived legends at that. Some modalities of speech as well as human (and Ancestor) interaction will not be true to real Japanese ways, and I ask that you do not interpret my legends too literally. I owe my deepest gratitude and respects to this extraordinary and beautiful society, lifestyle, and belief system. Thank you for allowing me to take inspiration from you and base this world off of your ways. I will do my best to pay it forward.

Of course, my greatest thanks must go to my family. To my father, John, for quite literally 'showing me how it's done.' Thank you for being my greatest writing role-model, forging the path of authorship, passing down your imaginative brain, and cultivating my love of stories. You will forever be my favorite storyteller. To my mother, Robin, for you unending support and countless sacrifices to help me be the best I can be, and for embodying the true strength a woman can possess. It is because of you that I have learned to value family as one of the most important things in this life. To my sister, Emilee, my first editor and forever roommate, for your professional expertise and natural talent as a writer. Thank you for consistently showing me some of the worst story content in the world.

To my dear friend and cover artist, Lorelei Fleishman. Thank you for some of my favorite days running around both Tokyo and Kyoto. Without you and your limitless talent, we would not be able to see the world through Mato and Kairi's eyes.

To my editor, Susan Helene Gottfried, thank you for taking my first child and believing in it! It was your keen eyes (I know, I know, I'm disembodying you – I'm sorry!), expertise, and warm encouragement that has given me the confidence that The Legend of Sosen no Tani is a story worth reading.

I want to give a warm thank you to my Japanese teacher, Shoko Ishida, for patiently answering my language questions and providing me with the context I lack on the Japanese culture. Although you will most definitely still find errors in this story (both intentional and not), I am so grateful to you, Shoko-Sensei!

To Kevran Lawrence, thank you for your ongoing support, listening to countless insecurity crises, and for dragging me into the world of anime, on which so much of this story is inspired. To my friend Hailey Lister, thank you for encouraging me to write every night in Kyoto and for hiking 26 miles with me in 48 hours across the Japanese wilderness filled with boars, snakes, and monkeys. Without it, I would have never experienced the wonder of Nachi Falls and some of the best days of my life on the Kumano Kodo. To my oldest friend, Gabe Brown, if you had not been willing to buy plane tickets with me that random Tuesday night in October, my world would have never changed so drastically.

To all of my friends who I have not mentioned by name, thank you for supporting both me and this book long before its creation, and for continuing to do so long after the final pages. To all of the amazing souls I met in my first journey across Japan, without you, the magic of Sosen no Tani could never exist.

For all who read this book, you forever have my gratitude for quite literally making this dream turn into a reality. Thank you for hanging in there with me through this first attempt. I hope we can watch this world grow together.

And finally, a thank you to my ancestors. If it wasn't for you and your knowings, this book would be nothing at all.

Manufactured by Amazon.ca
Bolton, ON

36287110R00129